MAKE YOUR CHANGE

ASTON ARCHERS
BOOK FOUR

CALI MELLE

Edited by Amy Pritt
Proofread by Amy Pritt
Cover Art by Essasketch
Cover Design by Cali Melle

PLAYLIST

YOUR GUILTY PLEASURE - HENRY VERUS
DANCING WITH YOUR GHOST - SASHA ALEX
SLOAN
JULY - NOAH CYRUS
LIE TO ME - ALI GATIE, TATE MCRAE
NICE TO MEET YOU- MYLES SMITH
SWEET NOTHING - TAYLOR SWIFT
I LOVE YOU - BILLIE ELISH
WHEN THE END COMES - ANDREW BELLE
WEATHERVANE - HUNTER METTS
ADDICTED - JON VINYL
HOME - GOOD NEIGHBOURS

this one is for the besties who love a man written by a woman
;)

PROLOGUE
CARSON

SIX YEARS AGO

A soft body collides into the back of mine. My spine straightens and my body tenses to retreat from the cold liquid now soaking the back of my T-shirt. Music bumps from the speakers throughout the club, the strobe lights above flashing in tandem with the beat, yet somehow, over all the commotion, I don't miss her velvety voice when she speaks.

"Oh, fuck." She lets out a breath that somehow comes across as both flustered and annoyed. "I'm so sorry."

I am in no hurry as I spin on my heels to find the owner of that voice who just soaked my back with her drink, and I'm delighted in what I find. At 6'4", I tower over her and have to tip my chin down to look at her, even with her feet shoved into a pair of white heels. Her cheeks are tinted pink, her high cheekbones sparkling beneath the strobe lights. Her long dark hair is slicked back in a high ponytail, not a single hair out of place. Her long lashes flutter, revealing the most beautiful hues of gold and green shimmering in her irises.

The best part of all?

The annoyance written in her expression. The way her dainty nose is scrunched, her dark eyebrows tugging together. She looks like someone spilled their drink on *her*. The black dress she's wearing hugs her curves in all the right places, stopping just along the middles of her tanned thighs.

Fuck, she's breathtaking.

Amusement washes over me and I cock my head to the side. "Did you spill your drink on me?"

"Yes. Some asshole bumped into me and knocked me into you." She closes her eyes, her nostrils flaring as her chest rises as she sucks in a deep breath. After a couple seconds, she blows it out and meets my gaze once more. "This place is packed tonight, there's barely any room to move." She shakes her head, like she's trying to shake away her irritation. "Can I buy you an apology drink or something?"

"There's no apology needed," I tell her, a smile lifting my lips. I do a quick survey of the room for my brother Caleb or Rowan, but I seem to have lost them somewhere. "But I'll buy you one instead."

Her red lips part, revealing her bright white teeth before she ducks her head and lets out a soft laugh. "I appreciate the offer, but I don't really drink except for the occasional glass of wine." She lifts her glass, shrugging as a sheepish look dances across her face. "This is just water."

"Aren't you refreshing?" I let out a low chuckle, and stuff my hands in my pockets instead of trailing my fingers across her exposed collarbones like I want to. I didn't come here with the intention of taking someone home, but I'm not opposed to entertaining that idea with her. "What brings you out to a place like this if you aren't drinking?"

She sucks her bottom lip between her teeth, dragging it back and forth along the top ones before releasing it. "I came here with some friends to dance and forget about my ex's engagement announcement." There's my confirmation that she's single. I catch her scanning the tattoos on my arms before she realizes what she's doing and snaps her attention back to my face. "What about you? Are you just here to drink?"

"Maybe I came here to dance too."

Her face cracks and she lets out a short burst of laughter. *She's fucking beautiful.* "I highly doubt that."

"Want to find out?"

She tips her head to the side, a decisive look in her gold and green orbs as she raises a manicured eyebrow. "You're rather brazen, aren't you?"

"I wouldn't say that," I tell her, my voice dropping lower as I inch farther into her space, standing close enough that I can smell the floral notes of her perfume. Warmth radiates from her body, but I don't dare touch her. Not without her consent. "Something caught my interest and I'm not in the habit of letting opportunities slip away."

Her plump lips part, demanding my attention as she lets out a ragged breath. "And what opportunity do you think presented itself?"

It's getting late and I might as well lay the bait now and see if she takes it. I'm not interested in anything other than a good time and, considering the fact that she's a bit jaded, maybe she's looking for the same.

"One that offers a few hours of distraction without any promise of attachment." My tongue darts out to wet my lips as I let my gaze roam over her body then back to hers. "The kind that will make you forget your ex."

Her eyes drag from one to the other, slow and seductive as the corners of her mouth lift just a fraction of a centimeter. "You are absolutely brazen."

"Maybe," I chuckle, shaking my head at her. "Or maybe I just know what I want and find it easier to be straightforward about it."

She stares at me for a moment, contemplating what I said before she takes my drink from me and sets it on the high top table beside me. She sets hers down next to mine, her arm grazing my shirt sleeve as she does. Her hand slides into mine, lacing her fingers with mine as she smiles up at me. "Come dance with me and we'll see where the night goes."

"Lead the way."

I let her lead me back into the crowd of people, pulling me deeper into the center before she finally turns around to face me. Her eyes find mine as she begins to move her hips, swaying them back and forth as she finds harmony with the beat that pumps through the speakers. I stand back for a moment, watching her, completely mesmerized by the way she begins to weave her body to the music.

Her head tips back, her eyes falling shut as she lifts her arms above her head, winding and twisting to the melody. I don't dare take my eyes off her, and as the crowd around us grows tighter, I immediately step closer in an effort to keep everyone else away.

When she looks up at me again, her eyes are hooded and a little dazed. She's drunk on endorphins, and a smile dances across her lips as she reaches for me. Her hands find mine and she tugs on me, pulling me closer. It's absolutely intoxicating and my god, I want to drink from her. I want to be intoxicated too.

My feet move without instruction, closing the distance until my body is almost flush with hers. My hands abandon hers, reaching for her hips instead to shift her closer. Her body moves, still swaying with the music and I start to move with her, letting myself get lost in her as our surroundings begin to fade away. I couldn't stop the blood that rushes to my cock even if I wanted to. And I don't want to. It throbs as it grows, pressing against the zipper of my pants.

Leaning forward, my cheek brushes against hers as my mouth finds her ear. "What's your name?" I murmur, my lips grazing the outer shell. A shiver ripples through her as she inhales sharply and rolls her shoulders.

She shifts away from me enough to lift her arms, hooking her wrists behind my neck. Her hands slide along my nape, her fingertips plunging through my hair. "Andi," she breathes, as her hooded gaze locks on mine. "What's yours?"

"Ford," I murmur, realizing I gave her my last name. "Carson."

She raises an eyebrow. "Which is it? Ford or Carson?"

A chuckle vibrates in my chest. "Carson Ford, actually, but you can call me whatever you want."

She stares up at me for a few seconds, as if deciding her next move, before dropping her arms away from the back of my neck. My hands never leave her hips as she shifts her weight, and spins around in front of me. I slide my palms over the silky material of her dress until I'm gripping her again. She shimmies back towards me, her ass pressing against my crotch as she begins to grind against me. There's no way she can't feel how hard I am already for her.

My cock pulsates as she moves against my length, only making it harder. I can't help myself as I shift my hips forward, grinding myself into her in tandem with her movements. My heart pounds in my chest at the thought of getting her out of here and out of this dress.

Taking someone home is always like rolling the dice, but our chemistry is off the charts. We've barely even spoken, yet I'm drawn to her like a moth to a flame. Perhaps it's the mysteriousness of her or her being a complete stranger. I don't really care, I just need to have her.

Fingers spread, I begin to move my palms around the fronts of her thighs, my fingertips drifting across her skin beneath the bottom hem of her dress. She presses back into me harder as I move my hands beneath the material, slowly dragging it up her thighs. We're in the middle of a room full of people, but the crowd is too thick and it's too dark for anyone to see what's happening.

Her dress is short enough, I could probably slide my cock into her right here on the dance floor and no one would even notice.

Andi's head falls back against my shoulder as my fingertips move to her inner thighs, just nearly brushing against her cunt. Heat radiates from her and a groan rumbles in my chest as she lets out the softest moan. Just as I skim along the outside of her panties, she abruptly spins in my arms, my hands now falling onto her ass.

She slides her hands around the back of my neck once more, pulling my face closer to hers. I stare down at her, watching her eyes as they bounce between mine and move to my lips.

I can't control my gaze as it homes in on her perfect mouth. My tongue darts out to wet my lips and I wait for her move. She lifts herself onto her toes, her lips nearing closer to mine before I meet her in the middle, my mouth immediately capturing hers.

The tension swirls in the air around us, growing thicker by the moment. Her lips move against mine and when I slide my tongue along the seam of her mouth, she doesn't hesitate to let me in. My tongue finds hers, soft like velvet as she kisses me with an intensity that rocks me to my core. *Goddamn, who the fuck is this woman?*

Her fingers dig into my skin, her nails cutting into my flesh. Intentionally slowing down the kiss, I nip, taste, touch, and tease her with every sweeping movement of my tongue. She matches my energy, equally torturing me until it feels like I could potentially come apart at the seams.

Abruptly, I pull away from her, both of us breathless as I search her eyes for permission.She's giving me all the signs that point in the right direction, but I need to hear her words. I need her to give me that verification that she wants the same thing I want.

Neither of us are looking for anything more than a good time.

Andi closes the gap between us, lifting back up onto her toes as she peppers kisses along the underside of my jaw. Her tongue is soft as it slides along my neck, her teeth sinking into the lobe of my ear before she gives me what I need. "I want you."

Goddamn, I love a woman who doesn't fuck around.

"Do you want to come back to my place?"

"No." She shakes her head, her cheek moving against mine. "I want to do something spontaneous that I've never done before." She pauses, her hands sliding along my biceps. "How do you feel about finding somewhere to fuck me here instead?"

Holy fucking shit.

She's trouble and I like it. I've been trying to stay out of trouble recently, but I am more than willing to bend that for her.

"You want me to fuck you here, where everyone can

see?" I murmur, my face dipping closer to her ear. "Does the thought of that excite you?"

"It does," she admits, her voice filled with lust as she presses her body against mine. "But I'd rather go somewhere a little private so people don't see us."

"Come with me," I tell her, my tongue tracing the outer shell of her ear before I pull away from her. "I'm sure there's somewhere we can go."

Andi follows behind me, her hand in mine as I pull her through the throng of people. We reach a break in the sea of bodies where it opens into a hallway. It's dark and the music is still loud, but it's a bit quiet. A little more private. I lead her deeper into the hall and farther away from the rest of the people. We pass the bathrooms and come across a few other doors. I test each handle until finally finding one that's unlocked.

The light flickers on when my hand finally finds the switch in the near total darkness. She spins around, her eyes wide. "I don't know if we should be in here." It looks like it's someone's office we slipped into. That door definitely should not have been unlocked.

"Maybe we should be in here then," I tell her, a smirk lifting my lips as I stalk closer. "We're somewhere private, but the risk of getting caught still exists."

Lust burns deeply in her green and gold eyes. "If that's the case, we're only wasting time with meaningless words."

"Tell me what you want, baby. You want me to bend you over that desk and fuck you?" My hands find her hips and I abruptly pull her flush against me. She gasps, her nails digging into my shoulders to steady herself.

"Or perhaps you'd rather I sit in that chair and you climb on top of me and ride me."

She stares at me for a moment. "We're not going to exchange numbers or anything after this, right? I want to walk out of that door with not a single string attached."

A chuckle rumbles in my chest as I lift my hand to the base of her neck. "I don't do strings, Trouble." My face dips down to hers, my teeth nipping at her lips. "I think we're both here for the same thing."

"I've never had a one night stand before."

Her words catch me by surprise, and I pull away, just far enough to peer down into her eyes. I wouldn't have pegged this to be her first time with how forward she's been with me. "You've come to the right person then." My fingers wrap around her neck, the other sliding along her collar bone before shoving the thin strap of her dress past her shoulder. "Let me show you how it's done."

My mouth finds hers once more, my hand plunging beneath the neckline of her silk dress as she opens for me. Tongues tangling, she moans into my mouth and I swallow the sounds as my fingers drift over her nipples. Her soft flesh pebbles beneath my touch and I take my time, touching and teasing each of her breasts while my other hand grips her neck.

Her hands drop down to the waistband of my pants, sliding the button through the hole before she begins to pull down my zipper. Cool air grazes the bottom of my abdomen as her soft fingers shove down my boxer briefs, freeing my throbbing cock. She moans into my mouth again, the sound vibrating directly to my balls as she wraps her hand around my length, slowly pumping her fist up and down.

If she keeps doing that, I'm going to fucking ruin this and come all over both of us a lot sooner than either of us wants.

Despite how good it feels to have her stroke me, I break away from her to take back control of this moment. My hand abandons her throat and I drop them both to her hips, spinning her to face the opposite direction. My arm is across her chest to hold her back flush to my front as my legs press against hers, the pre-cum on the tip of my cock undoubtedly leaving a mark on the back of her dress as I urge her forward. We don't stop until we reach the desk.

Leaning forward, I sweep everything off the surface, not giving a fuck about what tumbles to the ground. Andi lets out a soft chuff and raises that same eyebrow at me again as she glances at me over her shoulder. Without a word, I place a gentle kiss on her shoulder, my hands sliding beneath her dress to find the waistband of her g-string. I hook my fingers under the string, lower myself and the thin scrap of material to the floor to remove them before standing back upright, and setting her panties on the desk near us.

"Lift your dress and bend over the desk for me," I command, my hand pressing against the nape of her neck as I trail my lips over the tops of her shoulders. "Show me where you want me to fuck you."

Andi does as she's told, lifting her dress until it's bunched around her waist. She leans forward, pressing the front of her body against the desk as I step up behind her. My hand rubs her ass cheek, drifting across her crack before palming the other. Her body is taut and it's clear she works out. I'm fucking obsessed.

"Are you sure you want to do this?" I question her as I reach into my back pocket for my wallet. I keep an emergency condom in there in case a situation like this ever arises. I need to make sure this is what she wants before I proceed.

She doesn't hesitate and the word comes out breathlessly. "Yes."

My cock pulsates as the tip brushes against the center of her cunt. Warm and wet, ready and accepting. I flip open my wallet and begin to move the cards around, digging for the condom I could have sworn I put in there. I practically empty the entire fucking thing and come up empty handed.

"Fuck."

She lifts her chest, propping herself on her arms as she looks back at me. "What's wrong?"

My eyes fall shut and I huff out a breath as I run a hand through my hair. "I don't have a condom."

"That's okay," she says in a rush, her voice breathless. My eyelids flutter open, immediately meeting her gaze. "I'm on birth control. And I'm clean. It's not a problem."

Oh thank fuck.

Although it pulled us from the moment, we're both thrown back into the rush, into the lust as soon as she presses her ass back against me again. And fuck me, I need to be inside of her. Lifting my hand, I spit into my palm and wrap my fingers around my girth. I pump it a few times, getting myself wet before pressing against her again.

Andi bends back over the desk, her hands gripping the edges of it as she lifts herself up, granting me better access to her pussy. The tip of my cock slides through her already soaked lips, teasing her clit. "Fuck, you're so wet for me already." I press into her, pushing into her warmth. She inhales sharply, her head turning to the side as her lips part and her eyes widen.

"Goddamn, you feel so fucking good," I groan, sinking deep into her with one fluid thrust of my hips. Andi moans, her eyes rolling back in her head as I fill her to the hilt, my balls pressing against her.

"Jesus Christ," she breathes, half moaning as she white knuckles the edge of the desk.

"You can take it, baby," I moan, my hands sliding over her curves. I shift my hips and begin to move, thrusting in and out of her as slow as I can to give her time to adjust to my size. Andi's face is pressed against the desk, her eyelids fluttering shut as she lets out a soft cry. "You're doing so well, taking every inch of me."

She's soaked, her pussy gripping me as I slide in and out. Her body lurches forward and my hands slide down to her hips, gripping her as the desk groans beneath the force of my thrusts. What starts out as slow and teasing, quickly becomes something rushed and driven by urgency. My fingertips dig into her flesh as I fuck her harder, earning moans and soft cries from her as I fill her to the brim with every hard thrust.

Abandoning her right hip, I drag my fingertips

along her spine, making my way up to the back of her neck as I continue to pound into her. Her cunt stretches around me, sucking my cock in every time I press back into her. I grip the back of her neck, holding her down against the desk as I move my left hand around the front of her body, pushing my fingers between her legs.

"Open wider for me, Andi. I want to play with your pussy while I fuck you."

Andi's knuckles are white, but she does as she's told, parting her legs as she remains bent over the side of the desk. My fingers brush against her clit and she immediately tenses, her cunt clenching around my length. My movements become a bit slower as I pump my hips while finding a rhythm with my fingertips rubbing her clit.

"Don't stop, Carson," Andi moans, her ass pressing harder into me as she takes every thrust. I take a mental picture of her like this, storing it in my brain for a rainy, lonely day. "I'm so close."

Fuck, she's hot.

Applying more pressure, I roll my fingers, circling her clit as I feel her getting even closer. "That's it," I moan, my head tipping back as my face screws up. My eyelids slam shut, the muscles in my shoulders tightening as the warmth in my stomach begins to overflow. "Come for me."

I groan, my hand gripping the back of her neck tighter as I pound into her harder. She cries out, the walls of her cunt pulsating around my cock as she loses herself around me. Her orgasm sends shockwaves through her body, her pussy gripping me so fucking tight, it sends me over the edge. My cock fills her completely as I come, pumping her full as my thrusts turn slow and lazy, drawing out my own orgasm.

She's a mess of breathless moans by the time we're both done. I slide my hand away from the front of her body as I withdraw from her. Gripping her hips, I pull her away from the desk and help her to stand upright as she gets her bearings straight.

Shallow breaths escape her as she stares back at me. Her once sleek ponytail is disheveled, her cheeks tinted pink, her eyes glazed over, and lips swollen. Reaching down, she pulls her dress back down her thighs, covering herself.

"That was the best distraction I've ever had."

Bending down, I grab the box of tissues I knocked off the desk and hand them to her to clean herself. "You know, I could give you my number and be of service any time you want."

What the fuck am I saying?

She pushes away from the desk and clicks her tongue as she walks past me, stopping by the trashcan by the door as she disposes of the tissues. I wipe off my dick and shove it back into my pants as I get myself straightened.

Turning back to me, she shakes her head, amusement lighting up her expression. "That wasn't what we agreed to," she says with a wink and a lazy grin. I'm fucking captivated by her. "I'm only here for a week or so before I have to head back to Rome. I'm currently studying abroad there, but if we ever happen to run into each other again, I'm sure I can use another distraction."

"Consider it a deal."

"Thanks, Carson. You made my first one night stand an enjoyable experience," she says, smiling at me once more as she reaches for the door handle. She gives me one last lingering stare before pulling the door open. "Enjoy the rest of your night."

I watch her as she disappears through the doorway, leaving me alone in the office without another word. I'd enjoy the rest of my night a little more if I got to spend it still buried inside of her, but goddamn, I cannot complain one bit about what just happened. I know virtually nothing about her and I can't help but wish I knew more.

What a shame this was limited to a one night thing. We could have had a lot of fun.

Leaning back, my hands land on the desk and I feel the soft material beneath my palm. A smile dances across my lips as I lift it into the air and realize what I'm holding.

Her underwear.

A soft chuckle escapes me as I tuck them into my front pocket. At some point tonight, she's going to notice they're missing and they'll be long gone by then.

I exit through the same door and push my way through the mass of people that hasn't thinned at all until I finally make my way to the front of the building. The bouncers nod as I slip outside, walking to the curb as I pull out my phone to get an Uber. I secure a car and lift my gaze from my phone just as another vehicle pulls up a few feet away.

My heart pounds in my chest as I see Andi striding towards it. Just as she's about to lower herself into the car, her gaze meets mine. Eyes locked, her lips lift into a smirk and we share a moment, the particles crackling between us through the cool night air.

I could walk over and try to get in the car with her, but I don't. Tipping my chin, I nod at her once more, bidding her goodbye with her thong tucked in the front pocket of my pants. Andi's gaze lingers once more before she lifts her hand to give me a small wave.

She gets into the car, pulling the door closed behind her, and there's a pause before the vehicle begins to pull away from the curb, easing onto the street. She was only looking for a distraction and I was more than happy to give her exactly what she wanted. I've never been one to look for anything more than a hookup.

She was just a passing moment in time, but I know she's one I'm not likely to forget.

CHAPTER ONE

CARSON

PRESENT

S kating over to the boards, my blades cut through the ice as I come to a half stop and hop up the step to make my way down the tunnel and into the locker room. My brother Caleb is hot on my heels, anger radiating from him, but he doesn't speak a single word to me. I'm the reason we lost tonight. I got in Rowan's way and he wasn't able to see past me. My stick wasn't down on the ice and I couldn't block the shot that moved right past me, tucking into the right side of the net.

We're down to the wire right now. Playoffs are starting in two weeks. Even though we have a good position in the bracket going into it, we still can't afford to lose any games. Losing means we don't get points and if the other teams end up inching past us, we could potentially get bumped out.

The air in the locker room is a bit tense, but it begins

to dissipate as some of the guys start to talk, their chattering filling the void in the room.

I pull off my jersey and toss it onto the bench before reaching down to untie my skates. Once down to my jock pants, I rise to my feet and survey my teammates in various stages of undress around the locker room. I pause on my brother Caleb, who is also our captain. His furrowed brow and clenched jaw while he removes his gear lets me know he's lost in thought. I avoid his gaze, instead moving on to Lincoln Matthews and Nash Simmons, two of my closest friends who both play for the Archers.

Then finally settling on Rowan Taylor, our goalie and my best friend, who is staring down at the floor, sitting with his elbows propped on his knees and head resting in his hands. Loses are never good on any of our spirits and I know how heavily they weigh on him. He doesn't talk much about it, but it's next to impossible for him to not take on the brunt of the blame. He's the last line of defense to stop pucks from getting into the net.

But tonight—that was all me.

Rowan lifts his gaze to meet mine when I stop in front of him. Disappointment swirls in his irises and I immediately feel guilt for costing the entire team the game. He's blaming himself for it, but I need him to know that it wasn't his fault.

"I'm sorry about tonight, Ro," I tell him. My hand finds his shoulder and I give him a soft squeeze. Beside Rowan, Nash raises an eyebrow at me as I shuffle inch by inch into the small space between them, forcing him to scoot over to make a spot for me. I drop down onto the bench, my hand releasing Rowan's shoulder. "That was my fuckup. I was in your way and they used me as a screen."

"It happens," he tells me with a shrug, although I can see that it's not that simple. "Don't beat yourself up over it. I should have been able to stop it."

I shake my head at him, eyebrows lowering. "There's no way you could have stopped it if you couldn't see it coming." I pause, letting out a sigh, knowing my efforts here are futile. Rowan is still going to have his own thoughts regardless of what I tell him. "I just wanted to apologize again. It wasn't your fault and I don't want you to spend the rest of the night blaming yourself."

He tilts his head to the side, a ghost of a smile on his lips. "Thanks, kid." A shadow passes over us and I turn my head, catching my brother's eye as he looms over us.

"It was just one loss," Caleb says, his voice low as he directs his attention to Rowan. "Don't let it get you down, Taylor. Like Carsy said, he was in your way." He gives me a hardened stare. "We just have to make sure we do better next game and not fuck it up again."

The entire room falls silent as Caleb speaks and nothing about it is unusual. He's a natural leader and something about his presence demands everyone's attention. The way he leads and sets an example made him the perfect candidate for our team captain, and he's been holding that position for the past four years.

"Thanks, Ford." Rowan tips his chin at my brother

before glancing at me. "I know you didn't do it on purpose. We're both at fault, really."

I nod at him, but my brother interjects before I get a chance to speak. "None of this negative shit," he scolds the two of us. "Pick yourselves up and do better. That's all any of us can do."

Caleb changed when he lost his wife, Amelia, in a tragic car accident, leaving him and their infant daughter behind. Caleb's had his fair share of struggles, but ever since that night, there's a hardness to him that wasn't there before. He's always been a bit standoffish, even as kids, but now his guard is always in place.

He refuses to let anyone get too close.

"You're right," I agree, rising back to my feet as I stand toe to toe with my brother. There's a two year gap between the two of us, but the similarities in our features and height could have us passing as twins. "It won't happen again. I promise I won't let you guys down."

Caleb stares at me for a long moment, his gaze locked on mine before he shifts to Rowan and then around the room, and dives into a speech, trying to lift the spirits in the room. I make my way back to my area, tuning into Caleb's words. By the time he wraps it up, the entire room is chanting and hooting and hollering. I head to the showers with a smile dancing across my lips, the renewed energy practically vibrating within me.

Negativity will only bring us down further. We have to stand together and push through.

It's the only way we'll succeed.

———

I head back to my house alone, stopping to grab takeout on the way, just as I do almost every night. I grab my mail from the mailbox before stepping into the foyer. The door shuts on its own behind me and I make sure to lock it as I kick off my shoes.

The low hum of the refrigerator is my only companion as I step into the kitchen and flip on the overhead light. I set down the bag of food on the island and head to the fridge for a bottle of water.

There are times I wish I wasn't coming home to an empty house. The other guys go back to their homes where they have their partners and families. But not me.

It's always just me . . . alone.

I settle into the silence of the evening, the silence of my home. It's lonely at times, but I know this is how things are meant to be for me. Attachments were messy, it's just easier this way. There's no expectation anyone else is holding me too, and there's no one here to disappoint.

I've given everything to hockey and there's no way I could ever put another person ahead of that.

Hockey is my life.

And I'm meant to live it alone.

CHAPTER TWO

ANDI

"Are you sure you don't want me to come with you?"

Pushing my bag to the side, I make space for my brother, Vincent, to set the other one down beside it. I slowly stand upright, straightening my spine as I glance at him. The sun feels so good on my bare skin, the warmth a stark contrast to the cool spring breeze that drifts around us. "I think I should be okay."

"If you change your mind or decide you need any help, let me know," he tells me, a gentle smile lifting his lips. His dark brown eyes shimmer. "I'm always just a phone call away."

I appreciate the sentiment behind my brother's words, but I would never ask him to drop his life to come help me. Honestly, I'm not particularly happy about having to drop my own to go to Aston to take care of our Aunt Bella's estate, but I'm the one she left everything to.

After a long, hard battle with cancer, Aunt Bella's

last few months were spent in hospice care. Our mother went and stayed with Bella, her twin, so she wasn't alone, but it wasn't as easy for the rest of us to be there the whole time. Aunt Bella never married and never had any kids, so Vince and I were the closest thing she had to children.

Unwelcome tears spring to my eyes as the memory of her swirls around in my brain. It's been a good three months since we lost her and as much as it sucks, we've all had to move on with our lives. Bella wasn't ready to go, but she lived a good life and made peace with things before she passed on. I take comfort in knowing that she's no longer in pain and maybe one day we'll meet again.

"I still don't know why she left everything to me and not to you," I tell Vince, running my tongue across my top teeth as we turn back toward the house. Vince is the one who has been constant, not me. I left halfway through college for Rome and never intended on looking back. I ended up moving back home a little over five years ago, not long before Matteo was born.

Since moving back to Starling Ridge, it's never quite felt like where I'm supposed to be. I made the decision not to finish my master's degree in Rome and instead did it virtually while juggling the early years of motherhood.

I wouldn't have been able to do it without the support of my family. My parents have a small guest house on their property where Matteo and I live. I've had plans for the two of us moving out, but our current situation has been working out so far. Matteo is close to his grandparents and gets to see them frequently, while we still have our own privacy.

Eventually, I know things will have to change, but for now, I'm comfortable. I have a good job working for a historical foundation and Matteo will be starting kindergarten in the fall. The quiet and simple life I've built for us brings with it a sense of contentment.

Which is why the thought of upending our lives to head to Aston for the next few months is not exactly appealing. The plan is to stay at Aunt Bella's house so I can clean it out and see what improvements need to be made. Then I will oversee everything, making sure that it's ready to sell, and then that will be it. The house will be put on the market and I'll come back home to Starling Ridge.

"She left everything to you because you were always her favorite," Vince reminds me playfully as he bumps his shoulder against mine. "I wasn't as close to her and you know that."

"I know, but it just seems weird. You have a little more flexibility to move around."

He tilts his head to the side. Vincent works at the local university as an English professor, but he hasn't yet found anyone to settle down with. He's always claimed he prefers the solitude of being single. He doesn't have to worry about anyone but himself.

"I think she wanted to help you. It's her way of leaving something for you and Matteo." He pauses, rolling his lips between his teeth before releasing them. "She knows you don't need any help, but it's just her way of feeling like she's not abandoning you, you know?"

Emotion wells in my throat and I swallow hard in an effort to push it back down inside as I give him a curt nod. Pulling my gaze away from my brother, I glance at the house and spy Matteo sitting on the back of the couch, watching us through the window. I wave at him, before motioning for him to come outside.

He lights up, a smile breaking out across his innocent face as he treats the couch like a trampoline, then disappears from the window. He's my little bud. The sweetest little guy. He has a huge heart and is always so curious and inquisitive. He was an unexpected surprise who threw a little bit of a wrench in my life, but I can't imagine what it would look like without him now.

He's my entire heart.

"Hey, little man!" Vince calls out to my son as he comes bounding through the front door. He scoops him up into his arms, digging his fingers against his ribs, his smile stretching wide as Matteo wiggles against him, kicking his feet as a string of laughter escapes him. "One last tickle attack before you leave!"

"No! No!" Matteo giggles loudly, kicking his feet with vigor. "Stop, Uncle Vinny!"

"Okay, okay," Vincent laughs, immediately stopping when Matteo tells him to. He shifts my son in his arms, giving him a gentle squeeze before setting him back down on his feet. He crouches down to get on his level. "Your mom is going to need you to be good while you guys are away. Can you do that?"

Matteo straightens his spine, pushing back his

shoulders in an attempt to appear older and more mature. "Yes, sir," he says, bobbing his head. "I will be on my best behavior."

"You help her with whatever she needs help with, okay?"

"I will," he assures him, smiling at my brother. Matteo may only be five, but he's wise beyond his years. He's like an old, gentle soul. I wouldn't expect him to be anything but good. He has a very even temperament and normally doesn't misbehave. I really did get lucky with him, except for those horrid few months when he turned three.

I'm fairly certain the only word he knew then was "no."

Vince pats him on the head before rising back to stand in front of me. "Safe drive, little sis," he says softly, pulling me in for a hug. "Like I already said, if you need anything, call me. After the semester is over, I'll be off for the summer months since I decided to take a break."

"I think we will be able to manage, but I will let you know for sure."

Vince walks over to my car, opening the backdoor for Matteo. He climbs into his booster seat and straps himself in. I lean into the car, giving it a double check before pressing my lips to the top of his head.

"Let me know when you get there, okay?"

I move away from the car, Matteo giving Vince a final wave before I shut the door and turn to face my brother. "I will," I smile at him, shaking my head. "You weren't this concerned when I moved to a different country for a few years."

Aston is only a few hours from here and since we're leaving early enough in the day, we have time to swing by the grocery store on the way to Aunt Bella's house.

"Yeah, well, you didn't have Matteo then," he tells me with a shrug as he focuses on the car behind me. Vince is only three years older than me and we've always been close, but he's right. Things have been different since Matteo was born. He's back to being my overprotective brother, watching out for the two of us now.

"Fair enough." I give his cheek a little pat before walking to the driver's side, pulling open the door, and climbing inside. I look back at my brother one last time, giving him a soft smile. "Love you. I'll call you when we get there."

"Love you too." He directs his attention back to the backseat, giving Matteo a huge wave. "Bye, little man!"

I know this separation is only temporary, but leaving hurts my chest right now. Perhaps it has nothing to do with the place I'm leaving and everything to do with where I'm headed.

My Aunt Bella's house isn't the only daunting thing in Aston.

CHAPTER THREE

CARSON

My eyebrows lower in suspicion as I cock my head to the side. Why are there so many varieties of instant mac and cheese and mashed potatoes? I'm supposed to be going to Lincoln and Nova's for our first friends' dinner. It's something Riley and Nova decided they want us all to do once a month.

The only kicker is, it's supposed to be a potluck situation and I can't make ramen noodles without turning them to mush.

Pulling out my phone, I take a quick glance at the group text, realizing none of the guys were in charge of food. I see Rowan's name and tap on it. I trap it between my ear and my shoulder as I pull off a box of instant mashed potatoes to read the instructions. The ringing stops like he answered, but I'm greeted with silence.

"Did you talk to anyone about food tonight? No one said anything about what they were bringing and I was going to just bring mashed potatoes. Can I bring instant ones or will that be weird?" I ask, pursing my lips in contemplation. "I don't think anyone would be able to tell that they're not real."

There's still silence and I'm wondering if Rowan even actually answered my call. I set down the box, release my phone from my shoulder, and hold it out in front of me. It's connected.

"Hello? Did you fucking hang up on me?"

"No, Ford," he mutters in response, his voice seemingly disinterested.

"What are you and Hadley bringing? Did she talk to Nova or Riley at all about food?"

Silence again.

"Rowan?"

"Hadley isn't coming tonight." Rowan sighs, his voice trailing off at the end.

"Oh, is she sick or something?" I corkscrew my lips, shuffling down the aisle as I lean forward to inspect the boxes of pasta closer. I'm not so sure I should show up with instant mashed potatoes, but maybe something similar would suffice. Carb for carb, right?

"No." The word is vacant and flat as it comes through the speaker.

"Then why won't she be there?" I question him as I stand upright again, glancing around the aisle, not sure why the hell they put any expectation on someone like me.

"Ford."

My brain is still hung up on the food situation and I

don't even register what he said. "Can I just get a pasta salad from the deli counter or something?"

"Carson Ford."

"What?" I respond, holding my phone against my ear as I pause in the aisle, standing in front of the mac and cheese section again.

"I don't give a flying fuck what you bring to Lincoln and Nova's tonight. I don't plan on going."

My eyebrows pull together. "What? The girls are insistent on making this a thing." I let out a deep sigh, rolling my eyes in frustration. "You don't get to get out of this. You have to go tonight and if Hadley isn't sick, she should probably come too."

"Hadley can't come because she fucking left." He mutters a curse under his breath. "I just dropped her off at the airport and she'll be on a flight to California in an hour."

My entire body falls rigid. "You let her leave?"

"What the fuck was I supposed to do, Ford? Beg her to stay?"

"Umm, yes, you idiot." This time when I roll my eyes, it's because I can't reach through my phone and smack him. "If you love her, you can't let her go."

"I can't ask her to stay, Carson. She has plans, she has a life to live. I can't ask her to stay here when I can't give her the relationship she deserves."

I'm silent for a second as I chew on his words. "I'm confused why you think you can't give her what she deserves . . ."

He lets out a harsh breath. "My schedule is far too demanding and we're gone so often. I don't want her to be with me and feel like I just want her around to take care of Lucy."

Man, he really is dumber than I thought.

"Rowan, she already knows and understands your schedule." I pause, trying to figure out how to go over this without telling him he's stupid. "If you don't want her to feel that way, then don't make her feel that way. Tell her how you feel, tell her you want her here because you want *her*."

"It's too late," he mumbles after a beat or two of silence. "She's already in the airport and probably heading to her gate."

"Where are you?" I ask him, shifting my weight on my feet as I absentmindedly survey the boxes of mac and cheese again.

"Sitting in a drop-off area outside of the airport."

I thought he had more than two brain cells, but now I feel like I'm talking to a replica of my own brain.

"Rowan . . . bro. Seriously, what the fuck are you doing?"

"I was getting ready to come home but Lucy started crying, so I pulled over and then you called—" He rambles, his explanation a continuous string of words, but I abruptly cut him off.

"Turn the hell around and go get her. You cannot let her get on that plane," I whisper shout at him. "You need to find her and tell her how you feel, and then it's up to her whether she decides to go or not."

"I don't want to sway her decision."

Good Lord. How the hell can he not see what's right

in front of his face? It's clear as day that Hadley is in love with him. I sigh again. "Do you love her?"

"Yes."

"Have you told her that?" I question him again.

"No."

"Well, then, she's not making a well-informed decision, is she?" I say, shaking my head at how ridiculous this is. If he would have just communicated with her, this all could have potentially been avoided.

I also know how important Hadley has become to my best friend, and the last thing I'm going to do is let him fuck this up.

"Here is what you're going to do—you're going to go into the airport, buy a fucking bullshit ticket to wherever the hell the next plane is going, get through security, and find her. You're going to find her and you're not going to let her be the one who got away, do you understand me?"

Something pulls on my pocket. No, someone. I glance down at the small child tugging on my shorts, tilting my head to the side. His gray eyes meet mine as he gives me a sheepish grin. "Excuse me, mister."

"Oh, shit, hold on, Ro," I say into the speaker, smiling down at the little boy who doesn't look to be older than five. "What's up, little man?"

"Does this have milk in it?" He holds up a box of instant mac and cheese, trying to show it to me. "Milk makes my belly hurt but I wanted to show Mommy I can pick out my own all by myself."

"Well, let's see." I take the box from his small hand, and scan the list of ingredients. When I realize it's a gluten-free type, but not a vegan one, I frown. "Yeah, bud, this one has milk. Let's see if we can find one without it."

"You're right, Ford," Rowan's voice comes through the speaker. "I'm being a fucking idiot and I'm turning around right now. I'm going back to the airport and I'm not letting her go without telling her the truth."

"Wait, say that again." I drop one of the boxes I find on the shelf that says it's vegan. "Shit," I mumble, crouching down to pick it up. "Here, buddy. This one says it's vegan, so that means it doesn't have any milk in it." He reaches out with his left hand to take it from mine.

"That I'm going back to the airport?" Rowan asks, the confusion evident in his voice.

"No, the part where you said I was right," I chuckle, watching the kid as he tries to read the back of the box.

"Oh my god, there you are, *caro*."

My entire body falls rigid, my heart stalling in my chest. That voice—my god, I know that voice . . .

Lifting my gaze from the little boy, I'm momentarily transported back in time when my eyes collide with hers. Those gold and green eyes that have been swirling around in my mind since that one night almost six years ago. "Andi?"

"Carson." Her eyes widen with recognition, and a flush creeps up her cheeks as she tucks a lock of chocolate-colored hair behind her ear. "Hi."

My throat constricts as I look between her and the little boy, him smiling up at me with gray eyes that now seem eerily familiar. Panic passes across her expression, her hazel eyes locked on me as I connect the dots in real time. His hair isn't black like hers, but instead it's a dark brown, a few shades lighter.

There's no fucking way . . .

"Rowan, I'm going to have to call you back," I tell him, my voice sounding foreign and distant as my gaze settles on Andi's.

Her slender throat bobs as she swallows hard, her hand finding her son's opposite shoulder as she pulls him flush against her body, as if to protect him. He holds on to the box of mac and cheese, lifting it with his left hand for her to see.

None of this is making sense in my brain right now.

"Yeah, sure. Thank you for your help, bro," he says, the words not even registering in my mind as I pull the phone away from my ear without ending the call.

I cock my head to the side, looking back at the boy again, my stomach feeling like it's going to fall onto the fucking floor. "What's your name, little man?"

"Matteo," he says, his eyes bright and a grin spreading across his face. "What's your name?"

"Matteo, *caro.*" Andi's voice is soft and gentle as she directs her gaze to her son. "We should stop bothering Mr. Carson and let him get back to his shopping."

Mr. Carson.

I resist the urge to scoff at her formality. She says my name like she wasn't screaming it the last time I saw her.

"I'm Carson," I answer, ignoring Andi's interjection. It's been almost six years since we last saw each other. My heart is unsteady in my chest as I slowly ask him the next question. "How old are you, Matteo?"

His smile grows as he lifts his hand to show me his fingers, all spread apart. "Five!"

My eyes flash to Andi who inhales sharply. Her eyes widen as guilt, remorse and shame immediately flood her expression.

What. The. Actual. Fuck.

CHAPTER FOUR

ANDI

I'm frozen in place. The only thing moving is my heart pounding against my ribcage like it's trying to escape. My lungs refuse to work properly, and goddamn, I cannot get my brain to send the message to my legs that we need to get the hell out of here.

I knew coming to Aston was like rolling the dice on whether or not I would end up running into Carson Ford. After the night we hooked up, an easy search on the internet with his first name and location showed me a picture of his stupid, perfect face.

And the photo was straight from the roster of the Aston Archers.

Star defensemen for one of the best professional hockey teams in the country. I'm no stranger to the sport, since my brother played when we were growing up, but it wasn't something that ever really interested me. I learned how to figure skate and competed when I was younger, but when I left for college, I hung up my skates.

My life became busy with other things and I kissed skating goodbye. Now my time on the ice is pretty limited to when there's a pop up rink in the winter time or if I go out with any friends who can barely even skate.

When I discovered who Carson was, I realized I needed to try and reach out to him, but it was virtually impossible. I sent him a message on every social media platform, only to have my message sitting in his requests inbox. Finding an address for him was impossible and the same with a working phone number. It's like he had any way of discovering him scrubbed from the internet, which isn't surprising, given his status as a professional athlete.

There was no way for me to get a hold of him.

There was no way for me to tell him that I was having his baby.

I watch Carson for a moment, aware of what he's finding as he searches Matteo's features. The steel gray eyes that are an exact mirror of his own. The brown hair, somewhere between his shade and mine. The little boy is a perfect combination of both of our features.

"Well, it was very nice to meet you, Matteo," Carson smiles at him, still scanning my little boy's face as he holds his left hand out to shake Matteo's. Carson braces his hands on his knees and pushes himself back to his full height, the smile drifting away from his lips as his gaze collides with mine. "So, Trouble . . . What brings you back to Aston?"

Setting my basket down, I hand Matteo my phone, which is something I normally hate to do, but I have no idea where this conversation is about to go. "Here, *caro*," I say, opening up the app with kids videos on it. "I'm just going to talk to Mr. Carson for a few minutes and then we'll go."

"Okay, Mom," he smiles cheerfully, always agreeable, as he takes my phone and turns it sideways to watch the numbers that come dancing across the screen.

"My aunt lived here," I explain as I nervously shift my weight from one foot to the other. "She passed away a few months ago and left her estate to me. I'm staying here until the house is ready to sell."

His eyes are trained on mine, slowly nodding as he takes in my words. "I'm sorry for your loss," he says with an apology hanging in his tone. Sadness washing over his eyes before it vanishes quicker than it came. "As tragic as it is, I'm glad it brought you back to Aston. I wasn't sure I'd run into you again."

Heat creeps up my neck, blooming across my face as my mind is momentarily thrust back in time, back to that night with him in the club. "You're a hard man to track down."

The corners of his mouth twitch, his head cocking to the side. "You tried?"

Shit.

My throat bobs as I swallow over a dry lump, not sure what the heck I'm supposed to say. Is this the moment when I spill the truth? Where I tell him that I got pregnant that night and he has a five year old son? I can't tell if he's actually connected the dots or if he just had a second of doubt, where he questioned the possibility but ultimately waved it away because it's a terrifying possibility.

"I did," I admit, my voice soft so little ears don't hear as I glance at Matteo then back at Carson. "A few months after we saw each other."

Eyes cemented on mine slowly widen, his body becomes rigid. Shades of dark and light gray swirl in his irises as his drag back and forth between mine, almost as if he's searching for an answer. "If—" He pauses, his brows knitted with frustration as he lets out a breath. "We were together around the—"

He pauses again. I can't tell if it's frustration or torment written in his expression now, but this is the exact moment I've been dreading. This is him fitting the pieces together and doing the math. Despite his gaze locked on mine, his eyes are distant, like he's looking right through me.

I watch in real time as he thinks back on the night we were together. As he figures out how long ago that was versus how old Matteo told him he is. I'm not sure how much he knows about how pregnancy works and when due dates are calculated, but his eyes begin to focus on mine again, as if he's being drawn back into the current moment.

"This might be a wild question to ask." He pauses again, his brow furrows, a crease appears between them. His chest expands as he sucks in a deep breath, a shaky sound escaping him as he blows it back out. "Is he mine?"

There it is.

The question that holds a weight he doesn't even

know about. A weight I've been carrying around on my chest for the past six years since finding out I was pregnant and having no way to get in touch with Carson.

I need to be honest with him. He deserves to know the truth. Yet with that truth comes a lot of unknowns. A lot of scary things that I'm not so sure I'm ready to deal with yet. There are repercussions to every single one of our actions and this is the moment everything has led us to.

I'm a true believer in fate, yet I'm not sure how I feel about this chance encounter. This is what was meant to happen. This is how we were supposed to find each other again. This is how Carson Ford finds out he has a son he never knew about.

"Yes."

Our surroundings completely fade away. Carson doesn't move. He doesn't make a sound. His expression is fucking frozen and I can't help but wonder if I just broke him. He stares at me, his eyes not once leaving mine. I'm not so sure he even blinks.

"How do you know?"

I glance down at Matteo, who is completely oblivious to what's happening around him. I'm thankful for that because normally he would be fully engaged in the conversation, absorbing every single word like a little sponge.

"The timeline of everything," I tell him, keeping my voice low. "I hadn't been with anyone else around the same time and there was no one else after."

His eyes narrow on mine, his eyebrows lowering. "What about your ex?"

I'm shocked he even remembers that part of the equation. When I met Carson, I had just found out about my ex's engagement announcement. Maybe he has it all confused and thought I was with him around the same time. "We were broken up for close to a year when I met you." I pause, tilting my head to the side. "I hadn't been with him since then."

The muscle in Carson's jaw twitches, his Adam's apple bobbing as he swallows hard. His expression relaxes, but only enough to let the torment completely consume his features. Lifting a hand, he rakes it through his hair, partially tugging on his tousled locks as he tips his head back. His eyelids flutter shut, his black lashes grazing the tops of his cheek bones as he lets out a ragged breath. *Why do men also get the perfect long lashes?*

He straightens his spine, his head flips back upright as his eyes pop open again. "Fuck."

I stare back at him, not sure of what to say because I think he just covered everything with that very valid response. Fuck is right.

"Why didn't you come back to Aston? Why didn't you come find me and tell me?"

My heart stalls in my chest, a familiar guilt washing over me as he fires the questions at me, one right after the other. Swiveling my head, I glance around, realizing we're no longer the only ones in this aisle. "Can we not do this here?"

"Then where would you like to do this, Andi?" His voice is gruff, anger weaving itself through his words. "I'm sorry," he mutters, shaking his head as he drops his gaze down to the floor for a beat. "This is just . . . it's just—" His tongue darts out to wet his lips, his eyes filled with pain and conflict as they meet mine again. "It's a lot to process" He shrugs, giving me an apologetic smile. "You know?"

I get it. Maybe not to the same extreme as what he's feeling right now, but I understand.

"When are you free?"

"I'll clear my whole fucking schedule." His face is set in a neutral state, no smile or scowl, no anger or even sadness. It's as if he's shut off the part of his brain that feels emotions and is just focused on the business at hand.

"That's not necessary, Carson." I shake my head at him, the guilt piling up inside my chest. My lungs don't expand like I need them to and it feels like the walls of the store are creeping closer. "You don't need to stop your life."

His eyes are unreadable as he stares at me, the silence stretching. His nostrils widen as he runs his tongue over his top teeth. He breaks our star down first; his gaze drifts to Matteo before flashing back to mine. "Does he know?"

Drawing my bottom lip between my teeth, I bite down and shake my head at him. Matteo brought it up a few months ago, when he was starting to understand the world moving around him. His preschool had Dad's day and he was confused when the other men showed up and no one showed up for him. I've been able to field his questions, giving him minimal information.

When he asked about his dad and why he didn't

have one in his life, I just told him that he lived far away. He's far too young for me to tell him the truth and thankfully, he hasn't asked many questions since.

"I'm supposed to be at practice in an hour." Carson shifts his weight, clearly uncomfortable with his emotions and feelings creating chaos in his mind. The conflict is evident on his face and he speaks like he's considering finding a way to get out of it.

Him derailing his entire life is not going to be good for anyone.

"Did you want to come by after you're done?" I ask him, offering it as a solution, that way he doesn't end up missing practice. "We can talk about everything then."

He's silent for a beat, his eyes slowly searching mine. For a moment, he's caught in a daze before he snaps out of it. His head bobs up and down. "Okay, let's do that." He reaches into his pocket, pulling his phone back out. "What's your number? I'll text you and you can send me the address then."

I recite the number to him, watching as he types it in. A sound chimes from where Matteo is still standing, holding mine. He looks up at me, a smile dancing across his lips. "Here, Mom," he says, holding my phone to me. "You got a message."

"Thanks, *caro*. I'll look at it later." I look back at Carson and find nothing but the torment and pain he can no longer hold back as he watches Matteo and me carefully. "We'll see you later this afternoon then?"

Carson's attention snaps back to me, his lips parting as if he's going to say something, but instead, he rolls them between his teeth, biting back whatever words he almost spoke. "Okay," he nods, his voice barely audible. "See you then."

He lingers for a moment, studying us as I hold my hand out for Matteo. He slips his little palm against mine, wrapping his fingers around the side of my hand as I lead him in the opposite direction. I can still feel Carson's gaze on my back and it's like I carry it with me as Matteo and I continue on through the store.

I move on autopilot through the rest of our shopping trip and before I know it, I'm sitting behind the wheel of my car, staring at Matteo through the rearview mirror. It's been six years since I've seen Carson and that man has aged like the finest of wines. He looks a bit older but his features are still the same.

And as I study Matteo through the mirror, it's clear to see there was never any denying of who his father is. I've known it all along, but after comparing the two of them side by side, it's as plain as day.

Matteo *is* Carson Ford's son.

CHAPTER FIVE

CARSON

My skates cut through the ice, the edges of my blades shaving the top layer as I come to a halt next to my brother. I can feel his stare on the side of my face. "What's going on with you today, Cars? Something is up."

What the hell am I supposed to tell him? I set out this morning to grab something for dinner tonight and ended up leaving with the knowledge of potentially being a father.

This entire time, the woman I've been hung up on had a kid and I didn't even know about it.

"I—" my voice trails off, which is becoming a common trend today. It seems as though I cannot form a coherent thought or sentence to save my life. "Nothing's going on," I lie, the words bitter on my tongue as I shake my head at him. "I'm good."

He raises an eyebrow at me, pursing his lips with disapproval. My older brother knows me better than anyone else. He knows when I'm lying and can tell when I'm not good. "You're playing like shit. Our first playoff game is in two days, so you need to get your head out of your ass."

I nod, my chin dipping towards my chest and up again. He's not wrong. I missed every single shot I took today and got knocked on my ass multiple times. We need to be performing our best right now and I didn't do that today. It was only practice, but I know I let the team down and I can't have that happen during our playoff run.

Caleb leaves me where I'm standing on the ice and he begins to follow the rest of the guys to the door. When he gets a few feet away, my feet move. I don't know what the hell I'm going to tell him, but I need to talk to someone about this. It's eating away at me and it's only been three fucking hours since I ran into Andi and her son.

"Cale, wait," I call out to my brother, using the nickname I've used for him since we were kids, slowing to a glide when I reach him. "Can we talk after we get changed?"

He turns his head to the side, his all too familiar gray eyes meet mine as he gives me a single nod. "I'll meet you in the car park." He doesn't wait up for me as he heads off the ice, all of us making our way back to the locker room.

My brother isn't an asshole, he just has a rough exterior. He's always been very direct and to the point. He doesn't beat around the bush and he's a pretty simple person. When he lost Amelia a few years ago, he really struggled to get himself together. He was left with an infant daughter to raise alone and it really forced him to come out of his comfort zone a bit.

He's never been one to accept help from other people but when his life was turned upside down, he had no other choice. Everyone rallied around him, helping him navigate the different territory he was thrust into. There's a softness to him, but it's mostly only reserved for my niece. Tella is that man's heart and soul.

I don't imagine he'll ever get involved with someone else again, which is probably for the best for him. It takes a lot for Caleb to open up and even then, there's still a part of him he always keeps guarded. I see right through his bullshit, just like he sees right through mine.

Which is exactly why I know I need to talk to him about my current situation.

I'm the last in the locker room and find my spot as everyone's already stripping free from their gear. Nash and Lincoln are sitting next to each other, talking about whatever their women have planned for dinner tonight. I tune both of them out, making my way next to Rowan, who's removing his goalie pads.

I haven't talked to him since earlier this morning when I abruptly ended the call with him. "How did it go with Hadley?"

Hadley is his girlfriend or fake fiancée . . . or real fiancée? Hell, I don't even know what she is at this point. She's been living with him the past few months while he was sorting out custody of his daughter and adjusting to life as a new single dad. This morning,

Hadley was supposed to be getting on a flight to California for her next nursing assignment and Rowan finally had a come-to-Jesus moment where he realized he's madly in love with her.

It's been clear to everyone except for the two of them apparently.

"It didn't take much convincing," he admits with a smirk as he tips his head in my direction. "Really, it was just a big misunderstanding between both of us and it could have been avoided if we would have just told each other our feelings."

"Well, duh," I laugh, shaking my head at him after untying my skates. I slide my feet out, strip off my socks, and I stretch my toes. "I could have told you that."

"What happened to you at the store?"

Shit. I forgot about that part of our interaction earlier. "Um, there was just some kid who needed help." I shake my head in an attempt to dismiss the thoughts that push to the forefront of my mind. It's not just some kid . . . he might be *my* kid.

"Did you find what you needed for tonight?"

I shrug with indifference as I start to take off the rest of my gear. "No. I'll figure something out, if I end up going."

Rowan raises an eyebrow at me. "You gave me shit earlier about not going and now you're thinking about bowing out?"

I stare at Rowan for a moment, contemplating how many lies I should tell my best friend. As soon as I know the truth, I'll have to tell everyone else. I don't want to dig myself into too much of a hole right now.

My lips part and just as I'm about to give him an explanation, Caleb steps in front of me. I close my mouth, directing my attention to my brother instead. He's already changed and in his street clothes. "You ready?" he asks, his eyes surveying my half dressed body.

"Give me two minutes."

He nods and doesn't say anything. Instead, he crosses his arms over his chest, almost as if he's standing guard while I finish getting undressed. Rowan leaves the whole grocery store thing alone and when he finishes changing, he stands up and looks back at me again. "Text me later to let me know about tonight."

"Sounds good."

He walks over to Lincoln and Nash, saying something to the two of them before half rushing out of the room. Our lives are about to get insane with playoffs and I'm sure he wants to go spend time with Hadley and his daughter Lucy before we're cut off from the rest of the world. Lincoln and Nash aren't far behind him and I know Caleb would be doing the same if I hadn't told him I wanted to talk to him before we left.

Caleb waits until I'm ready and then we both head out to the parking lot together. It's not until we're at Caleb's car before either of us talk about anything that isn't hockey related.

"So, what's going on?" Caleb starts as he pulls open his car door and motions to the passenger's side. "Get in, we can talk in the car."

Nodding, I follow suit and we both get into the car before I respond. "I went to the grocery store today and ran into this woman I slept with a few years ago." I pause as he stares at me, giving me a look like he's not surprised by anything I'm admitting. He's waiting for me to get to the point. "She has a kid and based on the timelines, she would have gotten pregnant right around the same time we hooked up."

"Did she say it's yours?"

I swallow hard. "Yeah."

His eyes widen and he turns his head to stare out the windshield for a few moments. The silence stretches between us as he slowly turns on his car, his hands resting on the steering wheel. "Did she just come out and tell you?"

"No," I tell him, glancing out the window on my side as a few employees exit the arena. "I asked her after I started to put two and two together, after I saw him. She confirmed after I questioned her on it."

Caleb turns to look at me. "And you think it's your kid?"

I let out a breath, running a hand through my hair as I think back to my interactions with Matteo. His eyes. The hair color. His dominant hand was clearly his left, which is the same as me. Andi's right handed and dexterity is hereditary. The way there's a slight curve towards the end of his nose. My chest deflates, my heart racing inside my chest. "He looks like a Ford, Cale."

He's silent before letting out a sigh. "Shit," he mumbles, a frown tugging his lips downwards. "You're going to have to get a paternity test."

"Is that really necessary?" I nervously lace my fingers together, cracking my knuckles as I stare at my older brother, looking for some kind of direction. "I mean, if everything adds up and makes sense—and the fact that he looks just like we did when we were five."

"Do you know this woman other than the night you decided to sleep with her?"

I wince at his words that come out harsher than he probably intended. "No, I don't."

"Well, then I guess it depends on whether or not you want to take the word of a stranger or get a definitive answer." He closes his eyes, rubbing his temple like this is stressing him out. "If it were me, I would want a paternity test. You have to think about custody and child support and all the messy things that come along with having a child with someone you aren't with."

He shrugs his shoulders, an apologetic look washing over his expression. "You have to be smart about it and not be emotional. You don't know this woman and she could easily be trying to trap you for money or god knows what, especially with you being a professional athlete."

"If it had to do with money, don't you think she would have shown up sooner?"

Caleb raises an eyebrow at me. "Remember, you don't know her, Carson. You don't know what her motives are."

"So, I need to assume the worst until I'm proven otherwise?"

I don't like the way that sounds. It's not how I operate, but I know it's how my brother does. If I just assume that she's out to get me in some way, this won't go well at all. He's right with being smart and not acting from emotion, but I have to give her some benefit of the doubt.

"Not necessarily," he tells me, lifting his shoulders again. "Just stay vigilant and guarded." He shakes his head at me, snorting with disbelief as he stares at me. "And get a goddamn paternity test, for fuck's sake."

"I'm supposed to go over to her place now to talk to her about everything," I tell him as I unlace my hands and let them sit loosely in my lap. "How the hell do I bring something like that up?"

Caleb stares at me for a second before his face cracks. It isn't often that he laughs like this and I revel in the moment and the sound coming from my brother, even if he is laughing at my expense. "You have to tell her you want one." His face settles back into his stern, older brother look. "I know you, Carson. I know you don't like to be in uncomfortable and confrontational situations like this, but you should have thought about that when you decided to sleep with someone without using a condom."

"You don't know that," I argue, even though I don't have a damn leg to stand on. "Maybe we did use a condom and it broke."

He raises an eyebrow. "Did you?"

My mouth twitches. "No."

He lets out a breath that transforms into a laugh and he pushes the heel of his palm against my shoulder, pushing me toward the door. "Get the hell out of my car and go deal with the mess you've made."

My body shifts back into the center of the seat and I slowly open the door, both of us laughing as I begin to climb out of his SUV. "I'll let you know how it goes."

"Cars," my brother says, his voice making me stop before closing the door. I lean forward, looking through the opening at him. "I might give you shit, but I love you, bro. You're a good guy and I know you'll do the right thing." A slow smile creeps across his lips. "And I know if the kid is yours, you'll be the best damn father he could ask for."

My heart grows in my chest and a warmth washes over me as I smile back at him. "Thanks, Cale. I love you, too."

"Okay, you can go now."

Laughing at my brother and his apparent allergy to emotion, I let the door shut and step away, turning around to walk over to my car. My heart crawls into my throat and anxiety settles in my bones as I climb into the driver's seat. Sweat builds on my palms and I turn on the engine before reaching to buckle my seatbelt.

As much as I hate to admit it, Caleb is right.

This is my mess and I have to deal with it without taking the easy way out. This is uncomfortable as hell, but I need to know the truth. I have to confront my mistakes and take responsibility for them.

And if Matteo is mine, he's my responsibility now.

CHAPTER SIX

ANDI

The last time I was here, she was still alive.

It's been a few months since my Aunt Bella passed, yet it feels so strange to be back at her house without her here. When she took a turn for the worst, she came to Starling Ridge and left her house unoccupied. The place has remained untouched for the last six months, until now.

I'm not sure what Matteo and I are walking into here, but I do know that it's livable conditions. The house isn't in poor shape, it just needs some love and updating to get it ready to go on the market. My parents suggested doing some remodeling, although I won't know for sure what all needs to be done until I look things over and get a contractor involved.

Matteo runs ahead of me, his footsteps light on the front porch as he makes his way to the door. He shifts his weight from foot to foot, unable to contain his anticipation and excitement any longer, as I catch up to him. He's pretending this is all a grand adventure we're on, so I want to make it as pleasant and as enjoyable as possible for him.

Thankfully, Matteo is well adjusted and always goes with the flow. He's always been more advanced for his age, with his language and understanding of things. However, I was afraid to disrupt him and bring him away from everything he's used to. He's not being uprooted from his life completely, although this is a change of scenery for the next few months for both of us. We'll be going home as soon as we get the house listed for sale and then our lives can return to normal.

I slide the key into the hole of the deadbolt, slowly turning it until I hear the click inside the locking mechanism. I unlock both of the locks before reaching for the door handle. With a twist of my wrist, I push open the door. There's an eeriness to the silence as I step inside the foyer, but it vanishes as soon as I see that everything is just the way Aunt Bella left it.

There aren't very many belongings I will have to go through thanks to the very tidy woman who also happened to be a minimalist. For that, I'm grateful. When Aunt Bella was still here, she cut back on her belongings tremendously, virtually leaving nothing but furniture and a few things she needed.

At some point, I need to clear out her closets and as we begin to remodel things, I'll have to figure out what I'll be doing with the furniture. My stomach sours at the thought of discarding the last pieces of her existence, but I push the feeling away as I follow after Matteo.

"Which room do I get to sleep in, mom?" Matteo questions me as we step into the kitchen and he crawls onto one of the stools on the other side of the counter. The kitchen is spacious enough and could be opened up even more to the dining room if the wall between was knocked out. There's plenty of room for an island to be sitting in the center as well.

The home is outdated but it has so much potential. I know something like this won't last on the market long, and that's coming from someone who has no real estate experience.

"Let's get the groceries put away and you can go pick a room after," I tell him as I lift my arm full of bags and set them down. Matteo goes back out to the car with me and, after two trips of grocery bags and another for our belongings, we're back in the house for the rest of the day.

We work together, putting the food away while Matteo asks a million questions about what we're going to be doing while we're here, before we end up making our way onto the second floor. It's not a big house, but it's far bigger than Aunt Bella ever needed. Matteo checks out both guest rooms before settling on the one with the baby blue walls. It's his favorite color and since the rooms are all the same, it's the one he likes the best.

Aunt Bella's bedroom was on the first floor, so I end up in the second biggest bedroom in the house. It has a king sized bed, which I don't need, and a few pieces of furniture. It's more than enough for Matteo and me, but this is all only temporary anyways.

"Mom," Matteo's soft voice breaks through my thoughts as I'm unloading his suitcase and putting his things away. His eyes meet mine as I hand him a pair of shorts to place in the drawer of his dresser.

"Yeah, *caro*?"

"Will we be seeing Mr. Carson again while we're here? I like him."

He catches me off guard with his question. It's the first he's spoken of Carson since we ran into him earlier and if I'm being honest, I wasn't sure he would bring him up at all.

"He's going to be stopping by in a few hours, but he and I need to have an adult conversation, so I'm not sure that he'll be hanging out for very long."

A frown tugs his lips downward as he gives me a slow nod. "Can we maybe see him another time then? I want to show him my hockey stick."

Guilt washes over me. "He's very busy with his work schedule, but I will see if we can figure something out."

Matteo's face lights up and I'm drowning in the fucking guilt. "Thank you, mom!" He quickly climbs to his feet, brushing his hands against the fronts of his shorts. I stare at him for a moment, studying his ever changing features.

His steel colored eyes stare back at me before he looks around the room in a haste. "Can I go downstairs and get my dinosaurs?"

"I'll come down with you," I tell him, a smile forming on my lips, but it doesn't spread. It's no match against my guilt. Focusing on the past does nothing to change where we are today, but I can't help but wonder if I could have done things differently when I found out I was pregnant.

At the time I felt as though I did everything I could have done to get in touch with Carson, but maybe I should have done more. Five years have passed . . . five years worth of memories they could have had together.

And there's no one to blame but me.

―――――

My phone vibrates on the counter as I get everything ready to start cooking dinner. It's late in the afternoon and after the long day Matteo and I have had, I just want us to be able to get dinner done and start our evening routine in hopes that we can have a little bit of time to relax and adjust to the new house before heading to bed.

Even though Matteo easily adjusts, I don't want to throw him off our typical nighttime routine too much. I want to keep things as normal as possible for him and that includes making sure he goes to bed at a decent time. When he was littler, he would come into my bed most nights, but not as much anymore. It's become so infrequent, it only happens when he has a bad dream or when he's sick.

I pick up my phone from the counter, my heart thumping against my ribcage as I unlock the screen and see his message waiting for me.

CARSON

Is it okay if I head over to your house now?

A part of me wants to tell him no. I'm not ready to fully face him, although I feel like the hardest part is already out of the way. He knows that Matteo is his son, but I know that isn't going to be the end of it. I could see it in his eyes when we were standing in the middle of the pasta aisle at the grocery store.

He has questions. He wants answers.

And he has a lot of emotions about this.

ANDI

Now is a good time.

I sent him the address to Aunt Bella's house earlier when we exchanged numbers, so he knows where to go. I don't know where the practice facility is for the Aston Archers, so I'm not sure how long it will take him to get here, but I have a feeling the time is only going to stretch until he's here.

CARSON

I'll be there in twelve minutes.

Well, there's my answer. Twelve minutes is ultimately going to feel like twelve hours.

Turning around in the kitchen, I rest my hands against the counter behind me, my eyes surveying the space before landing on Matteo. He's sitting at one of the chairs on the other side of the counter, his left hand moving across the paper in front of him as he focuses on coloring in between the lines. My footsteps are light as I walk over to him, looking down at the paper, only to find he isn't coloring.

He flipped the paper over at some point and he's drawing a picture of his own.

"What are you drawing, *caro?*"

Matteo looks up at me, his smile stretching across his face as his gray eyes meet mine. "It's a hockey rink!" Matteo loves hockey and I can't help but wonder if it's in his DNA. He's been watching with my brother since he was old enough to hold his head up. Vince insisted I put him in skating lessons when he was three.

He's been obsessed with being on the ice since he got the hang of skating. This past year, we had him in a learn-to-play program, with the hopes of him playing on an in-house team this fall. "Do you think there is somewhere we can go skate here?"

I looked into rinks before coming here and found one that's only about twenty minutes from here. From what I saw on their website, it looks like they have a great program I can get him into for the spring, but I didn't want to sign him up for anything until I had a better idea of what things were going to look like here.

Staring at him and seeing the look on his face, I know I can never deny him what he asks for. "There is a rink that isn't that far. Maybe we can go to one of their public skates to check it out."

Matteo's face lights up. "Did you bring your skates too, mom?"

"I did," I tell him, nodding as I smile. It's been a long time since I've figure skated, but I've been on the ice plenty of times with Matteo. I just haven't really had the time to skate freely. When he was first learning, I was the one he clung to until he got his bearings. Now, he doesn't need me like that, but there's a part of me that's afraid to try anything.

Especially after the nasty fall I had in college that shredded the ligaments in my knee. I know my limitations now and doing the things I used to do just aren't possible anymore. It doesn't take away the enjoyment of skating, but I just haven't found the same love for it that I once had.

I'm more interested in nurturing Matteo's passions and love for the ice than my own.

Just as I'm about to look up the rink schedule to see when they have a public skate, the doorbell rings, drawing my attention away from what I'm doing. My heart sinks into my stomach and there's an uncomfortable tightening in my chest as my eyes widen.

"Mom, someone is at the door," Matteo tells me, pulling me back from my momentary spiral into panic.

I look at him, swallowing roughly as I nod at him. "Thanks, *caro*. I'll be right back."

"Okay!"

He's content at the counter with his drawing, so I leave him be. I walk across the floor in my bare feet and step into the hall that opens to the foyer. I suck in a breath, holding it for a moment as I count to three and expel it. My hand shakes as I reach for the door handle, but I push through. When I open it, I find Carson standing on the other side of the threshold, holding open the screen door.

His eyes find mine in a rush, worry furrowing his brow. "Hey," he says quietly, his voice almost sounding like a breath. He swallows and pushes his hand through his hair with a nervousness weaving into his features.

"Hi," I reply, a gentle smile lifting my lips as I watch the anxiety warping him. To save him from himself, I quickly step out of the way. "Please, come in."

His lips part. He doesn't move and shakes his head. "I don't know if I should right now."

"Why?"

"I just—" he pauses, conflict knitting his brows together. "I think out here is a normal neutral space."

I stare at him for a moment, a little taken back by the way he's acting. I know all of this is fucking with his head, so I'm not really sure what I should expect from him. At the end of the day, Carson Ford may be the father to my child, but he's also a stranger. A stranger I shared a mind-blowing moment with and nothing more.

Glancing behind me, I spy Matteo where I left him in the kitchen. Carson holds the screen door open for me to step out past him. The scent of his cologne infiltrates my senses as I do and I catalogue it inside my brain. He smells like the ice rink mixed with a hint of leather and bourbon.

Carson walks across the front porch and supports himself on the railing as he wraps his fingers around the edges. I study him, watching the way his body is rigid and stiff as he stares out at the front lawn. I slowly walk to him, not sure if I should approach or not.

As I step beside him, I see his chest deflates out of

the corner of my eye, his shoulders sagging in defeat. He doesn't look at me and the silence stretches between us before his gravelly voice finally breaks through.

"I would like to get a paternity test."

My breath catches in my throat. I'm not sure what I was expecting, but it wasn't for that to be his first sentence. "Okay."

His fingers tighten on the railing, his knuckles blanching. I watch him from the corner of my eye, afraid to fully look at him. He grinds his teeth, the muscles in his jaw clenching as he lets out another breath. The silence is fucking deafening, but I don't know where to start.

I don't know what to say.

"Tell me how this happened," he says quietly, his eyes laser focused on something in the distance. I try to follow his gaze, but there's only a line of trees along the front perimeter of the property. "Tell me how you had my child and I'm just now finding out about him."

There's nothing malicious in his tone. If anything, there's desperation and sadness. Like he's been searching for the answers for years, only to come up empty handed.

"It was almost two months after that night that I found out I was pregnant." I pause, letting out a shallow breath, my heart knocking against my ribcage as I attempt to collect myself. "My cycles have always been irregular and I was so busy with school that I hadn't even noticed. I took a pregnancy test just as a precaution and it was positive."

Carson still doesn't look at me. "And there was no one else?"

"No," I tell him, my voice soft as I shake my head. "I was there that night with a friend to blow off some steam and after that, I got on a flight back to Rome and was immersed in my studies."

He slowly turns his head to look at me. "What were you studying?"

Pulling my bottom lip between my teeth, I bite down, dragging them over my flesh before releasing it. "Ancient History." I let out a soft laugh. "It's a very niche degree and there's an amazing program in Rome for it."

His forehead creases. "Are you living in the states now?"

My lips purse and I nod. "When I found out I was pregnant, I tried to find you. A quick search on the internet brought you up as a player for the Aston Archers, but I couldn't reach you through your social media accounts." I let out a defeated sigh, and shake my head as I shrug my shoulders. "I tried to get a hold of you and everything I tried was a dead end . . ."

It's like a dagger in my chest as I think back to that time in my life.

He stares at me for a second, all the hurt, anger, sadness, and confusion written on his face. "You knew where I was, though. You could have come and found me in person."

"What was I supposed to do, Carson? Show up at a hockey game with a hand written sign that says 'I'm pregnant and the baby is yours'?" I let out a harsh snort, the air rough against the inside of my nostrils. "I didn't know if you were married or had a girlfriend. I knew nothing about your life."

Abruptly releasing the railing, he takes a step back, pushing both of his hands through his hair as he grips the top of his head. "Fuck," he mutters, shaking his head as he blows out a breath and looks back at me. "He's five years old, Andi. Five fucking years old." His face contorts. "How long were you going to let this go without me knowing?"

Shit.

My heart stalls in my chest and I stare back at him, my lips parting. I quickly shut them, emotion and guilt washing over me as I tilt my head to the side in a silent apology. "I don't know." I close my eyes, dropping my head. "I didn't think you would want to know," I whisper as I lift my head again. "Your career has been amazing and I didn't want to throw a wrench in your life at all."

The muscle in his jaw tightens. "Goddammit," he mutters again, his shoulders deflating. "I hate it and I'm fucking pissed, but goddammit, I get it. I fucking get it." His head moves from side to side in disappointment. "That doesn't mean I agree with it, but I understand the logic behind the choices you made . . . the choices you made for all three of us."

"I'm sorry, Carson," I say in a rush, my heart crawling into my throat as I turn to face him, my hands clasping together in front of my body. "I never meant to hurt you by it. I just did what I thought was right."

He's silent again, his eyes not leaving me as he

slowly searches my face. My heart beats erratically, the sound of my blood pumping filling my ears as I keep my gaze locked on his.

"It's okay," he finally says, in resignation. His expression is filled with such conflict, I'm overcome with an overwhelming amount of guilt. This is all my fault. He's right—if I would have just come back sooner. If I would have found him in person, we could have saved all this time and all this pain. "There's nothing we can do about what has already been done."

"Where do we go from here?"

His throat bobs as he swallows roughly. "I'd like to get a paternity test done and if he is mine, I want to be a part of his life, however that may look."

"I don't live in Aston, Carson. I live in Starling Ridge" Another wave of remorse feels like it's going to sweep me under. My hometown is two hours away. "How will we make it work?"

"I don't know, Andi. I don't know what the fuck any of this will look like, but if he is my child, I want to be in involved in his life." He lets out a breath, his eyes falling shut before he looks at me again. "I want to be his father and be the father he deserves."

"What about—" I start, but he abruptly cuts me off.

"We will figure it out, okay?" He takes a step closer to me. I'm caught off guard when his warm, soft hands find mine, squeezing them gently. The tenderness in his gaze as he stares down at me takes me by complete surprise. "Please let me be in his life. I don't care what I have to do to make that happen, but please don't keep him from me any longer."

My eyes burn as tears blur my vision. I never expected him to be this invested, for him to take such an interest like this. Having a child will only complicate his life, especially with it being devoted to his career. I don't know if he understands what all goes into being a parent, but he seems eager to step up to the challenge.

"I'm sorry I never came to find you."

"Shh," he murmurs, lifting one hand to catch my tears with the pad of his thumb. He brushes them away, his eyes slowly searching mine. "What's done is done." He pauses, a soft breath escaping him. "We can't go back, we can't change anything that has happened. All we can do is move forward and not repeat the mistakes of our past."

"Okay . . ." my voice trails off as I catch my breath, my heart still beating wildly inside my chest. "The paternity test."

"We have playoffs starting in two days." His nostrils flare, the torment marring his expression again. "If I get the test and do whatever I need to do, are you able to send it in?"

"Of course," I tell him, nodding in understanding. Carson is clearly at an internal war with himself right now, torn between the importance of playoffs and dealing with this curveball that has been thrown at him.

Carson releases me and takes a step back. I immediately feel his absence. He pulls out his phone, his attention directing to the screen as he types something and begins to read. "It looks like they have ones at the pharmacy that we can do and drop off at the lab." His eyes flash to mine. "They're just cheek swabs and it says the results take three to five days."

"Okay," I say slowly, nodding as the weight of the climate between us settles on my chest. He's visibly upset, although I can't tell if it's with me specifically. I wouldn't blame him for any negative feelings towards me.

"If you're not busy, I'm going to run to get one to do it now." He shifts his weight on his feet. "I'll drop off my swab and everything to do Matteo's."

"That works. I can do his swab tonight and I'll find out where to drop it off in the morning."

His tongue darts out to wet his lips. "Can you let me know when you drop it off?" His nostrils widen and his expression is unreadable. "Just so I can keep track of when I should get the results. I will fill out the paperwork and put my phone number on it, that way they will call me with the results."

"Whatever you need, Carson," I say, my voice soft as I give him a gentle smile. I know how hard this is for me right now—I can't even begin to imagine the conflicted feelings he's struggling with.

There is a piece of me that is hurt that he doesn't believe me, but I understand. I get it. He doesn't know me well enough to take my word, which is exactly why I'll be nothing but compliant with it all.

He needs proof that Matteo is his son.

And I'll make sure he gets that proof.

CHAPTER SEVEN
CARSON

I don't have the balls to face Andi again when I drop off the paternity test for her. I left her after our conversation, drove to the pharmacy, swabbed my cheek in the front seat of my car, and left the test on her front porch for her to do her part. This entire situation has me completely fucked up and this is the worst timing ever.

Playoffs start in two days. Two fucking days . . . and I'm practically useless.

I need to find a way to shut my brain off so I can perform. There's a certain expectation placed upon me and one that I've also placed upon myself. Pressure doesn't normally cripple me, but right now, I can feel my knees beginning to buckle under the weight of everything.

I can't let it happen now. I need to push forward and fucking get through this. What is done is done. Andi will swab Matteo's cheek and drop off the test in the morning. Then I need to forget about the fact that I have to wait and get my mind back in the game. We'll have the results sometime next week and then I'll deal with whatever shit storm comes with that.

After leaving her house, I get five minutes down the back roads before I pull off onto the side of the road. There's a gravel pull off area and I whip my car onto it, pressing on the brake as I slow the car to a stop. A pained breath escapes me as I put the car in park and shut it off.

My forehead falls against the steering wheel and my eyelids fall shut as I swallow hard over the lump lodged in my throat. I need a moment to let myself fall apart before I can continue on. Just a moment to spiral, to give some attention to the myriad of feelings running rampant inside me.

The silence settles around me and I sit with my eyes closed, forehead pressed against the top of the steering wheel, fingers threaded together as I hold my palms against the back of my head.

How the hell did this happen?

That night with Andi is one I'll never regret. If anything, I always regretted walking away and not getting her number. There was something about her that has stuck with me after all these years. She was like a mirage. Something shimmering in the distance that would always be a mystery to me.

It's like the light caught her that night and I've never been able to eradicate the memory of her. She's always been there, lingering in the back of my mind. A constant reminder of someone I let walk away. Someone I felt a connection with, a magnetic pull.

She was captivating and had my attention and I didn't bother to pursue her. Even after all these years, after all the other women I've been with, none of them ever caught my interest quite like she did.

And here she is . . . another opportunity to finally get to know her, except that isn't really the opportunity that is presenting itself. Instead, it's completely different and nothing like I envisioned.

She might be the mother of my fucking child. A child I never knew about until earlier today.

I can't blame her for the choices she's made, even if it tears me apart inside. I understand why she did the things she did. I understand why she didn't try to reach out to me again after failed attempts in the past. I can't imagine how these past six years have been for her, thinking there was never a chance I would have wanted to be involved.

How things could have been different if only I knew.

Then again, I don't know a single thing about her life. She doesn't have a ring on her finger, but I never bothered to ask her about herself. I don't know where she works, where she lives. I don't know if she's single or if there's another man in her life.

Hell, there could be another man that Matteo views as a father figure.

My fingers tighten as I grip the back of my head harder. I can't let my mind spiral like this when I don't know. I don't have all the information and the first step is getting the results of the paternity test.

After that is when I can worry about what comes next and what Andi's relationship status is.

On a ragged exhale, I slowly remove my hands from the back of my head, lifting my forehead away from the steering wheel as I open my eyes. It's well into the evening now and the sun is slowly beginning its descent beyond the horizon. Glancing at the clock on the dashboard, I let out a curse and grab my phone.

I was supposed to be at Lincoln's house twenty minutes ago for dinner. I'm sure they expected me to be fashionably late like I normally am, but the girl's wanted to eat early enough so we could all get some rest tonight. They know the life of playoffs and the importance of sleep and making sure there are no outside distractions.

So much for my life aligning with that right now.

I open the group chat with the boys and immediately wince when I see the string of messages I've missed from Rowan, Nash, and Lincoln. Caleb passed on the monthly dinner tonight, but there's still a message from him.

I open his first.

CALEB

How did it go?

CARSON

As well as expected. She agreed to the paternity test and I'll have the results sometime next week.

CALEB

Good. You'll be glad you had it done,
regardless of what the outcome is.

CARSON

I know. I just don't know what I'm going
to do after I know for sure.

CALEB

Worry about that when the time comes.
There's nothing you can do about it
right now, so you need to focus on
what you can control.

CARSON

Like how I play.

CALEB

Right.

Just let that be your distraction right
now. We'll figure out the rest of the shit
after we get through this.

CARSON

To war and back.

It's a phrase my brother and I have always said to one another since we were kids playing hockey together. We're not necessarily going to war, but when we all step on the ice together, we're all fighting the same fight. The guys are more than just teammates. They're like brothers and we all have each other's backs.

We win together and we lose together. We give everything we have and battle against the other team as if they are our enemy. Together we fight and together we protect.

CALEB

Always

Closing out the message thread with my brother, I open up the group chat and see a dozen messages from the three other guys. Caleb is in the chat, but he has it muted on his phone. I know he checks in periodically, but I think he'd rather not be bothered by the shenanigans going on in there.

LINCOLN

Carson, where are you? Nova is going to kill me if you don't get here soon.

NASH

Seriously, she's getting antsy.

ROWAN

Guys, chill out. I told you he's probably back at the grocery store trying to find something to bring.

NASH

Please do not bring instant mashed potatoes 🫣

I hate mashed potatoes.

LINCOLN

They are kind of gross, aren't they?

NASH

The consistency can be so weird. If they're lumpy, it just doesn't feel right.

LINCOLN

But if they're whipped, it's also strange.

ROWAN

I think he said he was going to bring
pasta salad.

NASH

Premade, right?

LINCOLN

God, I hope so. Ford can't cook for
shit.

I read over their messages, half stifling a laugh as I
decide to respond back to them.

CARSON

I'm not going to make it tonight.

ROWAN

We talked about this, bud. If I came, so
did you.

LINCOLN

Well, Nova's going to kill me.

NASH

I still don't understand why she would
kill you if it's not your fault he doesn't
show up.

CARSON

Something came up and I'm just not
really feeling up to it tonight.

ROWAN

Bullshit.

LINCOLN

Okay, she might not kill me, but she's not going to be happy. Don't tell her I told you, but she has little gifts for everyone before playoffs and she wanted to make sure everyone got one.

NASH

What did she get us?

CARSON

It matters if I'm not there, but it doesn't matter if my brother isn't?

ROWAN

Caleb automatically gets a free pass from everything and everyone, you know that.

CARSON

Fair enough.

Should I come by just for the gift?

LINCOLN

Tell me why you're not coming and I'll tell you whether or not it's a good enough excuse.

Fuck.

Do I tell them or do I keep it all to myself?

I don't want to fuck anyone else up before playoffs, but keeping this shit in is going to eat me alive. I'm not good at keeping secrets and I am certainly not good at keeping in the things that are bothering me.

They're my family. I can't keep them in the dark.

CARSON

I just found out I might have a five year old kid and just dropped off a paternity test with his mom so she can swab his cheek and send it in.

I probably could have worded it better, but might as well rip off the bandaid, right? I press send and wait for a response, yet suddenly the group chat goes silent. It's literally fucking crickets in there.

And then my brother decides to chime in.

CALEB

Well, that's one way to drop a bomb like that.

ROWAN

I have so many questions.

NASH

Holy shit, Ford.

LINCOLN

I thInk that's a good enough excuse.

I'll bring yours to the rink tomorrow.

CARSON

Thanks. You guys can tell the girls what is going on.

ROWAN

Do you think the kid is yours?

I swallow roughly, reading over his message. Rowan went through a similar experience when he found out about his daughter. He had to get a paternity test and then went through a whole ordeal to get full custody of her.

CARSON

Based on the timelines, the way he looks and other similarities—yes.

NASH

How the hell did you even find out about this?

CALEB

How about you all stop cackling like little hens and give the guy some space to breathe and time to process?

LINCOLN

Caleb is right, boys.

NASH

Sorry.

ROWAN

We're here for you for whatever you need.

LINCOLN

Anything you need.

CARSON

Thanks, guys. I'll tell you about it tomorrow.

NASH

No rush. Whenever you're ready to talk about it, we'll be here.

These guys are the best friends I've ever had and I'm eternally grateful to have them in my life. Growing up with Caleb, I've always known what it feels like to have that brotherly bond. That love from a sibling that you know you can always count on to have your back, regardless of what happens.

These guys are my brothers, but we aren't bound by blood and that connection is something unexplainable. You're not forced to be a family, but it's the one you choose. They're the people who will ride by your side through the good and the bad times.

They're always there when you need them and these guys continue to show up. We might give each other shit and bicker and argue sometimes, but at the end of the day, we still choose to stand by one another.

To war and back.

And this is the exact kind of familial bond I want my son to experience.

CHAPTER EIGHT

ANDI

Cold radiates from beneath my feet and its frigid tentacles wrap around my legs just above my skates as I swiftly guide Matteo around a small group of novice skaters. The way they hold onto each other or the wall and march along the boards around the perimeter for the rink lets me know it's their first time.

Matteo's soft, small gloved hand is wrapped in mine and he looks up at me, a soft giggle escaping him, his grey eyes bright with excitement as we continue to move around dodging other people. I love these moments with him—when we both get to share our love for the ice and skating upon the glistening surface.

With Matteo only being five, he isn't playing hockey at a high level and is still learning. The public skates are great for me to just get him on the ice and move his feet. And they're good for me too. I get to use the skills I neatly tucked away in a box when I hung up my skates years ago. It's nice to be back and to be skating with a purpose again.

As we round one corner and the crowd opens up, Matteo wiggles his hand out of mine, looking back up at me again, a huge smile spreading across his face. "Mom, watch what I can do," he says, and I watch as he attempts to transition to facing the opposite direction.

His blades catch a little bit in the ice, but he recovers without falling. His jaw is set, his eyes squinted a bit as he attempts to focus hard on what he's doing. He's been working on his backwards C cuts after he learned them during practice a few weeks ago.

I watch him as he attempts to create momentum and begins to glide backwards. He shifts his weight onto his left foot, pushing off the inside edge of his right, creating a C shape as he moves his foot outwards and then back to the center.

"Good job, *caro*!" I clap as I watch him shift his weight and move his left foot in the same motion he did his right. Matteo's gaze meets mine once more, another grin breaking out across his face as he does a little shimmy of his hips. He displaces his weight, guiding his body as he transitions back to facing the same direction as me, my hand finding his again. "Come on, little man, we only have a little more time left on the ice before we need to get home."

Their evening public skate goes a little later than Matteo's bedtime, but I promised him that we would come out just for a little bit, just so he could get back on the ice. We finish up and it's a little after 7:30 once we get off the ice. We find our bags on the bench outside of the rink and we sit down to get out of our skates. I wipe the slush from his skate blades, making sure they're dry so they don't rust. My fingers move to unlace his skates before unlacing my own.

Matteo helps me get them into our bags and as we make our way to the door. I pause at a message board with different pamphlets and information, and pull one out, reading over the front. It's a spring series of scheduled clinics and small area games. It's exactly what I'm looking for to keep Matteo busy and on the ice during the off season.

Tucking it in my bag, I hold my hand out for Matteo and he slips his into mine as we head out to the car. He lets out a yawn as I lift him into the backseat, making sure he's secure before I climb into the front. It's a short drive back to the house, and Matteo's soft voice fills the air as he talks excitedly about skating.

We pull into the driveway and the house is set farther back off the street. It's not a long drive, by any means, but it isn't right up against the road out in front. I pull up by the garage, putting the car in park and killing the engine. Matteo's eyelids are heavy as we catch each other in the rearview mirror and he gives me a sleepy grin.

"Come on, *caro*. Let's get inside and get ready for bed."

He doesn't disagree and nods as he unbuckles his seatbelt. I do the same with mine, making sure I grab our skate bags before meeting him by his door. He waits for me to get out, undoubtedly a little afraid because of it being a new place and how damn dark it is right now.

I don't know where the street lamps are, but I'm going to have to remember to turn on the exterior lights here when we're not home.

Matteo and I head inside and kick our shoes off just inside the front door. "Go upstairs and get ready for bed and I'll be up in a few minutes."

He doesn't argue before jogging up the stairs to the second floor. I hear him go into his bedroom to change before the water starts to run in the bathroom as he brushes his teeth. It's definitely past his bedtime and I need him to get some solid rest. The past few days have felt so long and overwhelmingly busy.

We drove here on Wednesday morning, so that was a travel day and one to get settled into the house. Yesterday, we ran more errands, which included dropping the paternity test off at the lab, before meeting contractors in the afternoon.

Today, we were able to relax a little bit, but not enough to make up for the hustle and bustle we've been caught up in the past few days. I'm hoping that things will slow down after we get the work underway here, but I don't fully know. This is the first time I've been hands on with trying to update a house.

I'm just thankful that it's a livable house. There really isn't anything wrong with the condition it's in now, but investing the time and money into fixing it up will definitely bring in more money. It was mapped out in Bella's will. One of her wishes was that I would fix the house up to either make it somewhere Matteo and I would want to live or to get more money selling it.

I head into the living room, stopping in the center in

front of the TV as I grab the remote from the stand and turn it on. With one hand on my hip, I shuffle through the channels, flipping from one to the next as I try to find something to watch. Matteo comes downstairs after brushing his teeth and I turn my head as he hovers in the doorway. I pause my channel surfing and watch him for a moment. I was planning on heading up to his room after he brushed his teeth.

His forehead creases and a slight tinge of worry flashes in his eyes. "Can I stay with you for a little?" he asks me, his voice a bit timid.

The fear laced in his tone instantly makes me feel guilty for uprooting him and bringing him here.

Our first night here, we were both too exhausted and I fell asleep in his bed while reading him a story. Last night, he started out in his bed, but he never actually went to sleep. He was in there for maybe thirty minutes before I heard his soft footsteps on the hardwood floors. He was excited about having his own bedroom when we first got here, although, this is a strange place to him. It's only natural for him to have some fear.

"Of course," I tell him, my arm extending for him to come closer to me. Matteo quickly shuffles across the living room floor, the feet of his footie pajamas sliding across the hardwood. He comes over to me, wrapping his arms around my leg as I rub my hand across the top of his back.

He turns his head, looking at the TV. "Oh look, Mom," he says, pointing at the television. "Hockey is on."

I look up at the TV, seeing no one other than the Aston Archers lining up in the center of the ice. They're already into the second period, but it looks like it's the start of the second. My eyes scan the screen, my heart pounding in my chest as I see his last name written across the back of his jersey as he gets into position.

The puck drops and another Ford who's playing center sends the puck back to him. From my research years ago, I learned about the Ford brothers who play together for the Aston Archers. Caleb Ford, captain and star center and Carson Ford, star defenseman. Caleb is the older of the two, but only by two years.

#8.

I didn't stalk him. I merely had to do research to figure out who he was after I found out I was pregnant. Naturally, I did a little bit of digging but it was all public information. Everything I know about his brother, his hockey career, and him was easily found by a simple search on the internet that anyone could perform.

"You know Carson, who we met at the grocery store the other day?" I question him, moving him away from my leg as I step closer to the television. Matteo nods and I point at the screen as the whistle is blown and play stops. "There he is, right there."

Matteo's face lights up, his eyes wide, mouth hanging open as he stares at the screen. "He plays hock-ey?" He quickly looks at me and my head bobs. His attention immediately leaves my face, his gaze glued to the TV as he watches Carson moving around on the ice, heading back to their defensive zone. "I want to be like him when I grow up."

A wave of guilt crashes against the shores of my heart. He met his father, yet he has no idea of the truth and I know I can't tell him yet. I don't know how Carson and I are going to navigate the future, but he made it clear that he wants to be a part of Matteo's life, so long as the results of the paternity test give him the confirmation he seeks.

"Do you want to stay with me on the couch for a bit and watch the game?"

Matteo's head whips around to look at me, nodding eagerly as he moves closer to me. "Can I, please?"

I stare down at my beautiful baby boy, his gray eyes searching mine with hope. A smile blooms across my lips, lifting the apples of my cheeks. "Come on," I tell him, my voice gentle as I guide him to the couch. He climbs on and I grab a blanket, settling down on the cushion beside him. He scoots closer and slips beneath my arm as he snuggles up against my side.

Pulling the blanket over his body and mine, I wrap my arms around him, holding him close as we both stare across the room at the television, watching as Carson heads back onto the ice for his next shift. Matteo is laser focused on him for as long as he can be until sleep pulls him into the darkness.

CHAPTER NINE

CARSON

I t's extremely difficult to not feel like I'm going to crumble from the insurmountable pressure right now. This isn't the first time we've made the play-offs. In the years that I've played for the Aston Archers, we've made playoffs half a dozen times. This year is a completely different experience for me because my heart just isn't in it right now.

This is the first year that I'm feeling the pressure from the outside world. It's the first time that I'm not able to completely shut off my mind from all the noise and all the distractions. It's the first time I'm dealing with a situation like the one I've found myself in with Andi and Matteo.

Rolling my wrist, I glance at my watch checking the time again. Yesterday was our travel day and today we're kind of just hanging out. We had an early skate this morning and practice earlier this afternoon. The time difference only has us two hours behind Aston so it's almost four right now. Today is day four of waiting for the paternity results.

The lab closes in 45 minutes and then I'll be left spending another night waiting.

I've been trying to not focus on the two different possibilities that results could be. It's so unknown, yet in my heart, I feel like I'm already certain of the truth. If I find out that Matteo isn't mine, I will genuinely be surprised after meeting him. Just from the small interaction I've had with him and his Ford-like features. It's undeniable.

But, even though I feel so certain, there is a part of me that is struggling with the possibility. I can't wrap my head around the idea of me having a child. Of me being a father.

I think it has to do with all the time that has passed. All the time I could have spent with him. I would be lying if I said I didn't feel guilty for her having to face raising a child as a single mother. But had I known, I would have been present.

She would have never had to worry about doing this alone.

The elevator dings and the doors slide open as I reach my floor. After our morning skate, I stopped along the street to grab some food from a vendor that had a food truck parked alongside the curb. The rest of the guys went ahead of me and they've been here at the hotel for a little bit now.

We normally have a pre-practice meal, but I didn't feel like I could wait until then. My appetite has been fucked up since I ran into Andi at the grocery store and the lack of nutrients is not helping me to perform at an optimal level right now. We only have one shot at play-offs every single season and I can't be the reason that we fuck this one up.

I get to the room that I'm sharing with my brother and find him curled up on the queen size bed on the far side of the room. He always takes the one closest to the window and there have been quite a few times I've caught him staring out into the distance, his mind drifting past the horizon.

In a way, it feels like he's still searching for some sign of Amelia . . . as if there's some way for her to come back to him.

I stare at my brother for a moment, my gaze drifting across his calm, relaxed features. His chest rises and falls in slow deep breaths. A frown tugs his lips downward, his forehead creasing as his eyebrows pinch together before relaxing again. Leaving him to sleep, I make sure I'm quiet as I slip into the bathroom.

After washing my face and my hands, I walk back into the room again and look at the clock. Only three hours until we have to be back at the rink. I have enough time to try and take a nap, but I'm not so sure I'll have any success.

At any opportunity, any moment of silence, the lingering thoughts about the paternity test that hang heavily in the back of my mind seem to have a way of working to the front of my mind. Sleep has been next to impossible the past few nights and it's just another strike against me fucking up my performance on the ice.

Walking over to my dresser, I pull out a change of clothes and strip out of my warm up suit to put on a comfortable pair of basketball shorts and a plain white T-shirt. As I pull my head through my shirt, my phone begins to vibrate on the top of my dresser. It immediately grabs my attention, my heart racing in my chest. It thumps to a face beat, violently racking against my ribcage.

My breath catches as I wrap my hand around the device, lifting it to see the screen. There's an unknown number that pops up and even though I don't recognize it, I have a very good feeling about who it is. My stomach sinks. I don't answer it until I'm sliding open the glass door that leads onto the balcony and stepping out into the hot sun. My finger slides across the screen to answer the call while I shut the door behind me.

"Hello?"

"Hi," a soft feminine voice sounds in my ear as I lift the phone to the side of my face and slowly sit down on one of the chairs facing the bustling city. "Is this Mr. Carson Ford?"

"Yes, this is him." My voice starts out as strong, but there's a hint of nervousness laced within my words.

"Hi, this is Janine from LabWorks. It was listed on the testing paperwork for us to give you a call with your results, along with emailing it to you."

My nostrils flare, my lungs only expanding halfway. "Yes, that is correct."

"Brilliant," she says, her voice quiet yet steady. "After conducting our thorough analysis of the samples, it is determined that they are a match."

I don't hear much of what she says after that. My hand still holds my phone against the side of my face, however, I stare off into the distance, everything becoming unfocused as my gaze is locked to the horizon line. It's almost as if my mind goes blank and the woman's voice is drowned out by the sound of my blood rapidly pumping through my body.

"Mr. Ford."

I hear her, but I can't respond. It doesn't fully register, like her words are simply floating past me.

"Mr. Ford, are you there?"

The second time she speaks my name, it pulls me out of the trance I'm caught in, abruptly pulling me back into reality. "I'm sorry, yes I'm here."

"Do you have any questions?"

Unless she can help me figure out what the hell comes next, then no.

"No," I tell her, my voice hoarse and thick with indistinguishable emotion. "Thank you."

"Of course. I will send over the results via email and you should have them within the next few minutes." She pauses for a second. "Thank you for using LabWorks. Please don't hesitate to reach out with any questions you may have."

I thank her again for her time, although the words are forced and feel robotic. She ends the call before me and I slowly lower my phone away from my face. Leaning forward, I plant my elbows against my knees, both hands holding the device between them as I stare out into the distance once again.

I'm not sure what I'm staring at or what I'm even

thinking about at this point. I can't even dissect any of my feelings right now. It's like everything kind of meshes together in this weird combination of feeling everything at once, yet feeling nothing at the same time.

This is a total mind fuck and I severely underestimated how affected I would be by learning this information.

I'm a father . . . to a five year old I just met a few days ago.

My heart continues to race, my breathing growing shallower with every breath I take. The anxiety washes over me, leaving me momentarily frozen in place before my instincts kick in and I know I need to get it under control. Inhaling deeply, I exhale even longer, doing it multiple times to calm myself.

Now calm enough for my brain to work again, I sit back upright. I move my hands off the screen of my phone, abruptly unlock it and tap on the messages app. I need to tell Andi the results. She needs to know so we can figure out what the hell happens next.

How the hell am I supposed to navigate this while we're on the road for playoffs? I don't know what I'm going to do. I don't know what to do. This is all so fucked and unfamiliar, uncharted territory for me.

At this point, I think I need to invest in a therapist again.

Instead, I send Andi a message.

CARSON

Hey. Do you have any time to talk today?

ANDI

Sure. Is everything okay?

CARSON

The lab called.

ANDI

I'm with a contractor right now. Give
me a few minutes.

CARSON

No rush. It can wait until later.

What a fucking lie. I would like to speak to her immediately, even though I have no idea what I'm going to say. It's like ripping off a bandaid and I'd like to do it sooner than later.

Time stretches and I rise to my feet as I wait for Andi's call. My heart has slowed down with the help of my controlled breathing, but my stomach still rolls with uneasiness. My feet eat up the small space of the balcony until my hands are resting on the railing.

My eyes scan the city streets beneath. The sun low in the sky reflects off the buildings and cars buzz down the roads. Everyone below moves with the hustle and bustle of their city lives and here I am. Watching life pass me by as I try to get a grip on my own.

My phone vibrates in my hand and I don't bother to look at the screen before answering the call and lifting it to my ear.

"Hello?"

"Hey," Andi's voice is tender and quiet as it sounds through the speaker. It slides across my eardrum, soft as silk. "What did they say?"

A lump is lodged in my throat and I let out a breath, my Adam's apple bobs as I swallow roughly. "Matteo is my son."

Andi is silent for a moment. "I know."

"You did," I agree, my voice catching in my throat again. My eyebrows pull together as I stare down at a car, hearing it honk at the one in front of it. "Why didn't you fight me for wanting to get a test done?"

"Because I'm a stranger to you and this is life changing information, Carson. You're a professional athlete and I didn't want you to think I was trying to take advantage of you." She lets out a soft breath. "I knew the truth, but I also knew that if there's concrete evidence, there's nothing to dispute then."

Her words swirl around in my brain, sinking deeply into the fibers of my mind. "I appreciate that," I say, nodding, even though she can't see me. I do appreciate it because she didn't insist on me accepting her word without knowing for sure. "What do we do next?"

"You meant what you said?" she questions me, hope and surprise mixing in her tone. "You want to be involved in his life?"

"Well, yes," I tell her without missing a beat. There's no hesitation or any doubt in my mind. "You've done this all by yourself and you don't have to anymore. Plus, I've got a lot of time to make up with him."

Andi is silent again for a moment before she speaks. "I'm sorry, Carson. I'm so fucking sorry that you didn't know sooner."

"Shh, it's okay. We don't need to worry about that because focusing on what has already happened changes nothing. Let's just worry about the future and what happens next, okay?"

"Okay," she says softly, her voice barely audible. "Okay," she says again, this time with more declaration in her tone.

"I want you to tell Matteo."

"Without you?" she asks, the inquisition heavy in her words.

My head bobs and I turn around, leaning back against the railing as I stare at the side of the hotel. There's movement on the other side of the glass, but I can't see what my brother's doing in there. "I think it would be best. I'm a total stranger to him and I don't want to scare him by telling him together."

"You're right," she agrees without hesitation. "I will find a good time to tell him and then when you're back in town, we can get together and figure out how we want to move forward."

"I just want to be involved. I want to be a part of his life."

"I want you in his life too," she admits, her voice tender, like a gentle embrace. "We can get a custody agreement, if that gives you a sense of security."

Her statement hits me directly in the chest. The consideration lifts an immense amount of weight from my shoulders. It wasn't something I had even thought about yet and she catches me off guard as she's the one who suggests it.

"We can talk more about it then."

She's quiet for a beat. "Whatever you need, Carson.

We will get this all figured out. You just put your head down and focus on the playoffs for now."

I snort. "That's easier said than done."

"I know but it's what you have to do right now."

"I know," I tell her, letting out an exasperated sigh. I'm exhausted from the emotional toll these last few days have taken on me. I feel better knowing the truth, but now I find myself desperately wanting to be home.

The cup is always the end goal of every season, so this is a really conflicting feeling for me. I should want to be here with the guys, fighting every battle . . . and I do. I just also want to be home.

"Can I be honest with you about something?" her voice breaks through my internal turmoil.

"Please."

"There was a part of me that was glad when I wasn't able to get in contact with you. The last thing I wanted to do was to throw a wrench in your life and your career. My brother played D1 hockey, but didn't make it pro. I know what you guys have sacrificed to get to where you are." She pauses, a soft sigh leaving her. "I didn't want to ruin your life then and I don't want to ruin it now."

"You're not ruining it," I assure her, my eyebrows inching closer to one another. "I promise you."

"Then I need you to go out there and get your head in the game. You have to pull through for your team and forget about Matteo and me. I will not let him be the reason behind you blowing a shot at the cup for you and your guys."

Goddamn, who taught this woman to talk like a hard-ass coach?

"I won't."

"Good," she says after a beat, her tone softening. "If you want to see Matteo or talk about anything, we're both here. I just don't want you worrying about the logistics of everything until after the playoffs."

"I appreciate that," I tell her, my voice barely audible as emotion washes over me again. She's more concerned about my feelings and my mental wellbeing than I think anyone ever has been in my life. Well, maybe except for my therapist, but I was paying her to care.

The glass door slides open and my brother pauses in the doorway, tilting his head to the side as he scratches his forehead.

"I'll call you when I'm back in town." I pause, lifting my shoulders at him as he steps out onto the balcony and closes the door behind him. He walks over to the chairs, taking a seat in the closest one. "Let me know how it goes when you tell him."

"I will." She falls silent. "Bye, Carson."

"Bye."

Caleb watches me carefully as I pull my phone away from my ear, locking the screen before slipping it into the pocket of my shorts. "Was that her?"

Running my tongue across my top teeth, I nod. "The lab called me."

"Oh, shit."

I walk over to the seat next to him, lowering myself

down onto it as a ragged breath escapes me. "The kid is mine."

Caleb is silent for a moment. "Are we happy about it?"

"I think so," I tell him, swallowing my emotion. "A little shocked and a lot fucking terrified, but I think I'm happy, too."

Caleb sighs and reaches over to clasps his hand over my shoulder and give me a squeeze. "It's okay, Carsy. It will be okay."

"I have no fucking idea what I'm doing here, man." I shake my head, Caleb removes his hand and I drop my head down into my hands. "I don't know how to raise a kid."

"Well, thankfully you don't have to do it alone," he says quietly as sadness is injected into the atmosphere around us. "What I meant is you have me. I've been doing this long enough to know a thing or two. I got your back, little bro. You'll never have to do anything alone, as long as I'm still here breathing."

Lifting my head, I turn it to the side, my eyes finding my brother's. "Thanks, Cale."

"That's what I'm here for," he says, nodding his head at me. "How did your call with her go? What is her name?"

"Andi," I tell him, pausing to chew on the inside of my cheek. "The call was fine. She's actually quite pleasant and understanding . . . and feels guilty for me not knowing sooner."

"As she should," he says with simplicity and a bit of

hardness in his tone. "Is she someone you think you'll be able to co-parent with?"

I nod. "She suggested getting a custody agreement so we have things set in stone and to also give me peace of mind."

Caleb watches me, a look of surprise passing through his irises. "Okay, that's a good start. It sounds like she wants you to be in the kid's life."

"I think she does."

The muscle in his jaw tightens. "Just proceed with caution, okay? You still don't know what her true motives are."

I stare at my brother for a second. "I know."

He could be completely wrong about Andi, but I don't say that to him. Caleb has always struggled to trust people and after losing Amelia, it only got worse. I don't think he'll ever attach himself to another person again. A serious relationship has never been in the plan for me, especially after watching what my brother went through when he lost his wife. Andi and I have a kid, but it doesn't mean that we'll be walking down the aisle to the altar together.

We have a situation that we need to navigate together and nothing more.

CHAPTER TEN

ANDI

Matteo sits across from me, his mouth open as he shovels in a fork full of spaghetti. It's nothing like the dish Aunt Bella used to make, but I think she'd be proud. Our family roots have strong ties back to Italy, especially because my mother and Bella lived in Italy until they were of college age. They both left their families to move to the states, which is where my parents met.

My father's family is also from Italy, but the past two generations were born and raised here. After him and my mother met in college, they married and the rest is history. Aunt Bella never moved back to Italy either, although we have been plenty of times to visit family and the country itself.

Matteo knows so much about my family and there's so much neither of us know about his father. I have to tell him the truth about Carson, and I still haven't found the perfect way to do it. It's been a whole day since

Carson called with the results, and I'm beginning to wonder if there even is a perfect way. *Here goes nothing.*

"Matteo, do you remember when we talked about your father before and what I told you about him?"

Nothing about this is easy. I immediately want to pause the conversation. I don't want to make this a big thing and upset him in any way.

Matteo looks up at me, chewing his food as he nods eagerly. "He lives farther away so we don't see him."

Fuck. I swallow over the lump lodged in my throat, trying to choose my words carefully. Speaking in facts and matter-of-factly might be the best approach. Limited facts, but the truth, nonetheless.

"Right. So, when I first met your father, we were in very different places in our lives. I was living in Italy at the time and we didn't live anywhere near each other." I pause. I want to be honest with him, but there are certain adult things he doesn't need to know. "Things are complicated, *caro*. That's just how life is when you grow up and sometimes things are just hard and don't always make sense."

I'm losing the plot here and starting to ramble because I don't know how the hell to tell my son about his father when he's staring at me with those gray eyes. There's no judgement in his gaze, just pure curiosity.

"I know we've never really talked about your father and I want to tell you about him and who he is."

"Okay," he nods eagerly, giving me a gentle smile as I watch his expression brighten. He stares at me while he shovels another mouthful of food into his mouth. "Do I get to meet him sometime?"

My heart breaks. This is the first real, open conversation we've had about this. Granted, he is only five years old, so I need to remind myself to keep it to his age level. The guilt of not telling him about Carson sooner sits in my stomach like a boulder.

"You have actually already met him, but we didn't want to scare you at all. He lives here in Aston." My throat bobs, nostrils widening as I straighten my spine. "Carson is your father."

Matteo's jaw drops, his eyes widen, and his fork clatters onto his plate. "Hockey-player Carson?"

"Yes." I let out a breath, half sighing in relief as his face transforms into something that resembles excitement. "We talked about it and felt it would be better if I told you without him because we didn't want to scare you or upset you at all."

He shakes his head, moving around in his seat as he tucks his legs underneath him. "I'm not upset or scared." He tilts his head to the side. "I like Carson. He's really nice and really good at hockey."

"He is, isn't he?" I agree, a soft laugh escaping me as the anxiety begins to wane. He's five, so thankfully I think he may be too young to be affected negatively by this. Time will tell when he gets older, as I'm sure he'll have more questions then.

For now, I'll take his ability to accept things and adapt.

"His team is playing tonight, if you want to watch some of it before bed."

"Oh, yes!" He exclaims, clapping his hands with

excitement. He settles back in his seat again. "Do I get to see him again?"

"Of course, babe. They are playing in the playoffs right now, so his schedule is a little crazy, but when he's back in town, he plans on coming to see you first thing."

"Good," Matteo says, nodding his head in approval. He gets up from his seat as we're both finished. He walks over to the sink with me and hands me his plate as I begin to wash them. "I want to see him. Do you think he will skate with me?"

Tears prick the corners of my eyes as I turn my head and glance down at my sweet boy. "I'm sure he would love to do that with you."

"I'm going to ask him when I see him."

The excitement that radiates from Matteo as we finish up in the kitchen is palpable. It wraps itself around me and I hang on to every word he says as he chatters about hockey and skating with Carson.

———

After Matteo's bath, we settle on the couch to catch the first period of the game before it's time for him to go to bed. He cuddles up next to me, dragging a blanket from the back of the couch and pulls it over his body. I wrap my arm around him and pull him close to my side. He rests his head against the side of my chest as I turn on the television.

By the time I find the channel with the game, we've missed the opening face-off and the first minute of play.

The whistle is blown as the ref calls offsides on the other team and they head to the dot in the neutral zone, closest to where the call was made for another face-off.

Matteo sits up a little straight, moving away from me as I tuck the blanket around him. His leg is pressed against mine and I pull my feet up onto the couch, settling deeper into the plush cushions. "Look, mom, there he is!" Matteo exclaims, pointing at the TV as Carson hops onto the ice, skating towards the play.

Within the next five minutes, they end up scoring, only to have the other team score right after them. The energy is visible and the aggression is in full force on the ice. I lean forward, sitting up as anxiety knots my intestines. Now is the time of the season where they want to avoid penalties, but the tension is so thick, it's almost impossible.

Personally, I hate playoffs. They're fun to watch when you're not watching someone you care about on the ice. Saying I care about Carson is nothing more than being a good person. From what I know of him, he's a good man. He's the father of my son. Our connection is weird, given the circumstances of having a one night stand and the resulting child that he recently found out about.

Regardless of our relationship—or lack thereof—I care about him and his well being.

Carson's brother wins the next face-off, sending the puck back to Carson. He pushes it around another player with the blade of his stick. He sends it back across the ice to their other winger who sends it to the older Ford brother.

Carson crosses over the blue line, receiving a sauce pass from his brother and heading directly to the net. One of the defensive players from the other team attempts to check Carson. Carson dodges out of his way, losing possession of the puck in front of the net. His brother is there and steals the puck back, taking a shot that their goalie ends up catching.

When I find Carson on the screen again, he's holding his right forearm. I scoot farther in my seat, my eyebrows pulling together. *Oh no, is he okay?* I was following the puck and not Carson so I missed what happened to him.

They show the replay and that's when I see it. He got tripped up and his wrist hit the goal post as he went down. He didn't stay down on the ice but for a split second before he was back on his skates, holding his arm.

Shit.

"Is he okay?" Matteo asks me quietly as the television cuts to a commercial break right after showing the instant replay.

"I hope so," I tell him, giving him a gentle squeeze against my side. Sometimes the injuries that don't look bad can be the most detrimental. This is the playoffs. This is the time of the season where players are pushing their bodies to the limit.

The commercial break ends quickly. The camera pans to the bench and I see Carson sitting there, which is a good sign, but not necessarily a great sign. Matteo is quiet, watching as the game starts again. My chest constricts and anxiety builds in the pit of my stomach.

There's a line change and Carson hops over the side of the boards. "Look, *caro*, he's back on the ice," I tell Matteo as we watch him rush over to where the play is moving.

Just because he's on the ice doesn't mean he's okay. Hockey players are borderline insane. They'll play with broken bones and serious injuries unless someone removes them from the ice and they physically cannot play.

"I can't wait to skate with him," Matteo says quietly, the excitement evident in his tone. "Maybe he can help me work on my shot."

I sit silently, squeezing him to my side again as he nestles back into me. Seeing him excited like this makes my heart swell while simultaneously splintering. There's regret and guilt that still lingers in the back of my mind, but I know I can't hang on to it.

Knowing what I know now, I would have done everything differently.

Carson has forgiven me and Matteo doesn't seem to be bothered by any of this.

So, why can't I seem to forgive myself?

CHAPTER ELEVEN

CARSON

F uck. Fuck. Fuck.

I stare at the doctor, my arm throbbing as I cradle it in my lap. "I can't get surgery right now. We're in the middle of the playoffs."

A frown tugs his lips downward. "I'm sorry, Mr. Ford. If we don't operate, it could lead to some serious issues and complications. If you continue to play without the operation, or even immediately after the operation, you could cause serious damage and it could implicate your career."

This is not what I want to hear right now. Quite frankly, this might be the worst possible news I could have received. When I hit my wrist on the goal post, I knew it wasn't good. The contact lit my arm on fire immediately. I knew it was broken the instant it happened.

This isn't the first time I've broken a bone while playing before. I broke my jaw a few years ago and played through that. This is different. So much is required of my wrist and my arm and my hand. I understand everything the surgeon is saying.

That doesn't mean I like it at all.

"We can get you into the OR first thing in the morning."

"What does recovery look like?" I question him, staring down at my limb that has committed the ultimate betrayal against me. "Is there any chance I could play within the next month?"

He purses his lips, shaking his head as disapproval washes over his expression. "Absolutely not. Even if there are no complications with surgery, recovery, and rehab, you're looking at a minimum of 12 weeks off. I cannot, in good conscience, clear you to play before then."

Fuck.

Clearance from him will be my first step at getting back into the game. After that, comes clearance being granted from the team's medical staff. They won't allow me to play without the surgeon okaying it first.

My hands are tied. Figuratively and almost literally.

Disappointment floods me. I'm officially out for the rest of the season.

"Okay," I tell him, resignation sagging my shoulders as I lie back against the hospital bed. "Surgery it is."

He rises to his feet, holding his hand out to shake my left. I reach for him, shaking it swiftly. "We'll get you settled in a room for the night and take you first thing in the morning."

"Just do whatever you have to do to get me back on the ice."

He gives me a look—a look that says I better not push my fucking luck, before nodding and leaving the room. I may not always make the best decisions, but I'm not an idiot. I know better than to do something that will jeopardize my entire career . . . even if it means I have to sit out the rest of the playoffs.

———

The pain medications weigh my body down and I slowly inch up farther in the bed, careful not to disturb my casted arm. I laid awake most of the night last night and they took me in for surgery bright and early this morning. They discharged me after things were determined to be stable and Nate gave me a ride back to my hotel room.

According to the surgeon, surgery went as well as they expected. It was performed as an outpatient procedure, which is why they discharged me hours after cutting me open. They were able to repair the fracture in my wrist and secured things with a few pins. .

The pain meds are strong and my brain swirls with them, my eyelids heavy as I stare at the coffee table. Nate left to go pick up food, since he's under strict orders to stay with me for 24 hours. Because of the anesthesia and medications, I'm not supposed to be alone, although I don't need him.

My flight back to Aston is tomorrow around noon. I won't be flying with the team because of time sensitive schedules, so Nate is planning on flying back with me then too. He's a bit like a thorn in my side right now. I just want to be alone so I can sit with my fucking feelings over this whole ordeal.

It's a bit of a mindfuck. We work so hard all season to make it to the playoffs, if we are lucky. It's such a battle, a fight, and it feels so defeating to be forced to throw in the towel right now. Sure, our team still has a fighting chance, but not being there to help the guys feels like a blow to the chest and I'm not sure what to do with the whirlwind of emotions I'm feeling currently.

This is the first time in my career that I'm being forced to sit out during the most important part of the season.

My phone vibrates on the bed next to my leg, immediately gaining my attention and pulling me away from my spiraling thoughts. The screen lights up and the room shifts for a second. Closing one eye, I pick up my phone, squinting both eyes against the harsh light.

There's a message notification, but it's hard for me to make out the name on my screen. Tapping on it, my phone uses Face ID and unlocks the screen, directly opening up the message. My heart immediately skips a beat when I see who it is, a grin sliding across my lips.

ANDI

> Hey. I saw you're out for the rest of the playoffs with an upper body injury. Are you okay?

Shit. I didn't say anything to her about my injury. Hell, the only ones who knew I had to get surgery were the guys on the team. I'm not used to having someone

I'm supposed to check in with—not that that is the case with Andi, but for some reason it feels like maybe that's the way it's supposed to be.

Holding my phone in my right hand, it feels unnatural and awkward as hell as I attempt to move my thumb across the screen to type out a response. It takes me three different tries to spell out a single word before I let my hand drop with a defeated sigh. Someone probably should have just taken my phone because between the after effects from the anesthesia and the pain meds, I don't think this is a great idea.

But Andi texted me and, given what has happened in the past, I don't want her to think I'm dodging her again.

Lifting my phone back up, I tap on the screen, tapping on the video button in the corner. I watch as my face pops up and my eyes are barely open. *It's fine, I'm sure she won't notice.* My brows rise as I try to open them farther, attempting to not look fucked up from the medications. I stare back at myself at what looks somewhat wide eyed.

Andi's face pops up on the screen, the sound ringing from the phone as my face slides to a smaller box in the corner. I can't help myself as a smile lifts my lips, lazy and comfortable as her hazel eyes search mine, her brow furrowing. "Are you okay?"

"I am now," I tell her, my words slurring as I blink slowly, my eyelids half sticking together.

"Are you sure you're okay? You look . . . off."

"Yeah, yeah," I tell her dismissively, my eyes rolling

back before I focus on her again. "You don't look off. I like looking at you, actually."

Her brows lift. "Well, thank you," she says, a soft laugh following. "Are you drunk?"

"No, no," I shake my head at her, the room spinning for a fraction of a second as I let out a sigh. "I had surgery this morning so it's just the pain meds and shit." I move my phone to show her my sling holding my casted arm across my chest.

"Oh my goodness! Are you okay?" Worry washes over her features and my insides feel like they're melting with the way she's staring at me right now. Goddamn, she's beautiful. "I saw you go down at the game, but you went back on the ice so it was hard to tell if you were severely injured or not."

"Adrenaline and modern medicine are a beautiful thing," I tell her, a harsh laugh escaping me. "Or not. I mean, I don't know. I played through the pain, but they won't let me now."

She narrows her eyes. "You just had surgery. You have no business being on the ice."

"Yeah, yeah, I know," I huff, rolling my eyes with annoyance. "I fractured my wrist so they went in and fixed it and put in some pins. They said eight to twelve weeks for recovery."

"When are you coming home?"

"I fly home tomorrow around noon," I tell her, attempting to readjust in bed. A dull pain slides up to my shoulder, causing me to wince. "Fuck," I mutter, grunting as I get into a comfortable position. "Sorry. You don't realize how much you take for granted having two working arms until you only have one that works."

Andi nods, her lips pursing. "I'm sorry. Do you have anyone to stay with you and help you when you get home?"

A smirk lifts the corner of my lips and I cock my head to the side. "Are you offering?"

Her face scrunches, a soft laugh leaving her again, but this time it's a bit nervous. "I mean, yes and no. If you need someone, I will help you."

"I should be okay."

She's silent for a moment. "How good is your memory with the pain medicine?"

My brows furrow. "What do you mean?"

"If I tell you something right now, do you think you'll remember it?"

"I remember everything you tell me, Trouble."

She snorts and rolls her eyes. "Yeah, okay." She shakes her head. "I wanted to let you know that I spoke with Matteo and told him about . . . things."

My heart stalls in my chest. "You told him I'm his father?" I let out a breath I didn't realize I was holding. "How did he take it?"

"Better than I expected," she says, the relief laced in her words. "He normally adjusts well and adapts when needed, but he's also a child so I wasn't sure how he was going to take it. He asked a lot of questions and is excited to see you again now." She pauses for a moment. "I'm not sure if he'll be angry with me one day when he's older or not."

"He won't be," I assure her, my words slurring as I

shake my head from side to side. "Hopefully, we won't ever have to explain the specifics to him, but when he's old enough to understand, I'm sure he'll see it clearly. You did nothing wrong, Andi. You can't beat yourself up over it."

She's silent for a moment, her expression unreadable as her eyes burn holes into mine. "Thank you for that, Carson. I'm trying." She gives me a half smile and a shrug. "That's all we can do, right?"

"Right," I tell her after a beat. "Can I come by when I get home?"

She raises a perfectly sculpted eyebrow. "Are you allowed to drive?"

"Are you worrying about me?" I question her, biting back my grin.

"What?" She shakes her head, a mischievous look in her eyes. "I have other things to worry about than you, Carson Ford."

"Of course . . ." I smirk, shaking my head at her. "So, can I come by or not?"

"Fine," she says, biting back a grin. "Get some rest, Carson. If you need anything before I see you, please let me know, okay?"

I tip my chin, my eyelids growing heavier as a grin slides across my lips. "Goodnight, Trouble."

"Goodnight, Carson."

CHAPTER TWELVE

ANDI

"Miss Rossi, can I borrow you in the bathroom for a second?"

Turning off the water at the sink, I slowly turn around to look at Henry as I dry off my hands. He's the contractor I've hired to do most of the remodeling in the house and today is the second day of real work being done. There are some parts of the home that are fine, like the flooring and the general structure of the house. The bathrooms and the kitchen are the most in dire need of remodeling.

Henry's standing in the doorway, his bright blue eyes finding mine. His lips part, the corners reaching upwards as he flashes his straight, white teeth at me. He's in his early thirties, his angled jaw covered in stubble. His dirty blonde hair is pushed away from his face, although a stray wave hangs down just above his eyebrow.

"Of course." I smile back at him, pulling my hair back into a ponytail as I walk over to him. His gaze is warm and doesn't leave mine. "Is there something wrong in there?"

"No, no," he says with a soft chuckle as he spins on his heel. I follow him upstairs to the main bathroom, which he's about to get started on. "Although, you never know what you're going to find until you start tearing things up."The old, outdated linoleum floor is already half torn up to expose the plain plywood subfloor. "You didn't tell me which color you wanted to go with for the tile in the shower."

"Oh, yes, of course," I say, nodding eagerly as I pause in the doorway. My head tilts to the side as I try to picture what it will look like when it's finished, however, I can't quite seem to conjure the image. "I was thinking about white, but I'm afraid that will be too much white." I turn my head to look at him. "What do you think?"

"Personally, I think white is a great choice," he says, nodding his agreement. "It's a very clean look and can make the space actually appear bigger."

I scan the room once more, contemplating how bright this bathroom would look with white tile. "You're right. Let's do white."

He beams at me and claps his hands together once. "Perfect!"

"Mom, someone's at the door," Matteo calls out to me as he comes trotting down the hallway. His hair is a tousled mess and he's holding an armful of dinosaurs that he was trying to decide which to bring downstairs to play with. I guess he settled on all of them.

My forehead creases. I didn't hear the doorbell ring,

but then again, I'm not even sure if it works here anymore. "Did someone ring the doorbell?"

Matteo shakes his head, dropping a pterodactyl onto the floor. I bend down to pick it up and hold it in my hand as I wait for his response. "Someone was knocking and I looked out the window and saw a car."

Anxiety courses through me and then I remember the text from Carson earlier this morning. I told him we could come over, but he insisted on stopping by instead. My heart speeds up in my chest and I glance back at Henry. "If you need anything else, let me know."

"Of course, Miss Rossi," he says, smiling brightly at me as he tips his chin and turns back into the bathroom to get back to work.

"Come with me," I tell Matteo, gently pressing my hand against his back in an effort to guide him down the stairs. "Carson is supposed to be stopping by. Do you want to answer the door with me?"

A wide smile breaks out across his face. "Yep," he giggles, his footsteps moving quicker. "Race you there!"

"Be careful, *caro*!" I call after him as I follow him down the stairs. He runs as fast as he can down the stairs and I'm holding my breath the entire time because I do not need him falling and hurting himself.

I reach the front door after he does and he's already waiting there, hand on the door and a shit eating grin on his lips. "I beat you!"

"I couldn't keep up with you!" I laugh softly and ruffle the hair on top of his head. Matteo does a happy, little celebratory dance, spinning around in a circle. Laughter fills the air and my hand finds the doorknob.

Slowly turning it, I pull the door towards me and reveal our visitor on the other side. My eyes meet his and a slow smile creeps across his perfect lips.

He looks at me, then down at Matteo, and then back to me again. "Hey," he says softly with a nervousness evident in his tone.

I'm immediately drawn to the sling around his neck, holding his arm across his chest. My gaze travels back to his, searching for any indication of pain or discomfort.

"Hey, how are you? How are you feeling?" I fire off a round of questions. My eyebrows tug together, contorting my expression in concern before relaxing again.

"I'm good," he says, smiling at me as something dances in his irises. His gaze drops down to my lips before slowly drifting back to my eyes. "Much better now." His voice a gentle caress and my stomach flutters as my breath hitches. I immediately shelve the feelings. That's not why he's here. He probably just means he feels better since surgery.

Carson bends his knees, lowering himself into a crouching position in front of Matteo. "Hey bud. I'm Carson. I don't know if you remember or not, but we saw each other at the grocery store when you were helping your mom."

Recognition washes over Matteo's eyes. "You helped me find the one that won't hurt my belly."

"Right," Carson smiles, nodding eagerly. "What's that you got there?" He motions to the dinosaurs Matteo holds in his arms.

Matteo pulls one hand out, showing him the pterodactyl as excitement transforms his features. "I brought my dinosaurs downstairs to play. Do you want to play with me?"

Carson nods with equal excitement, his smile lighting up his entire face. "I would love to," he tells Matteo. Matteo reaches for his good hand, giving him a gentle tug. Carson slowly rises back to an upright position.

I hold the door open for him and step out of the way. "Please come in," I offer, as Matteo leads him into the house. "You'll have to excuse the mess," I explain as I follow them into the living room. "They just got started on the renovations today."

Carson turns to look at me, his eyes scanning my face with an unreadable expression on his. "It's not a mess, Andi."

My lips part to argue, but I close them as I watch the two of them settle on the floor around the coffee table. Matteo unloads his armfuls of dinosaurs and Carson takes a seat on the ground next to him. I keep my thoughts to myself as Matteo's voice fills the empty space.

He starts to show Carson his different dinosaurs and tells him all their names. Carson watches him intently, nodding along as he takes each toy that Matteo hands to him.

There's an armchair across from the couch and my eyes never leave the two of them as I lower myself into the chair. It's a candid moment I never thought I'd get to witness. Carson hangs on to every word Matteo says, his eyes glued to Matteo. Matteo talks excitedly and I love seeing him like this.

He's getting to share pieces of himself and the things he likes with Carson. My heart splinters a bit as I watch them knowing that this is something that they could have had for years now.

"What happened to your wrist?" Matteo asks Carson after a brief break in their conversation about dinosaurs.

Carson moves one of the dinosaurs across the table, knocking over one of the ones on Matteo's side, another smile pulling across his lips. "I broke it playing hockey the other day," he explains, lifting his shoulders before letting them fall. "It happens sometimes."

Matteo tilts his head to the side. "We were watching when that happened." His forehead creases. "You came back on the ice, though."

"I shouldn't have," he smirks with a wink. "I had to finish out the rest of the game and just worked through the pain. I'm all fixed up now, though. They put a few pins in my arm." Carson leans closer to him, lowering his voice to more of a whisper. "I'm pretty much a robot now, but don't tell anyone."

Matteo's face cracks and he erupts with laughter. The sweet sound fills the air as he tilts his head back. His body shakes and his eyes are bright as he straightens his spine and looks back at Carson. His expression is so serious. "I want pins so I can be a robot too."

Carson chuckles, his head moving from side to side. "What if I told you that you can be a robot without pins?"

Matteo's eyes widen. "Wait, really?"

"It's top secret and it isn't easy." Carson glances at me, a playful glimmer in his eyes. "I'll tell you sometime."

Matteo moves one of his dinosaurs, making it roar before it trots across the table. "Matteo, *caro*," I say, breaking through the sounds of him playing. "Can you go pick up your other toys in your room while Carson and I talk?"

Matteo looks at me, setting down his dinosaurs before nodding. "Okay, Mom." He's such an easy kid and never cares to argue. He walks over to me, pausing as he looks back at Carson and then back to me. "Am I allowed to call him Dad?"

His words pull at my heart. I look at Carson, my eyes widening in the slightest before looking back, waiting for him to give me something, anything. Carson's eyes are equally wide. After a moment, he nods. I look back at Matteo. "You can call him whatever you'd like, *caro*."

Matteo smiles and nods, looking over his shoulder at Carson. "I'll be back soon, Dad."

Carson's lip part and a shallow breath escapes him. I watch as conflict washes over his expression. It mixes with other emotions. His tongue darts out, he lets his lips. "I'll be right here, bud."

Matteo disappears from the room, leaving Carson and me alone with our thoughts for a second. The heaviness hangs in the air, and he watches me carefully from across the room. I rise to my feet, closing the distance as I move over and sit down on the couch.

Carson moves from the floor to sit on the other side of the couch.

"How are you actually feeling?" I question him, pulling my legs up underneath me.

He purses his lips, his nostrils widening. "Not being able to play sucks."

"I meant your wrist."

"Oh," he says, dropping his gaze down to his arm before looking back at me. "Okay. It's sore, but manageable with medication."

"That's good." I stare at him for a second, letting out a breath. "I think we should talk about custody things." I pause staring at him for a moment. "I have a few reservations about the entire situation."

His eyebrows tug downward for a second before relaxing, not giving anything away. He tucks his lips between his teeth, nodding again. "Okay."

"I think we need to develop a plan to present to our lawyers, but I don't feel comfortable doing that until I know that this is going to be a good thing for Matteo." I fold my hands on my lap. "I'm not saying I don't think Matteo will be safe with you, but I need to know for sure before agreeing to anything."

I don't know Carson well enough to determine whether or not my child is fully safe with him. I know nothing about his life, other than his extremely demanding work schedule.

"Okay," he says after a few seconds pass. His expression is unreadable, and I don't dare to dive into what could possibly be going on inside of that beautiful head of his.

"I have no intention of keeping you from your son," I assure him again. "But I think we need to take things slowly. I think it would be best if we get to know each other better and I want to make sure that Matteo is comfortable."

"How long are you planning to be in Aston?"

I swallow. "Just for a few months, until we get the house ready to go on the market. With Matteo starting school in the fall, I don't imagine we will be here all summer."

Carson adjusts in his seat. "Okay, so we can take things slow while you're here in town, but what happens after you leave? How do we go about things then?" There's a touch of worry in his tone and I just want to wash it away. He doesn't have to worry about any more missed time with his son.

"Honestly, I'm not sure because of how often you have to travel and how demanding your schedule is. It's not like we can do a normal agreement where you get him every other weekend and a few days during the week." I let out a sigh. "This is not home for us, Carson. And I don't know if driving back and forth is going to be best either."

Carson stares at me. "I'll drive however far I have to, whenever I have to."

Those words alone and the seriousness in his tone makes my heart stall inside of my chest.

He lets out a sigh and drops his head. "Fuck," he mutters. He's silent again, and it stretches between us. I wring my hands in my lap, unsure of what to say or what to even do.

My life isn't here in Aston, but it could be if I wanted it to be. I could keep Bella's house and move us here. We could establish a whole new life so he can have a relationship with his father.

It's always an option, but on the other side of that coin, it means that I am disrupting, uprooting, and upending my entire life and the life that I've built in Starling Ridge.

I don't know what I'm supposed to do. I don't know what the best option or best solution is. "Do you think we should get a mediator involved?" I ask him, a frown tugging my lips downward. "Perhaps an outside party could offer us a different perspective."

Carson lets out another breath before he lifts his head and shakes it. "No. I think we can figure it out ourselves." He pauses, leaning forward as he rests his tattooed arms on his thighs. I want to study them and the intricate designs, but I know that now isn't the time. "You're only about two hours from here, right?"

I nod. "That's correct."

"I'll drive back and forth to see him."

My eyebrows draw inward. "How will that work with practice and games?"

"I'm willing to try whatever I have to do, Andi." His expression cracks. "I just want time with him. I just want to get to know him, to watch him grow up. I just —" He pauses, letting out another ragged breath. "I just want to be a part of his life."

"I want you to be a part of it too," I tell him with nothing but honesty. "I could always move here to

Aston." The words tumble from my lips before I even realize what I'm saying.t

Carson immediately shuts that idea down. "I can't ask you to do that. It's not fair to you."

"None of this is fair to anyone."

"I'll come to you guys." He tells me, nodding with resignation. "I can find an apartment there and I'll drive back and forth. I'll stay in Aston when I have to."

"That won't work with your schedule and you know that," I remind him again.

"I don't fucking care, Andi." He says his voice dropping to a tone that's almost unrecognizable. It's laced with pain and fear, regret and remorse. "Sorry, I'm frustrated and shouldn't be projecting onto you."

"It's okay," I tell him as I lean forward and reach for his hand. I give him a gentle squeeze as he wraps his fingers around mine. His palm is soft and warm against my skin. "I think tensions are high right now and maybe we both need to take a step away from this for a bit. We can each write down how we would like custody to look and when it's time, we can take it to our lawyers."

He's silent for a second. "Okay." His Adam's apple bobs as he swallows roughly. "I have no choice but to trust you right now. The last thing I want to do is make Matteo uncomfortable and for you to feel as if he's not safe with me, so I will do what I have to do to show you that you can trust me too."

My heart fractures. "I don't want to keep him from you."

Emotion swims in his eyes and he gives me a curt nod. "I know."

I slowly rise to my feet, reaching for his hand to pull him with me. "Come with me."

He doesn't resist and stands up, letting me lead him towards the kitchen doorway. It registers in my mind that I'm still holding his hand and I quickly drop it, heat creeping up my neck and spreading across my face. "Can I get you something to drink?"

"Water would be nice."

I motion for him to sit at the island as I grab him a bottle and set it in front of him. He takes a seat, unscrewing the top as I open the drawer in front of me and pull out a pen and a notepad. I rip off one sheet and hand it to him along with a writing utensil and give one to myself.

"Let's write down our plans." The corners of my lips lift as I momentarily get lost in the gray hues of his eyes. "I want this to work. I want you and Matteo to have the relationship you both deserve to have."

"He's a great kid," he says softly, his voice barely audible as his eyes burn holes through mine.

"He is." I slowly nod, my smile stretching. "He's your kid."

"I still can't believe it," he admits, his eyes growing damp as a mixture of emotions conforms to his features. "It's crazy, you know?"

"I know."

"Would the two of you want to come to the next playoff game that's a home game?" He pauses, nervousness encapsulating him. "I don't know if you have plans or anything . . ."

My heart clenches in my chest, the same moment my stomach does a somersault. "We would love to."

Matteo's footsteps are heavy on the stairs as he comes bounding down them, the sound breaking up our conversation. He comes racing into the kitchen and pauses in the doorway when he sees the paper and pen on the counter. "Are you guys drawing?" he says, excitement in his voice. "I want to draw too."

Carson looks at me, then down at the papers, and back at me. "Can I do this on my computer and send it to you and we'll go from there?"

I nod, watching him as he turns back to Matteo. "Come on, bud," he says, pulling out a seat for him. "Come draw with me."

"I'll get some crayons," I offer, leaving the two of them as they settle into an easy conversation again. I linger in the doorway a moment to just watch the way they interact. It's as if they've known each other this entire time. There's such an ease and comfortableness to them, as if their souls are tethered.

There's an undeniable connection between Carson and Matteo.

And I can't wait to watch it grow.

CHAPTER THIRTEEN
CARSON

"Hey Dad," Rowan says with a smirk as I walk over to him and take a seat on the bench beside him. They have a home game tonight and if they win this one, they win this series.

Since I'm injured, I'm not traveling with the team, but I'm still expected to be here on game days. Even if I wasn't supposed to be here, I still would be. This is my team.

I slowly look around the room, my eyes scanning over Nash and Lincoln, over my brother Caleb and Rowan before I lift my gaze to the logo on the ceiling.

This is my family.

"I wish I were able to go out on the ice and battle with you guys tonight," I tell Rowan, my voice low as I drop my attention down to my dress shoes. It feels weird sitting in the room with them, still dressed in a suit, while they're all getting ready to go out without me.

"It fucking sucks, but it's not your fault," Rowan says, clasping his hand over my shoulder. "We wish you were about to play too, but shit happens. You know how it goes."

"I know," I agree, nodding reluctantly. It's the cold hard truth about playing a contact sport, but it doesn't change the way I feel about it.

Caleb steps in front of me as Rowan removes his hand from my shoulder. I slowly tip my head back to look up at my brother. His expression is hopeful and he gives me the smallest smile that I would have missed if I weren't staring at him.

"How are you, Cars?"

"I'm good," I tell him, tipping my chin down before raising it again. "As good as I can be."

"Having you here makes things feel normal. The energy has been off in the locker room without you," he says, his voice reaching me through the rest of the commotion in the room. "It's not the same without you on the ice, but you need to focus on healing so you can get back with us next season."

"If they'd let me play, I wouldn't let this stupid thing keep me from being out there," I admit, raising my stupid broken wrist to show him. There's a heaviness on my chest and I need it to disappear immediately.

Caleb gives me a look of disapproval. "You need to stay off the ice, Carson," he scolds me with a shake of his head and fist against my chest. "Do not fuck this up and ruin your entire career."

An exasperated sigh escapes me, my shoulders

deflating. He's right. This isn't worth fucking up my entire career. There will be other chances at the playoffs. I'll get to play with them again as soon as we get back into the groove after the off-season. "Okay."

"Did Andi and Matteo come?" Caleb questions me, abruptly changing the conversation. My brother and I talk daily, even if it's just a quick text to check in. It became a habit after Caleb lost Amelia. I didn't want to crowd him at the time, but I needed to know he was okay.

I nod, a few pairs of eyes slide in my direction as I respond. "They were in the wives room and I'll be meeting them upstairs for the game."

"I'd like to meet them soon," Caleb adds, a gentle smile lifting his lips again.

I haven't been keeping them a secret, but I don't want to overwhelm Matteo in any way. I do want him to meet his uncle, though. I want him to meet all of my family, blood or not.

"We'll make it happen." I nod again and glance around the room, taking in the sight of my guys.

Caleb holds up a paper in front of my face. "Will you do the honors tonight?"

It's the line up list. I take it in my hands and slowly rise to my feet. A smile tugs at the corners of my lips as I meet his gaze. "I'd love to." I look around the room as everyone begins to quiet down. "All right, boys. Tonight is an important night and I know you all are going to go out there and fucking fight your asses off for that *W*."

The guys erupt in hoots and hollers.

"Here we go," I start, pausing to clear my throat. "We've got Ro between the pipes." They all clap, the sound echoing throughout the room. "We've got Cale." *Clap.* "We've got Nashy." *Clap.* "We've got Matthews." *Clap.*

I continue through the entire line up, everyone clapping in between the names until we get to the very end. The room breaks out into more commotion, the guys all hopping off the benches as they get their helmets and gloves on.

I hang out for a moment, moving to the side of the room, standing by the door as I watch them all. Coach Landry steps up beside me and watches with me. "They needed that from you tonight." His voice is low. "They've been playing their asses off but you know how that is when you're missing a vital part of the team."

Hearing him say it hits me in the chest like a ton of bricks, except it's not a negative. Pride blooms inside me. He can be a tough coach at times but every now and then, he approaches issues from a tough love stance. He doesn't hand out empty or meaningless compliments. You only hear those things from Coach Landry when he means it.

"Thanks, Coach."

"How are you doing? How is the wrist healing?"

The cast is heavy around my arm. "It's healing well. It's not easy having to sit back and watch everyone, but I'm doing well, all things considered."

"I get that," he says, nodding in understanding.

Coach played professionally until he was in his late twenties. A knee injury made it difficult for him to continue to play so he retired and began coaching instead. "Well, we look forward to you getting back into the game, Ford."

"I'm looking forward to that as well."

Coach leaves me standing by the door alone as I watch my teammates all lining up. The music sounds from out in the arena and the energy buzzes in the air around us. It's electric and everyone feels it.

"Here are your Aston Archers!" The announcer's voice echoes throughout the stadium and the guys all start heading down the tunnel to the ice. I hang back, wishing I was following them.

My footsteps are heavy when I force myself to turn around and head in the opposite direction. I find the elevator down at the other end of the hall and I step onto it, catching glimpses of the guys as they skate past the end of the tunnel.

———

As I walk through the suite, moving past everyone, I see the top of her head. She's in one of the seats in the front row. Andi leans over toward Matteo as he says something to her, pointing out at the ice below.

We have a suite that the wives and family members use, but during the playoffs, it's just the wives and kids in it.

"I like her," Nova, Lincoln's fiancée says as she steps

up beside me. I look over to her and find her watching Andi with a soft smile on her face. "She seems really nice."

"She is," I say softly, turning my direction back to Andi and Matteo. My eyes roam over the side of Andi's face, memorizing her features. "I'm still getting to know her, but that's been my assessment so far."

Nova laughs quietly. "You like her, don't you?" She pauses. Her soft smile has morphed into a sheepish grin. "I mean, clearly you liked her when you first met her or else you guys wouldn't have a kid." She laughs again, shaking her head.

"Well, yeah," I choke out, covering up my fumble with a laugh. "She's attractive and nice. There's nothing not to like." I roll my lips between my teeth. "We're just trying to figure out how to co-parent, I guess."

"Right, right." She bites back a grin. "So, you wouldn't want anything more with her than co-parenting."

"Relationships aren't really my thing," I tell Nova in a hushed voice so those around us don't overhear. I would be lying if I said the scenario hadn't crossed my mind. In a perfect world, Andi and I together would make so much sense. The three of us, living that family life together.

However, this isn't a perfect world.

"Things can always change." She gives me a small shrug as she taps her hand against my shoulder. "Just keep an open mind, kid. You might surprise yourself."

My eyebrows pull together. "Surprise myself with what?"

She shrugs again, holding her hands up in an innocent gesture. "You think you know what you want now, but you might decide you want something different." She inches closer, her voice dropping lower. "I promise you, relationships aren't as bad as you think they are."

A laugh escapes me, loud enough that Andi slowly turns around in her seat, her eyes searching for me. Nova retreats, moving back to where her daughter Posey is sitting, and I'm left under Andi's gaze.

My throat bobs, a warmth building in the pit of my stomach as my heart flutters inside my chest. My body betrays me when she simply looks at me. Goddammit. I'm drawn to her in ways I can't even begin to understand.

And just like that, my feet move without instruction, leading me directly to her.

"Hi."

Andi's still staring at me, her nude colored lips twitching. Her hazel eyes stand out against her dark mascara, but her face appears to be free of makeup, except for the pink tint across her cheeks and the bridge of her nose.

"Hi."

Matteo whips his head to the side, a smile lighting up his face when he sees me. "Hi!"

"Is there room for me here with you guys?"

Matteo nods eagerly and I smile at him then look at Andi, waiting for her approval. Her eyes burn holes through mine, her lips parting as a breath escapes her. Her tongue darts out to wet them and I wish it was mine instead. As her tongue retreats, my gaze drifts back to those hazel eyes that have lingered in my mind for years.

My heart skips a beat as she smiles at me, like I'm the only one in the damn stadium.

"We were hoping you'd join us."

CHAPTER FOURTEEN

ANDI

Carson and Matteo are both sitting on the edge of their seats, Carson's elbows propped on his knees, Matteo craning to see over the ledge. They watch the game intently as Carson explains some of the plays to Matteo. I sit back in my seat, unscrewing the lid of my water bottle to take a sip and watch the two of them.

My heart swells in my chest and I see the way Matteo hangs onto every single word Carson says to him. I didn't realize what was missing until seeing the two of them together.

There's a stoppage in play and Carson glances over his shoulder at me as a tender smile crests his lips. This isn't the first time I've caught him looking at me while talking to Matteo within these first two periods of the game.

It's the ninth time, but who's counting?

"I'm going to use the restroom quickly," I tell Matteo

and Carson as I finally rise to my feet. There's only four minutes left in the second period and the Archers are up by two goals right now.

"Okay," Carson nods as he stands up to grant me access to pass Matteo and him. Matteo moves out of the way, moving into my seat as he watches the players getting into position for a face-off.

As I walk past Carson, his body shifts towards mine and I end up brushing against him. The warmth from his chest radiates against my arm and I pause to inhale his scent. Blush creeps across my cheeks and I force myself to keep moving, clearing my throat as I duck my head. I don't miss Carson's low chuckle so I move my legs faster, forcing myself away from him.

He's been looking at me all night long and it's bringing back thoughts of that one night we shared together. I was immediately drawn to him after I collided with his back that night, and I can feel myself once again being pulled into his orbit.

I liked Carson Ford more when he was an enigma. When he was unreachable and a memory.

Having him close like this is dangerous to my heart. We need to focus on co-parenting and finding a balance, yet I find myself incredibly distracted by him and his presence.

I slip into the bathroom, relieving myself before stepping in front of the mirror to wash my hands. I stare at myself, my eyes roaming over my face as I work the soap into a lather between my fingers. My hazel eyes stare back at me and the pink tint on my cheeks lingers.

Damn him for what he does to me, especially when I

know it can never be anything more than a fleeting moment or a lingering feeling.

He made it clear that night that he doesn't do relationships. He specifically said that he doesn't do strings and unfortunately for both of us, I'm no longer at a place in my life where I don't want strings. I want more. I want a love that rivals the types you read about in fictional stories.

And I don't think that's something Carson will ever want.

When I come back out of the bathroom, there's less than a minute left in the second period. I step closer to the stairs, but movement to my right catches my attention. It's Nova, Lincoln's fiancée, and she waves me over to the table where she's sitting.

I briefly met all the women earlier, but Nova was the one I talked to the most. She seems to be more of the leader of the group. Riley, Nash's wife, sits to her left, holding her son and I see Hadley, Rowan's girlfriend, walking around patting Rowan's baby girl on the back.

"How are things going?" Nova questions me as she gets up from her chair, leaving her daughter and Caleb's daughter, Estella, with a coloring book. She looks over at Carson and Matteo. "He seems like such a natural with him."

Carson and Matteo stand up as the period ends. I can't stop the smile that takes over my face at how similar they are. "He's great with Matteo, and Matteo is obsessed with him."

"I'm glad the two of you ran into each other again."

She pauses, her eyebrows pulling together. "Can I ask you something?"

"Sure." I swallow back my anxiety about what she might ask. There's something heavy behind her eyes, but I don't dare try to figure out what the emotions may be.

"If you wouldn't have run into him, would you have tried to get in touch with him?" She corkscrews her lips. "I know it's none of my business and I don't know what all has gone down with you and Carson, but he's family."

"I tried to get in touch with him when I found out I was pregnant." I swallow the lump in my throat. "He was completely unreachable. I planned on trying to find a way after we got settled in Aston."

"There you are," Carson says softly, his voice a warm embrace as he instinctively presses his hand against the small of my back. My body instantly relaxes against him, reveling in the warmth of his palm through my shirt.

"Hey," I say, my voice catching in my throat as I turn around to face Carson and Matteo. "I was just talking to Nova about the two of you."

Carson looks at Nova, raising an eyebrow in question at her. She doesn't give anything away as she glances out at the ice and then back at us. "I didn't even realize the period was over." She steps over to her daughter and Caleb's. "Come on, girls. Let's go get dessert."

"Dessert?" Matteo's face lights up. He looks between Carson and me. "Can we go too?"

Nova walks back over. "He can come with us, if that's okay with you two. They have dessert options during the second intermission. We were going to go grab something and come back up."

"Do they have anything without dairy?" Carson questions her before I get the chance to say anything. "Matteo doesn't tolerate dairy well." He glances at me. "Right?"

I nod. Carson and I haven't talked about it, but when we saw Carson at the store, he helped Matteo pick out a vegan mac and cheese. Matteo told him that milk hurts his stomach. "He's lactose intolerant."

"They have some options," Nova smiles, glancing at Matteo and back to us. Her daughter pulls on her arm. "Hold on, Posey." Nova looks at me again. "I promise he won't have any dairy and I'll bring him right back."

"I'm fine with that," I smile and turn to Carson. "Are you okay with that?"

He stares at me, emotion filling his eyes as I wait for his approval. He gets to have as much of a say as I do. It's not just Matteo and me anymore.

"I am," Carson says softly, tipping his head at Nova. She looks between the two of us before motioning for Matteo to follow along with her and the girls. I watch him as he falls in step with Estella, the two of them looking almost as if they could be siblings. "Thank you for that."

I turn to Carson. His eyes slowly search mine, gratitude and perhaps awe linger in his. "He's your son, too. You get as much of a say as I do."

"Was it hard?"

My eyebrows pull together. "Was what hard?"

Carson's Adam's apple bobs as he swallows roughly. "Doing everything as a single mom." He lets out a breath and rakes a hand through his tousled hair. "I can't imagine it was easy and if I'm being honest, I feel like an asshole thinking about you doing it all alone while I was just out living my life."

Emotions well in my chest and cause my ribcage to constrict around my heart. "Don't feel like an asshole, Carson. You didn't know." I pause, shifting my weight on my feet. "It was hard at times, but my family is very supportive and they helped me when I needed it."

He chews on the inside of his cheek for a beat. "Good," he says, tipping his chin. "I'm glad you had them."

I stare at him for a moment. Though he tries to hide it, I catch the torment wash over him. I close the distance between us, reach out for his hand and squeeze gently when mine finds his. "I know that you would have been there if you knew."

"Fuck," he mutters, then sighs out a breath after a moment of silence passes. "I wish I would have known."

"Me too," I tell him, my voice barely above a whisper as I squeeze him again and nod. "I'm glad you know now and that we—I mean, he has you in his life."

His eyes crinkle with the ghost of a smile dancing across his face as he shifts his hand, wraps his fingers around mine, and squeezes back. "Me too, Trouble." Electricity crackles in the air between us. "Me too."

My heart crawls into my throat and I force it back

into my chest. He doesn't release my hand and I revel in his warmth. It spreads up my forearm like wildfire. He may be agreeing with me on Matteo, but his eyes imply he's not only talking about our son.

The lingering stare, the way he caresses my hand . . .

Maybe he feels it too—or I'm severely delusional.

CHAPTER FIFTEEN

CARSON

"Dad."

The sound of his voice. The single word that falls from his lips that holds more weight than anyone will ever understand. My heart stumbles over itself in my chest, my eyes immediately flashing to Matteo's as I pinch the laces of his skates between my fingertips.

"What's up, bud?"

"Do you think you might come out on the ice too?" The hopeful smile on his face dissolves as he glances down at the cast still wrapped around my wrist. "I forgot," he says quietly, his eyebrows pulling together as a frown tugs his lips downward.

A lump lodges itself in my throat and I release his foot after tying his skate. "Well, I'm not supposed to be playing." I don't mention the fact that I was told to stay off the ice until further notice. I can't stomach the disappointment etched in his features. "But if I just come out, I'm not technically playing."

Matteo's eyes widen and a huge smile cracks across his face. "So, you might come out?"

I tip my chin towards my chest and lift it. "I'll talk to the coaches before the clinic starts."

Matteo's beams at me. "Okay." He rises to his feet and slides his helmet over his head. "Can you help me with my straps?"

I get to my own feet and reach for him, pulling the straps from his cage back to the snaps behind his ears. I press them in on each side, listening for the snapping sound. I grab his chin strap, connecting the two pieces before tapping him on the helmet. "Go get 'em, kid."

He tilts his head up, looking at me once more with determination set deeply in his features. He slides his hands into his gloves, gives me a nod, and marches out of the locker room. I stare at the door, my heart swelling in my chest. I still have so much to learn about this little guy, but goddamn, he's my kid without a doubt.

My arm is heavy from the cast and instinctively, I hold it across my chest as I follow him out. I see Matteo's number on the back of his practice jersey, lost in a sea of little people crowded by the door. One of the coaches blocks their way, keeping them out as another coach gets the equipment ready for their drills.

It looks like they're the only two here today, so I head over to the one by the door. He pushes it open, letting the kids hop onto the ice.

"Excuse me, Coach," I say as I reach him. He looks over at me, eyes widening with recognition as he scans my face. "I'm not sure I can be of much use, but if you need another helper on the ice, I'm more than willing to."

His throat bobs. "We would love to have you out there." He pauses. "You're Carson Ford, right? Aston Archers defensemen?" He holds out his hand. "Coach Dan."

"In the flesh," I tell him with a smile and take his offered hand. My gaze drifts past him in time to see Matteo wipe out along the blue line. A chuckle escapes me as he pops back up like a spring. "That one is mine," I say, pointing to Matteo as he starts to skate around the rink with the rest of the kids.

I'm in awe as I watch him begin to move. He's a little unsteady at times, but he's a complete natural. It's as if the kid was born with a pair of skates on his feet. Then again, it's in his DNA.

"Do you have skates with you?"

I nod. "In the car. I'll be out in a few minutes."

"Awesome," he nods eagerly, a smile brightening his expression. I leave him where he's at, head out to my car and find my spare pair of skates I keep in the trunk. It's a strange habit, but then again, it comes in handy sometimes.

The kids are all lined up to start their first drill when I step onto the ice. Pushing off with my inside edges, I bend my knees, heading in their direction as I hold my arm across my chest. It feels fucking weird, but it's manageable.

I shift my weight, my blades cut through the ice and create a layer of snow as I come to a stop by Coach Dan and the kids. Matteo's eyes are glued to mine, watching me with enough admiration to pull my heart directly from my chest.

Coach Dan introduces me to the other coach, Coach Jackson, before turning back to the kids.

"Kids, this is Coach Carson. He plays for the Aston Archers and was so kind to offer to help us today." Whispers break out within the crowd of kids and I swear I hear Matteo say something about his dad. Coach Dan pauses, nodding to the other coach. "We're going to start with a little game of red light, green light on the other half of the ice."

Coach Jackson glances at me and gives me a quick nod before directing his attention back to the group of kids. They're all chatting, racing down towards the other goal line, where they are supposed to start the game. I don't miss the way they all glance at me, their little mouths moving a mile a minute as they line up along the red line.

"Coach Jackson, can I get you on one side and Coach Carson on the other?" Coach Dan looks at the kids. "All right, everyone. Coach Carson and Coach Jackson are going to watch to see if we have any cheaters. When I yell 'green light,' skate as fast as you can toward the neutral zone. When I yell 'red light,' you have to stop. If you don't stop or we catch you moving, you go back to the goal line."

Their little voices break out into chatter again and although I can't make out the words, excitement and anticipation charges the frigid air around us.

And then the game begins.

He yells "green light" and they all begin racing,

their little legs attempting to carry them quickly across the ice. A few lose their footing and another catches an edge in the ice and topples over. Laughter fills the air, Coach Dan yells "red light" and they all attempt to stop.

By the time he says "green light" for the third time, they're down to five out of thirteen kids left playing. Matteo is one of them. Determination is set in his brow and his knees are bent, his body anticipating the next time he's supposed to move.

Pride fills me and I watch with my stomach twisting in anxiety as they start to move again. He's inching closer to the neutral zone and after another call for them to stop, just Matteo and one other kid are left.

"Green light!"

They take off racing to cover the last few feet. Matteo's legs move as quickly as they can, his ankles unsteady beneath his weight as he moves one foot in front of the other. He reaches the blue line and crosses it two seconds before the other kid does.

"Yes!" Matteo exclaims, pumping his fists in the air as he ends up losing an edge and falls onto one knee. The other kids cheer for him and we all meet in the center of the ice.

I skate over to him, sliding to a stop as I pat him on top of his helmet. "Good job, bud. I'm proud of you."

Matteo looks up at me and all I see is his grin through his cage. "Thanks, Dad," he says softly, his voice filled with excitement as he nods.

"All right, kids, time to get back to work!" Coach Dan calls out as he begins to skate towards the opposite end of the rink. I reach for Matteo with both hands when I feel the weight of my cast around my right hand. I can't do that—not yet. My good hand finds his, and I pull him onto his feet.

The other kids are already forming two lines and we skate over to where they are, but Matteo doesn't get in line at first. He hangs back for a moment, worry knitting in his brow as he watches Coach Jackson run through the drill as he explains it to everyone.

"You good?"

Matteo glances up at me. "I'm not very good at crossovers," he says quietly as he turns back to watch.

"I wasn't very good at them at first, either," I tell Matteo, my voice soft as I let my hand rest on his shoulder.

His head whips to the side, his chin tipping upwards so he can see me from under his helmet. "You weren't?"

I shake my head at him. "Nope. Every time I would try to go to the right, I would trip over my own feet and end up falling head first on the ice." A chuckle rumbles in my chest as I remember those moments. I used to watch Caleb skate and just wanted to be as good as him. "Coach made me keep doing it, over and over."

"What happened after that?"

"I learned how to do it." I give him a gentle nudge, pushing my hand against his shoulder to urge him forward. "And I know you will too."

Matteo stares at me for a beat, as if he's absorbing my words. He gives me a nod. "Okay. I can work hard and learn how to do it too." There's determination in his voice and confidence in his stance as he skates over to the other kids.

I hang back and head over to the boards to keep an eye on the one section as the kids skate through. I watch Matteo the same way I've watched game films countless times before.

Except this time it's different.

It isn't about stats or scouts or contracts.

It isn't about my performance and ability to produce.

It's just about being here.

I can't play. I can't help my teammates as they battle through the playoffs. Hell, I can't even open a water bottle without help right now. But this? Hanging out at our local rink, helping with a youth clinic while watching my kid skate?

This is something I can do right now and honestly—this is more than enough for me.

This is everything I didn't realize I was missing . . .

And it's everything I don't want to lose.

CHAPTER SIXTEEN

ANDI

I stare at Henry, my eyes wide with disbelief. This entire remodeling project for Aunt Bella's house has been headache after headache. If we were gutting the house and redoing the inside completely, I could understand why that would happen.

This is entirely unexpected . . . and highly inconvenient.

"How is there mold in the duct work?"

Henry screws up his lips. "It can be caused by numerous things, but I wouldn't be surprised if there were some leaks in the roof before it was repaired."

My eyelids fall shut, a sigh deflating my lungs before I look back at Henry. "Okay, so there is mold in the duct work. What happens now?"

"Well, it depends on what you'd like to do. I would recommend getting a remediation company involved. They will advise whether you should replace all the duct work or have it cleared out." His brow furrows as he frowns. "You and Matteo shouldn't be staying here in the house. It's not safe."

Well, shit.

"For how long?"

Henry shrugs. "Depends on how quickly the company can get out here." He tilts his head to the side, sliding his hands into the front pockets of his jeans. "I would say anywhere from two to four weeks."

"Shit," I mutter, the muscle in my jaw tightening as I silently curse the situation. Matteo and I are going to have to find a hotel that isn't too far away that we can stay at for an extended amount of time. Maybe we should just go back to Starling Ridge and I'll come back after the entire house is done.

I'm not stupid. I know we can't stay in the house and I'm not going to jeopardize Matteo's health. Guilt pricks my skin for staying here this entire time and for both of us breathing in the harmful mold. Matteo's been exposed to it and I can't help but feel like a horrible parent for a moment.

"I'm sorry," Henry tells me with an apologetic gaze. "I hate to be the bearer of bad news."

Shaking my head at him, I uncross my arms and let them hang at my sides. "No, I appreciate you finding it and telling me. I don't want to endanger Matteo at all." I give him a small smile. "The 'inconveniences' are just a little too inconvenient, you know?"

"Oh, I get it," he agrees, nodding. "Life can be full of inconveniences." He pauses, glancing around the living room for a second. "Do you need any recommendations for a remedial company? I know a guy who owns one, so I can always call him and give him your information."

"That would be amazing," I tell him, smiling a little brighter. Relief settles over me. I'm fully capable of making a call myself, but having Henry take that weight from me while I figure out where Matteo and I are going to live is so helpful.

Henry pulls out his phone at the same time mine vibrates in my back pocket. I slowly pull it out and direct my attention to the screen as Henry holds his up to his ear.

There's a message from Carson and I hate the way my stomach flutters when I see his name.

CARSON

Hey. If you're not busy later, would you and Matteo want to get Italian ice?

ANDI

I'm sure he would love that.

CARSON

I can come pick you guys up. What time should I come?

Shit. Screwing up my lips, I gnaw on the inside of my cheek as I watch Henry ending his phone call. He walks over to me and I release my cheek, waiting for him to tell me the news.

"I spoke to the owner of the remediation company, Max. He said they can get you in in about two weeks. He's pretty confident that replacing the entire HVAC system won't be necessary. If it isn't, it will be about two weeks from start to finish for removal of the mold and cleaning."

I stare at him for a moment, processing the information. "So from today until the end of that, it will be roughly a month?"

"Yes."

Shit. What are we supposed to do for an entire month? We could go home, but then what about Matteo and the hockey clinics? What about him and Carson spending time together?

"Thank you, Henry," I tell him, ignoring the turmoil that's running rampant inside of me. "If you're able to schedule that with him, I would really appreciate it."

"Absolutely," he nods. "I'll get that squared away and then I'll wait to hear what's going on before continuing the renovations."

"This really derails everyone's plans, doesn't it?"

"Welcome to tearing into old homes and never knowing what you might find." He lets out a light chuckle. "I'll send you Max's contact information after I talk to him. If you need anything before then, let me know, okay?"

"Thanks, Henry."

"Can't we just stay with my dad?"

I spin on my heel, my heart pounding in my chest as I see Matteo standing there with his little hands tucked in his front pockets. "Oh, *caro*. You scared me."

"Sorry, mom."

"It's okay." I force a smile onto my lips as I wave him over. "I'm going to see if I can find somewhere for us to stay for now."

"Why can't we stay with Dad? He has a house, doesn't he?"

I nod and roll my lips between my teeth. "Well, yes, but I don't know if we are able to stay there right now or not."

"You could ask him."

My heart splinters as I stare at my little guy. He's right, I could ask Carson, but I don't want to bother him. I don't want to ask him for any help. "Why don't you go get your things packed and I'll see what I can do."

After Matteo leaves the room, I direct my attention back to my phone. I need to find somewhere for Matteo and me to stay here in Aston. I won't let him and Carson lose out on any additional time together.

ANDI

We can meet you.

CARSON

Nonsense. I'll pick you guys up to make things easier.

ANDI

I appreciate the offer, but we'll meet you there.

It isn't but five seconds after the message is delivered that my phone starts to ring and Carson's name shows up on the screen. Damn him.

"Hello?" I say as I answer the call and hold the phone up to my ear.

"What is Andi short for?"

My eyebrows pull together in confusion. "Andalina."

"Thank you. That's a beautiful name," he murmurs in approval. "Why the hell are you being difficult, Andalina?"

I purse my lips and my forehead creases as I switch the call to speakerphone so I can start looking at hotels. "I'm not. It's just going to be easier for me to meet you."

"I disagree, but I'd love to hear your reasoning."

Frustration overwhelms me and the words tumble from my lips before I get the chance to wrangle them. "Because we can't stay at the house right now and I'm not sure where we're going to be staying yet."

Carson is quiet for two heartbeats. "What are you talking about? Why can't you stay there?"

A sigh escapes me, deflating my lungs. "They found mold."

"Shit."

"Yeah," I say in a defeated tone as I scroll through a list of shitty motels outside of Aston. "The remediation company can't get to us in two weeks and they're estimating two more weeks after that until it's done. It isn't safe to stay here, so I'm trying to find a hotel or somewhere for now."

"Come stay with me."

My heart stalls in my chest. "What? No, we can't."

"Yes, you can." There's a rustling sound that comes through the speaker and I'm not sure what he's doing. "I have two guest rooms that you both can use."

The thought of staying with him has my stomach doing somersaults. My heart kicks into overdrive, thumping against my ribcage. "I appreciate it, Carson, but we can't impose on your life."

"Andi, this isn't up for debate," he says, his voice low and tone demanding. "My son and the mother of my child will not be staying at some bullshit run down motel."

"There are actually some decent hotels in Aston," I retort as I finally get to some nice ones in my search.

He's quiet again. "Pack your shit, Andi. I'll be there in thirty minutes."

"You shouldn't be driving and I'll need my car too."

"Okay," he says in resignation. "Get your stuff together, get Matteo in the car and drive to my house where you will be staying until you can safely return to your aunt's."

My stomach does another flip and my heart goes on a mission of its own, racing inside of my chest. It's fine. This will all be fine. He's simply being kind and offering his home to us. It's nothing more.

A text message flashes across the top of my screen and I see it's from Carson. I tap on it and it's his address.

This will never be anything more. He's simply the father of my child and that's it.

"Don't make me beg, Andi." His voice is hoarse, thick and low as it breaks through my thoughts.

A shiver runs down my spine, simultaneously sparking a fire in the pit of my stomach. "Okay. We'll be over in a little bit."

"Good," he says, his voice low yet smooth like silk

as it dances across my eardrums. "I'll see you both soon."

A nervousness inside of me mixes with excitement as we end the call. It's one thing having Carson Ford inserted in my life the way he has been as we navigate co-parenting together.

But living together?

Even if it's temporary, I don't see this being as easy as co-parenting . . . especially when he keeps looking at me like he has a little secret he's keeping from me.

And fuck me for wanting to know what it is.

CHAPTER SEVENTEEN

CARSON

My footsteps are light as I walk through both of the guest rooms on the second floor, checking to make sure that there isn't a single thing out of place. Andi and Matteo will be here any moment and I just want things to be perfect for them. I hadn't yet thought about making one of the bedrooms into Matteo's so this will be fun. I have so many ideas, I can't wait to share them with him and see what kind of ideas he might have himself.

Just as I'm coming down the stairs, the doorbell rings, followed by a knock on the door. It's a bit erratic and I smile to myself, knowing that it's the exact two people I've been waiting for.

My hand finds the doorknob and I slowly turn it, pulling the wooden door towards me. Andi and Matteo are standing on the other side. Andi's hand rests on the handle of a small suitcase and Matteo has an even smaller one beside him.

"Hey Dad!" Matteo smiles up at me, rocking onto

his toes with excitement as he looks past me and then back to my face.

"Hey Matteo," I greet him, smiling back before meeting Andi's tired eyes. "Hey, Trouble."

"Why do you call her that?"

I look back at Matteo. "Because when I first met your mother, she was nothing but trouble."

"Hey, that's not true," she cuts in with a playful tone. Her eyes are laser focused on mine as she pulls her sunglasses from the top of her head. "You were the one looking for trouble."

A smirk pulls on my lips. "Well, it looks like I found her." Andi's lips part and I cut her off before she gets the chance to retort. I reach for both of their suitcases. "Come on, let's get you guys settled in." I glance down at Matteo. "I want to show you your room and we can figure out how you want it to look. How does that sound?"

His eyes widen. "I get my own room here?"

"Of course," I nod, moving out of the way for the two of them to step inside. "This is your home now, too."

He glances back at Andi. "Do I get to stay with both of you?"

She rolls her lips between her teeth and tips her chin at him. "Yes. We'll talk all about it later, okay?"

"Okay!" Matteo bounds into the foyer, kicking his shoes off at the front door before patiently waiting for me. I abandon their suitcases by the bottom step and motion for them to come farther into the house.

"Let me show you both around."

Andi and Matteo are both quiet as I show them around the first floor. The living room, an office, kitchen, dining room, and bathroom. We breeze past the laundry room and the door that leads to the garage.

We head upstairs and I carry both of their suitcases as we make our way up the staircase. Matteo is hot on my heels with Andi following along behind us. She's quiet, taking it all in as we head down the hall. My room, the primary with an attached bathroom is on one side end of the hall and on the other is two guest rooms, each with their own private bathroom.

"Which room do you want to be yours?" I ask Matteo as we stand in the center of the hallway, near the doors that lead to each room. "You can pick and we can design it however you'd like."

Matteo's entire face lights up. "Really?"

"Really."

Matteo looks back and forth between all the rooms before he moves and ducks his head into them. Andi moves closer to me, the scent of her perfume infiltrating my senses. "Thank you for doing this for him."

"You don't have to thank me," I tell her in a hushed voice. "This is only a small fraction of all the things I want to do for him."

Her eyes flash to mine, slowly scanning my face. Understanding passes through her expression, mixing with something else. She studies me for a moment, her lips part just as Matteo comes running over to us.

He grabs her hand and then mine, pulling us to a room. "I want this one," he declares with a bright smile. He beams up at me. "Can we paint it blue?"

"This is your room, bud. We can do whatever you want to do."

He abandons both of our hands, runs over to the bed and hops onto it. I can't take my eyes off of him as he flops onto his back, spreading his arms and legs out wide. "I love it."

Andi lets out a soft chuckle before she follows him in. She glances at me over her shoulder, her hazel eyes immediately finding mine. "I fear he may never want to leave now."

She flops down onto the bed next to him and I take a moment to just watch the two of them. There's such a strong pull in my chest, like a string stretched taut between the two of us, drawing me towards her. Getting to know her was part of the plan, but there's something else festering inside my chest.

Something deeper. Something scarier.

Andi is the mother of my child, but the connection between us is undeniable. It's electric and magnetizing. Andalina Rossi is under my roof and creeping under my skin.

And I fear I may never want either of them to leave.

———

After all the excitement, we opt out of getting Italian ice and instead settle in for the evening. We end up ordering delivery pizza because I overlooked the fact that my cupboards and fridge are almost completely bare. Welcome to the life of a bachelor who can't cook a damn thing.

"Thank you for letting us stay here," Andi says softly as she comes out of the bathroom that Matteo is in. She helped him get into the bath and wash his hair before coming out to me waiting in the hallway so he can dry off and get dressed. She tilts her head to the side when she finds me on the floor, but instead of questioning me on it, she walks over and sits down next to me.

"My home is both of yours," I tell her, my voice low as I stare down at my hands clasped in front of me. "I want this to feel like a home to him."

"It will," she says, her voice quiet as she turns her head to look at me. "The more time he spends here, the more comfortable he will be." She pauses as I turn to look at her. "I think we should send our plans to our lawyers to have them look over things. That way we can decide on a plan that works best for all of us."

The custody agreement, right. I slowly nod. I haven't typed them up, but I will get it over to her tonight. "I was thinking that I could come to Starling twice a week and every other weekend, depending on my schedule?"

"I'm fine with that," she agrees, offering me a tender smile. "What were your thoughts on holidays?"

I roll my lips between my teeth. "Would we do every other holiday?"

"That would be fine with me." Her tongue darts out to wet her lips. "We can modify things for the summer months after we see how everyone adjusts." She pauses and blows out a long breath. "I don't want to keep him from you, but the thought of not being with him all the time has me frightened. I—I've never really been apart from him much."

I stare at her, tilting my head to the side. "He's safe with me, Andi. I won't let anything happen to him."

Her eyes rest on mine, relief washing over her expression. "I don't think you would."

"You know, you can always come stay with me too . . . you know, so you don't have to be far away from him."

Her eyes widen slightly as heat creeps up my neck and spreads across my face. I don't know why the hell I suggested something so stupid. Andi has her own life, but the thought of having her here too has my heart skipping over itself inside my chest.

I don't know what the hell she's doing to me and why the hell I want her around.

"Well, that might make your love life a little awkward." Her laugh breaks through the silence and tension. "I'm not sure how anyone you're dating would feel about your kid's mother staying at your house too."

Goddamn, I love the sound of her laughter. The way the corners of her eyes crinkle and the apples of her cheeks lift. I run my tongue over my teeth, my gaze not leaving hers. "I'm not dating anyone, Andi."

The laughter dies down, and I don't miss how her lips part before her tongue darts out to wet them. Her throat bobs as she swallows hard. "I didn't know."

"Well, now you do," I tell her, my voice hoarse as my heart pounds harder against my ribcage. "What about you? Do you have anyone in Starling Falls who's been occupying your time."

She shakes her head. "Nope," she says, popping the *P* sound at the end.

My chest expands as I suck in a deep breath and hold it a second before blowing it out. Lifting a hand, I drag it through my hair. "I've always kind of lived by a 'no strings attached' mentality."

She stares at me for a moment, then her face cracks as laughter spills from her perfect lips again. "So much for no strings, huh?"

I join in with her, my own chuckle vibrating in my throat. "I'm beginning to wonder if they might not be such a bad thing after all."

The bathroom door opens, almost as if on command, and Matteo comes bounding out, already dressed in his pajamas. He comes galloping over to us and jumps onto Andi's lap.

"Speaking of strings," Andi giggles, her eyes finding mine again before she turns her attention to Matteo. "Are you ready to brush your teeth and get settled in a bed for a story?"

"Yep!" Matteo pops the *P* sound, just like Andi did. I smile to myself. "Can my dad read me a story tonight?"

My chest constricts as they both look at me, waiting for an answer. I stare back at them in shock, my eyes shifting between my son and his mother. "I'd be honored."

Matteo climbs off Andi's lap and runs back into the bathroom like a fire has been lit under his ass. Andi stands up and tilts her head down at me as she holds her hand out to me. My heart betrays me again, stumbling over itself as I slide my palm against hers and allow her fingers to caress my hand as I rise to my feet.

Andi's hand lingers in mine. Her skin is so soft under my fingers. I don't want to let her go, but she releases me and heads into the bathroom. I watch the two of them from across the room as butterflies flutter to life inside my stomach.

I don't know what she's doing to me, but I can feel her creeping beneath my skin, crawling in between my ribs and infiltrating my heart . . .

And fuck me—because it's beginning to feel like that's exactly where she belongs.

CHAPTER EIGHTEEN

ANDI

"Are you sure you want to go with us?"

Carson tilts his head to the side as he stands inside the foyer and slides his feet into his sneakers. "Do you not want me to go?" He purses his lips. "I don't have to."

"No, no, that's not it." I shake my head as I grab my purse and sling it over my shoulder. "I just don't want to bother you. I don't want you to feel like you have to come along with us." I pause when I realize I'm rambling. I take a deep breath and blow it out to slow myself down. "I don't want us to be a bigger disruption in your life than we already are."

He rolls his lips between his teeth and pulls his eyebrows downward before his face relaxes. My breath catches in my throat as he lifts his tattooed arm and his hand reaches towards my face. His fingers graze my skin as he brushes a piece of hair away from my cheek and tucks it behind my ear. "What if I told you I want you to disrupt my life?" His eyes find mine. "You aren't bothering me, Trouble. My time belongs to the two of you."

My heart stalls in my chest. His fingertips linger along the skin just below my ear. My stomach performs an acrobatic routine inside my abdomen.

"Matteo, I get, but why me?"

His stare is so intense it feels like his eyes are burning holes into mine. He lifts his shoulders in a shrug and drops them with a sigh. "Because you're you." A ghost of a smile dances across his lips.

His gaze doesn't falter and if he doesn't stop looking at me like that, I'm afraid I'm going to melt into a puddle by his feet. Carson Ford is smooth with his words, but I have to remind myself that's all they are. He doesn't do relationships or attachments.

He's the type of guy you have your fun with and then he sends you on your way for another man to swoop in and meet you at the altar.

Carson finally tears his gaze from mine and crouches down to help Matteo tie his sneakers. I watch them for a moment and again, I'm afraid I'm going to melt. I love these tender moments between the two of them. The way Matteo's gaze is fixed on Carson's face, hanging onto every single word that falls from his beautiful mouth.

And the way Carson is captivated by our son. Always watching, studying, admiring him. It's like he's constantly trying to memorize his expressions and his facial features.

"All right, I think we're ready to go." Carson stands

back upright and tips his chin to look at me. "Are you ready, Mom?"

My stomach does a flip. "Ready when you are."

Matteo is the first at the door, pushing it open before breaking out into a run across the yard. Carson holds the door open for me, although he doesn't leave much space. I'm forced to brush against his body as I walk out onto the front porch. His hand drifts against mine as I move past him and my fingers instinctively twitch towards his.

I pull them back as if I'd been burned. My pace quickens as I step away from him. Goddammit. Every moment around him is a test against my self control and I'm not sure how much longer I'm going to be able to keep it together here.

————

Matteo steps out onto the ice and immediately begins to skate as his blades hit the surface. Carson follows after him and I'm right behind, all three of us moving one after the other. Matteo skates out ahead, not even bothering to stay with the two of us as he begins to race around. I watch his little legs and a smile lifts my lips as I laugh to myself.

Carson spins around to face me. He lifts his hat from his head and positions it backwards. *Why is that so sexy?* His blades cut into the ice and he moves with precision, skating backwards as I skate towards him. He scans my body with narrowed eyes. "This isn't your first time on the ice."

"Of course it isn't," I laugh, shaking my head at him. "I figure skated growing up, but I stopped competing when I went to college."

"And your brother played D1 hockey, right?" he questions me and I nod in response. "Is that why Matteo started to play?"

"It's clear he's a natural," I tell him. Matteo continues to move around the rink without us. There aren't many people yet at the public skate, so it's easy to keep track of him for now. "My brother suggested it and Matteo had already been skating with me before I signed him up. He fell in love as soon as he stepped on the ice."

A smile transforms Carson's expression. Goddamn him for looking as good as he does right now. "It's in his DNA on both sides then."

I bite back my own grin. "I suppose it is."

"I'd like to meet your brother and your family some-time." He pauses, his eyes slowly searching mine. "I want my family to meet you and Matteo, as well."

My heart crawls into my throat. "I'd like that."

"Good," he says softly. His strides slow as I move closer to him. As I come up beside him, he turns around to face the same direction as me. His arm brushes against mine. "I would too."

A gentle laugh escapes me. "You already said that," I say as I turn to the side to look at him. He's much closer than I realized and the heat radiates from his body. Both of our strides slow more. He shifts his body slightly so his chest faces me more as his head tips down closer to mine.

"I did, didn't I?" he murmurs. A new fire ignites in his eyes. I never noticed the three small freckles in his left pupil until now. And just beneath his left eye, close to his temple is a small mole.

His gaze drops down to my mouth and my lips instinctively part. My tongue darts out to wet them, and my head tips back as he inches closer.

And then a body collides into both of our legs.

"Whoa!" Matteo yells out before he falls onto his bottom and laughter erupts out of him. My skates abruptly shift, throwing me off balance. Carson's arms dart out, injured one and all, and he grabs me as best as he can with his fingers wrapping around my biceps.

"Your wrist," I say, as I grab onto his shoulders to steady myself instead. His right hand isn't secured around my arm at all because of his cast. I glance down at it before looking back at him.

"I'm okay," he says, his voice low. "Don't worry about me, trouble. As long as you and Matteo are safe, that's the only thing that matters to me." He winces, but quickly recovers as he looks down at Matteo and slowly moves his hands away from my arms.

I drop my own from his shoulders and let out a breath while I go to check that Matteo didn't hurt himself. Matteo bounces back up, ignoring the two of us as he starts to skate again.

Carson and I stand still, facing each other as I reach for his casted hand. I take it in my own and gently hold it while I search his face for pain.

"Are you sure you're okay?" My fingers slowly trail over the plaster material, inching closer to his exposed fingers. Concern knits my eyebrows. "Please don't lie to me."

His throat bobs as he swallows roughly. "It aches sometimes. Movements like that and the pressure make it feel sore."

A frown tugs my lips downwards.

"It's okay, Trouble," he says softly. His fingers sweep against my palm. Electricity slides along the nerve endings in my arm, my stomach quickens as my heart beats harder.

My eyes flash to Carson's and he stares back at me with a hooded gaze. His lips part, a ragged breath escaping him.

"Andi . . ." His body inches closer to mine and my breath catches in my throat. His fingers trace the lines in my palm again. His other hand reaches for mine.

Tension sizzles in the air between us. My heart forgets how to pump blood and my lungs forget how to breathe. His tongue darts out to wet his lips, the smell of his cologne infiltrates my senses.

Suddenly, Matteo inserts himself between the two of us, immediately severing the tension. My hands fall from Carson's and Matteo sandwiches himself between us, me on his left and Carson on his right.

"Come on, Mom and Dad," he urges with a tug on both of our hands. "You guys are skating too slow."

"Sorry, bud," Carson chuckles. "You took off without us, so we were waiting for you to circle back around."

I glance down at our son as the three of us skate

together, hand in hand. "Sometimes you move too fast, it's hard to keep up."

"You're a liar," Matteo giggles, the sound penetrating my eardrums as his smile lights up his face. "You guys were just too busy talking to each other."

"Maybe I like to talk to Carson."

I glance up at him through my lashes. He's already staring at me, watching me over the top of Matteo's head. He doesn't care that I've caught him staring at me. His mouth twitches and after a second, he winks and then directs his attention back to Matteo.

Butterflies flutter in the pit of my stomach as my heart thumps erratically in my chest. At this point, I may need to go see a cardiologist because I'm afraid I've developed an arrhythmia.

And Carson Ford is one hundred percent to blame.

CHAPTER NINETEEN

CARSON

"Well, if it isn't my son with the secret child who has finally decided to call me."

I wince at my mother's words. Normally, there would be a playfulness in her voice while talking shit, but not right now. All I can hear is the disappointment radiating from her tone.

"Cale told you?" I question her, gritting my teeth as irritation rolls through me.

It sounds like she blows a breath through her nose into the speaker of the phone. "He did." She pauses for a moment. "He was adamant that he didn't want to upset you, so play nice with your brother, Carson."

My eyebrows pull together and I relax them. I shut my eyes as I roll my head from side to side to stretch the muscles in my neck. "I wanted to be the one to tell you and Dad."

"Well, you're on speaker phone now, so go ahead. Tell us."

"Lise, be nice," my father scolds. He comes through

loud enough that I'm sure he's sitting next to her. After Caleb lost Amelia, they moved to Aston to be closer and to help Caleb with Estella. They both retired two years ago and after some serious insisting from Caleb, they decided to spend this entire year traveling.

They're on the west coast right now, which is exactly why my mother is calling me at eleven o'clock at night.

Andi and Matteo both went to bed a little over an hour ago, so I retreated to my bedroom. They've been here for two days now and I've been trying to give them some space to get settled in. Andi had a busy day today with virtual meetings for work, so I took Matteo to the park and kept him out of her hair.

She seemed stressed when it was time for dinner. I picked up takeout again because I haven't had time to go to the grocery store since they arrived. Over our meal, she explained that there were some issues at the museum with some ancient scripts, but she didn't go into much detail after that. It seemed like she didn't want to talk about work, so I didn't push the issue.

Although, I am interested in hearing more about what she does. Hell, I think I may just be interested in anything she wants to tell me.

"Carson, are you still there?" My father's voice cuts through my thoughts. "Your mother went to get a drink real quick. She's obviously upset by this whole situation, but you know how stubborn she can be. She's not going to admit her feelings, so I'll go ahead and tell you what it is now."

My mother is the most caring, most pleasant person I've ever met. It takes a lot to make her mad and even when she does get angry, it's like pissing off a preschool teacher, still sweet and gentle. When she feels hurt or betrayed is when she seems to be the most triggered.

I can understand why she's upset with me right now. I mean, I would be upset with myself too. It's been two weeks since I've found out about Matteo and this is the first conversation I'm going to have with my parents about him.

"It's my fault. I should have come to you both before Cale did."

"What did I miss?" My mother's voice comes through instead of my father's. "Anything important?"

"He was just getting started," my father tells her, buying me another second to collect my thoughts.

"I'm not sure what all Cale has told either of you, so I'll just start from the beginning." I take a deep breath before diving right into it. I start at the beginning, when Andi and I first met up to when I ran into them at the store. I don't hold back a single detail and wrap things up with a neat little bow when I tell them that Matteo and Andi are temporarily staying with me.

"Well, that's a lot of information to take in," my father mumbles, almost as if he's not sure what else to say.

"Have the two of you discussed custody and what happens after they go back to Starling Ridge?"

"Yes, Mom," I tell her, running a hand through my hair as I adjust in my bed. "We have things figured out and are getting them taken care of legally."

"Good," she says, her voice dropping to a tender tone. "When do your father and I get to meet them?"

I swallow roughly over the lump in my throat. "When do you want to? I would like to check with Andi to see how Matteo is adjusting to things. The last thing I want to do is bombard him with a bunch of new people. It might be overwhelming."

She's silent for a beat. "That's completely understandable," she agrees, her softness returned."Whenever you are all ready, your father and I will be on the next flight home. We could use some time back in Aston, anyway."

"I'm sorry for not telling you sooner," I tell the two of them, but mainly my mother. My father is a pretty agreeable guy. He goes with the flow and doesn't get too bent out of shape about things. If anything, he only gets bothered when my mom gets bothered. "I was in shock when I first found this all out and needed time to process it myself."

"Not to mention you getting injured and having surgery," my father adds in, as if he's trying to soften things in my favor.

"Yeah, that's been a bit of a setback, but also feels like it's forcing me to slow down in life. It's giving me more time with Matteo, so I can't fully be mad about it." I pause again and suck in a breath. "I felt a little embarrassed by the whole situation and then I also felt guilty, which I'm trying to not let myself feel that anymore."

"There's nothing to be embarrassed by or to feel guilty for," my mother says, her voice warm and comforting. "There's no sense in holding on to the 'should haves' or 'could have done.' No one knows what things would look like now if the past were different and no one can change what has already happened. Adapt, move forward, be kind to yourself and Andi, and don't take any moment for granted."

"Lise, is your edible kicking in?"

She giggles after my father calls her out. "I think it might be. I usually start to get philosophical when it does."

"Are the two of you high right now?" I ask through the chuckle vibrating in my chest as I shake my head at them. They've never been big drinkers or anything like that, but recently, they've both taken a liking to eating edibles in the evenings.

"No." "Yes." They say simultaneously before breaking out into louder laughter.

"Dammit, James," my mother chuckles. "Carson, honey. It's true, my edible is kicking in, but that doesn't mean anything, really. I owe you an apology and I'm sorry for the way I spoke to you earlier. It wasn't far for me to project like that."

"It's okay, Mom. I understand why you were feeling upset by this."

"That's still no excuse," she says softly. "You may be an adult, but I always want you to feel safe and comfortable with us."

A smile lifts my lips. "I do feel that way with you and always have."

"Good," she says. "Your father and I are going to let you go since it's late there. Send me a picture of that sweet boy and please let me know as soon as you talk to Andi, okay?"

"Yes, mom."

"Goodnight, honey. I love you," my mother says.

"Goodnight, Cars. Love you," my dad chimes in.

"Goodnight. I love you both."

We end the call and I roll over, scrolling through my pictures to find one to send to my mom. There aren't many of Matteo, yet, but I find one of him on the ice, his smile stretching from ear to ear through the cage of his helmet and I send that one to her.

My finger accidentally moves to the right and it opens the next picture. My stomach flutters, my heart pounding a little harder as I take in the image. Andi was crouched down in front of Matteo with his skate positioned against her thigh as she untied his skates. Her chin was lifted, her gaze trained on Matteo, her cheeks raised, lips parted as laughter escaped her.

I don't remember what he said to make her laugh, but I remember the way she sounded. The way she looked at him. I knew I needed to take a photo of the two of them. Whether I send it to her eventually or keep it to myself, it's at least a memory I have for myself.

And it's one I want to hang onto for a little while longer.

CHAPTER TWENTY

ANDI

"Kale, like the lettuce stuff?"

My eyes widen and I cover my mouth with my hand as I choke back my laughter. Carson's gaze flashes to mine, a grin spreading across his face as he shakes his head. I follow his eyes back to Matteo.

"He's not a lettuce," Estella, Carson's niece says, her ponytail shifting as she tilts her head to the side to give Matteo a weird look.

Caleb is sitting on the couch in front of him and smiles back at his nephew. "I mean, the sound is the same. My name is Caleb, but your dad calls me Cale, so it's up to you."

"Uncle Caleb," Matteo says, testing it out, as his eyebrows pull together. "Uncle Cale." He rolls his lips. "I think I like Uncle Caleb better."

Caleb nods and winks at him. "Me too."

"I have another uncle. Uncle Vince," Matteo explains, switching gears. "He used to play hockey."

"That's fun," Caleb says. He shoots a glance at me before looking back at Matteo. Caleb and Carson have very similar features, the shape of their jaws and noses. They have the same color hair, but Caleb's eyes are blue instead of gray. "Maybe he can come to a game sometime next season," he adds with his smile drifting.

The Archers were knocked out of the playoffs two nights ago in game seven. They fought hard and I know the guys must be feeling the loss, although Carson has yet to comment on it.

"He would love that!" Matteo exclaims. "He works teaching people now or something."

"He's an English professor," I explain, offering Caleb a small smile.

"Very cool," Caleb says. There's a slight smile still on his face as he looks from Matteo to his daughter Estella. "Tella, why don't you and Matteo go see if you can find that frog in Uncle Cars's pond again."

"Oh!" Estella claps her hands then reaches for Matteo's hand and drags him with her. "Come on, Teo. There was this little frog jumping around the last time I was here and he was so cute!"

The sound of their voices and feet drift through the house before they disappear through the backdoor into Carson's fenced in backyard. In the back right corner of his property, there's a small man made pond with a little waterfall. It isn't very big, but when I wandered over to it yesterday morning, I didn't see a frog anywhere.

Carson walks toward me and takes a seat on the couch beside me. "Is he a Ford or is he a Ford?"

Caleb's gaze meets his brother's and he chuckles. "Oh, he's definitely a Ford. It was clear in the picture you showed me of him, but it's in his mannerism too."

"So, the two of you are hard headed then as well?" I ask, a playful smile on my lips as I glance back and forth between the two of them. Caleb chuckles as he lifts a bottle of water to his lips to take a sip.

"No, Trouble, he must get that from you."

Caleb half chokes on a mouthful of water he just took. "Trouble?"

"It's nothing," I say dismissively at the same time Carson speaks.

"It's something I like to call her."

Shit. My face burns and I glance at Carson who studies me carefully. His expression is unreadable and I see his brother glancing between the two of us from the corner of my eye.

"Interesting" Caleb muses, his voice low. The back door abruptly opens but there's no footsteps running through the house. Anxiety washes over me and I immediately sit up straighter and crane my neck to see what is going on. *What if something happened to Matteo and she's afraid to tell us?*

"Daddy!" Estella calls out loudly with excitement. Matteo is jumping up and down behind her and relief floods me. "We found the frog and there's another one. Come look at it!"

Caleb is already on his feet, his smile broad as he heads in the direction of the kids.

"Mom! Dad! Come too!" Matteo's voice calls out after them.

I rise to my feet, my lips parting to respond, but I stop the moment Carson's hand wraps around my wrist. Spinning on my heel, I find him standing behind me, his eyes glued to mine.

"Wait." Carson says softly, his voice hoarse. I nod and he calls out to Matteo as he steps closer, his hand still on my wrist. "We'll be there in a minute, bud."

"What's up?" I question as I tilt my head to the side and ignore my heart thumping erratically inside my chest.

Carson loosens his grip and the tips of his fingers begin to absentmindedly trace invisible patterns on the inside of my wrist. He's standing close enough that I can smell him–a combination of leather and bourbon–and I have to tip my head back to look at him. "Does it bother you when I call you 'Trouble'?"

My eyebrows pull together. "No."

"You told Caleb it was nothing." He pauses. His throat bobs and nostrils flare as his unwavering gaze penetrates mine. "It's not nothing to me, but if you don't like it, I won't call you it anymore."

My breath catches in my throat. "That's not what I meant." I pause and attempt to calm my heart, but my heart is rarely calm around Carson Ford these days. "I like it."

"Are you sure?" He releases my wrist and I immediately miss his gentle touch. He's close enough I can feel his warmth. One step forward and our bodies would collide into one another. "I don't want to make you feel uneasy or anything."

"Too late," I murmur, my involuntary drive to

breathe suddenly ceasing to exist. I didn't mean to say that out loud.

His forehead creases and concern washed over his gray irises. "I make you uneasy?"

Shit. "Not in the way you meant."

He doesn't look any less concerned. "In what way do I make you feel uneasy?"

"In every other way," I laugh, shaking my head at myself. I'm already too far into this, I have to explain now. Although, I'd much rather the floor open up beneath me instead. "You don't make me uncomfortable, if that's what you were worried about."

His eyes slowly search mine, as if he's contemplating his next move. Like he's asking me for permission. I let out the breath I didn't know I was holding and wet my lips as he reaches for my wrist again. This time, he lifts my hand in between us now. "May I?"

I don't know what he's doing, but I nod anyway.

He takes half a step closer, the distance even smaller between us now. He uncurls my fingers, pressing my hand against his chest, palm flattened over his heart. "Do you feel that?" he murmurs, his eyes burning holes through mine.

His heart pounds hard and fast beneath my palm. "Yes," I breathe. A warm tingling sensation washes over every single nerve ending in my body.

"You make me uneasy too." A ghost of a smile dances across his perfect lips. "You make me uneasy in a way that feels as though my heart is going to burst through my chest. In a way that feels like my brain can't remember how to function properly. Like I don't know how to regulate my breathing." The corners of his mouth twitch, his hand shifting away from mine. "So, yeah. You make me uneasy in the best way possible, Trouble."

A shallow breath escapes me and my lips part, drawing his attention to my mouth. He lifts his hand and slides his knuckles beneath my chin. "So do you." The pad of his thumb is soft against my chin, tipping my head back farther as he takes another fraction of a step closer to me. "Carson," I whisper.

"I'm going to kiss you, Andi," he admits, his voice hoarse. "If you don't want me to, now would be the time to tell me."

My breath catches in my throat and my lungs constrict. "And what if I do want you to?"

"Fuck," he groans. His nostrils flare as he sucks in a deep breath. He runs his thumb across my bottom lip. "You're going to be my undoing, Trouble."

"Are you guys going to kiss?" Tella's voice shatters the moment, immediately severing the electrical current flowing between us. "You totally look like you're going to kiss."

Carson whips his head to the side, the same moment I pull my hand away from his chest and take an abrupt step backwards. "Tella. What are you doing in here?"

"I could ask you two the same thing," she retorts, raising an eyebrow at her uncle. She's only six, but the sass this girl has is frankly admirable.

Heat blooms across my face. "Carson was looking at something on my face."

Carson raises an eyebrow at me while simultaneously stifling a grin. "Yeah, she had a chin hair that needed to be plucked."

"Gross," Tella says, crinkling her nose as she scrunches her face. "Matteo wants to show you guys the frogs."

"On our way!" I chime, my voice unusually off pitch as I begin to move farther away from Carson. I step around the couch and breeze past Estella as she heads to the bathroom.

Carson is right there with me. "It's a shame she interrupted," he murmurs as we step out onto the patio. My footsteps are light, my heart thrumming in my chest.

"Yeah," I glance at him as a smirk pulls on my lips. I shoot him a quick glance over my shoulder. "I guess I'll just have to get that chin hair myself then."

Carson chuckles. "Nonsense," he says with a mischievous glimmer in his eyes just as we reach Matteo and Caleb. "We can pick up where we left off later."

"What took you guys so long," Matteo lets out an exaggerated sigh.

"Yeah, what *did* take you so long?" Caleb questions, raising an eyebrow at his brother.

"She had a chin hair," Tella calls out from behind us as she skips through the yard. "Show them the frogs before they hop away!"

Caleb looks even more confused. "Chin hair?"

"It's nothing," Carson tells him and winks at me before he crouches down to look at the frogs. I have to duck my head and bite back my grin before I direct my attention to the two amphibians.

I stare at the frogs sitting on a rock along the perimeter of the pond, yet they don't have my full attention. I'm too busy attempting to will my heart back into a steady rhythm while my brain fixates on *nothing*.

What a contradicting word . . .

CHAPTER TWENTY-ONE

CARSON

"Okay, I'm not sure what you like to eat, but I figured tacos would be easy enough for tonight."

The sound of Andi's voice drifts from the front door as she lets herself in. Matteo and I are sitting in the kitchen looking through some of my old hockey cards I collected as a kid. Caleb and Tella left just before dinner and Andi insisted on running to the store to get some things for the house since I've been living here with virtually no food except for snacks.

I rise to my feet and meet her right inside the foyer, on the other side of the door that leads into the kitchen. "Let me get that," I insist, taking the two bags from her. "Is there anything else that needs to be brought in?"

"There are a few more bags, but I can get them."

"Nonsense," I tell her and shift my body around her so I'm half ushering her into the kitchen with the bags. She looks over at Matteo, smiling at him before stopping by the island. "I'll get the rest of the things."

"Do you have a certain way you want the groceries put away?" she asks as she takes the two bags from me and begins to unload them. "I don't want to put anything in the wrong place."

I shake my head at her. "Wherever you put them is good with me."

Leaving the two of them in the kitchen, I head back out to Andi's car to grab the rest of the groceries and head back inside. Matteo is up from his seat, helping her to put things away as she arranges the ingredients she needs for dinner by the stove.

I step up to her, her back facing me as she glances over her shoulder. "What can I do to help?"

She raises an eyebrow at me and slowly turns around to face me. "I thought you don't cook?"

"I don't," I admit, lifting my shoulders in a dismissive shrug. "How am I supposed to learn if no one ever teaches me?"

Her expression softens as her lips begin to lift into a warm grin. "Fine, I'll teach you."

Internally, I feel like I'm about to come undone, but on the outside, I'm able to allude to nothing but being cool, calm and collected. My heart is beating a million beats per minute, stumbling over itself as the butterflies in my stomach flutter uncontrollably.

Andalina Rossi was supposed to be a one night stand and after learning about Matteo, she was only supposed to be the mother of my child. But lately, things just feel different. The attraction that's always been there grows deeper with every passing moment together.

"Can you chop up that onion for me?" Andi asks, motioning to it rolling away from her on the counter. She looks over at Matteo and thanks him for helping. "*Caro*, why don't you go play in the living room while we cook?"

"Okay, Mom," he says with the brightest smile and gives her a gentle hug.

I grab the onion, peel away the outer layer and Andi hands me a cutting board I never knew was tucked away in a cabinet. I find a knife and get to work. Andi gets the skillets she needs and sets them on the stove to heat while she starts to prep the rest of the food.

My eyes start to water, but I power through. I'm not sure the last time I've chopped a vegetable, although I've watched enough people doing it, so I think I'm doing it right.

Lifting the board, I walk over to Andi who's standing by the stove. "Here you go," I say, my voice soft as I hand it over to her. She tilts it over the skillet and the oil sizzles as she drops the onion in.

I cross my arms as I lean against the counter and watch her as she continues about her business in the kitchen. My heart pounds erratically in my chest, the aroma of sweet onions fills the air as I watch Andi. She preps another skillet and carefully slides the meat into it.

She grabs a spatula and slides it through the ground beef, her movements slow and elongated as she presses it in and out.

Goddamn, she makes cooking look like foreplay.

"You're hovering," she says softly, the corner of her

lip curling as she glances at me from the corner of her eye. "You're supposed to be learning."

"Oh, I am," I murmur. "I'm learning so much."

She pauses her stirring of the beef, the tension between us snapping as she turns her head, hazel eyes flashing to mine. Her pupils constrict and my heart flutters inside my chest.

"Grab that tomato," her voice is husky and she nods to it on the counter. "Be gentle and dice it. Try not to accidentally turn it to mush," she says as she hands me the cutting board again.

My breath quickens and I step in beside her, close enough to feel the warmth radiating from her body. She smells like lime and honey and something sharper—like a memory. Like her skin on mine in the darkness, six years ago, before either of us knew where that moment would lead us. Before Matteo.

Our arms brush and she sucks in a sharp breath, the sound catching in her throat.

"Am I doing it right?" I ask, slicing the tomato, aware of her watching. *Acutely aware.*

Andi steps in closer, her body angling so she's positioned behind me. "You're pressing down too hard," she explains, then her hand covers mine. "Let the knife do the work."

Her voice drops lower and becomes breathier. Her palms are warm against the back of my hand and I fall still.

"Am I doing it right now?" I murmur, my breaths growing shallow.

Andi's silent for a moment and the tension stretches

between us. Her hand doesn't leave mine, neither of us moving, the air between heavy with tension and something messier—regret, maybe. Or *want*.

Her fingers slide away. "You're getting better."

She turns back to the stove but my eyes are glued to her, watching the flush creep up her neck. She pulls her bottom lip between her teeth, biting down as she stirs the meat.

I step behind her again, too close now. She doesn't move; her body stills, her slender throat bobs as she swallows hard.

"This feels familiar," I say quietly, my mouth close to her ear, my voice but a whisper. "Us . . . like this."

Her spatula slows in the pan, steam rising between us as the silence stretches again. The heat radiates from the stove and from her—two different kinds, one making it incredibly hard to think straight.

"This isn't something we've ever done before."

She's right. We've never cooked together. We've never stood like this in the kitchen, bodies close with the heat growing and history hanging in the air.

This feels much more intimate than that night we had together. Slower, closer, more tantalizing.

"No, it isn't. We've done a lot of *different* things together though."

She reaches forward and turns off the burners. "Don't start something you can't finish, Ford."

"I'm just learning how to make tacos," I tell her, my voice husky and low. "Mostly."

Her breathing hitches, the sound subtle but I don't miss it.

She turns her head slightly, just enough for me to see the smile dancing across her lips. "Then stop standing so close."

I don't move.

"Then tell me to move."

She doesn't.

The silence stretches, the tension between us rivaling a forest fire that could burn down everything in its path.

Without a word, she lifts the skillet and holds it out behind her, her fingers wrapped around the handle. I reach around and take it from her. Our fingertips brush, slow and unhurried, they linger for a second longer than they have to.

"The table's over there," she murmurs, still not turning around.

My voice is just as quiet as hers. "I know."

I turn away from her and carry the heat away with me—in the skillet, in my fingertips, and in the space she didn't ask me to leave.

———

"Well, I think it's safe to say that your taco lesson was a success," Andi smiles at me from where she sits on the back patio as I step back outside. Matteo fell asleep on the outdoor sectional a half an hour ago. I just carried him into his bed and he didn't stir awake, most likely exhausted from the long day we all had.

"I had a great teacher," I tell her with a wink and I settle on the chair next to her at the table.

"What do you want to learn next?"

I tilt my head to the side and raise an eyebrow as a smirk pulls on my lips. "Are you offering to teach me how to cook something else?"

"Did you have something else in mind that you'd rather I teach you?"

Holy shit.

My heart skips a beat in my chest, the same moment that blood rushes between my legs. "Teacher's choice." My cock twitches. "You continue to surprise me, Trouble, so please, don't stop now."

Andi sinks deeper into her seat, both of her brows drawing inward. "Hm." She purses her lips.

"What's wrong?"

She lifts one shoulder in a noncommittal shrug. "If I had to guess, I'd say you've probably already been taught everything you could possibly need to know."

"That's not true," I tell her, my tongue darting out to wet my lips. Leaning forward, I grab the legs of her chair and abruptly drag it across the patio until it's almost flush against my chair. "There's never been any opportunity to learn with anyone else," I admit, my voice low as I peer up at her, slowly sitting back upright. "I don't do this kind of stuff, Andi."

"What kind of stuff?"

"Let people in." I swallow roughly, my chest constricting. "I don't let others occupy my space or my time or my fucking thoughts like you do." I let out a breath. "I don't know what I'm doing here with you, but I know I don't want to fuck it up."

Her eyes widen slightly before they drift back and

forth between mine, slowly searching. "There's nothing here to fuck up."

My legs are spread wide with hers tucked in between. The sunset is beginning to fade in the distance, but the glow of the light behind her illuminates the perimeter of her head, creating a halo effect. "No?" I question, trailing my fingers along her bare thighs. She inhales sharply, her pupils dilating. I stop them just as I reach the bottom hem of her shorts. "Nothing doesn't mean what it used to, does it?"

She pulls her bottom lip between her teeth and bites down as she shakes her head. "It's become quite a contradicting word."

"So, tell me, Trouble." I pause, lifting a hand up to cup the side of her face. I don't do relationships or attachments, but it feels like there's an invisible thread that has us tethered to one another. There's a constant tug, always pulling me closer and closer to her. "What am I supposed to do here? This is uncharted territory for me and I need some guidance."

Andi shifts closer, her legs press against mine as she tips her head back. The light from the setting sun shifts across her eyes, illuminating the gold and green tints that swirl together. "I think you're supposed to kiss me."

Time is momentarily suspended as my fingers drift across her skin. Her hair is soft like silk. It slips between my fingertips as I plunge them into her locks, cradling the back of her head. A gentle breath escapes her, her neck craning, chin tipping up. I inch closer, watching the way the colors shimmer in her eyes.

"I think I'm supposed to, too," I tell her, my voice hoarse and thick with lust. Closing the distance between us, I lean toward her. The smell of her perfume invades my senses and I take the time to inhale her deeply as her eyelids flutter shut. Her long, black lashes brush against the tops of her cheeks.

My eyelids fall shut just as my mouth brushes hers. Time ceases to exist and our surroundings fade into the background as my lips slowly move against hers. It's soft and gentle, sensual, yet tranquil. A serenity washes over me, as if sunlight is seeping into my pores, filtering directly into my soul.

Andi's lips begin to move with mine, melting into me as she kisses me back with a tenderness that has my toes curling. She lifts her hands to fist the front of my shirt, drawing me in closer to deepen the kiss. My tongue sweeps along the seam of her lips, urging her to let me in. There's no hesitation from her. She parts her lips and her tongue meets mine.

Our mouths melt together, our tongues tangle together in a slow dance. I breathe her in, drawing her deep into my lungs, into my heart, and into my soul. Something about Andalina Rossi just feels right.

She feels like home, like a place I'm certain I never want to leave.

We break apart, coming up for air as both of our lungs scream for oxygen. I suck in a deep breath as my eyes open and adjust to the dimming light as I study every inch of her face. Her hands fall away from my shirt and reach for my waist instead. My hand slowly moves away from her neck to trail down her arm before resting on her forearm.

My eyelids flutter shut and I lean forward to rest my forehead against hers. "What am I going to do with you, Trouble?" My voice trails off.

Keep you—that's what I should do.

I should keep her and Matteo here with me until the end of time.

I absorb the moment, the way she feels this close to me. The way she smells, the way she sounds. I want every last piece of her tucked away in my brain for safe keeping, because at the end of the day, I know I can never give her what she deserves.

Andi deserves a man who will be there for her through every moment and that man isn't me. Hockey was my first love and it's what will always come first. Relationships always have a way of forcing you to choose and when that time comes, I know I will be nothing but selfish.

I'll want the three of them to myself—Andi, Matteo, and the sport I've devoted my entire life to—and I'm not so sure that's even a possibility.

CHAPTER TWENTY-TWO

ANDI

"What the hell kind of reality TV show are you living in right now?"

My eyebrows pull together as I dry my face and glare down at my phone on the counter that is on speaker phone. Matteo went to sleep a little while ago and my brother called while I was getting ready for bed. "Vincent, don't be dramatic. It's not that bad."

My brother is a total softie and a hopeless romantic, which normally I find comical . . . until it's my life that we're talking about.

My brother lets out an exasperated sigh. "Okay, maybe not. Although it does sound like you're telling me the plot of a romance movie."

My face relaxes and laughter spills from my lips. "Yeah, right. Carson doesn't do relationships and he doesn't really strike me as the type to settle down with someone."

"Why do you say that?"

"Well, for starters, the first night we were together

he told me as much." I pause, blowing a breath through my nose. "From what I know, he's never been in a serious relationship."

"Maybe you're the one who changes it all for him," my brother chimes in, a chuckle breaking up his sentences. "Maybe you're the one who makes him think differently." He pauses, laughing again. "And then you all live happily ever after. The end."

"You're an asshole," I laugh, leaving the bathroom and slipping back into my bedroom. "You know I'm only staying here until Aunt Bella's house is ready to be listed."

Vince is quiet for a moment. "You could move there. You're able to work remotely and it could be good for Matteo. He hasn't started school yet, so now would be the perfect time to make a life change like this."

I'm momentarily rendered speechless by my brother's suggestion. "You think we should move to Aston?"

"I didn't say that," he counters. "I'm just saying, if you're going to do it, now would be the time."

I kick my slippers off and pull back the comforter on the bed to slip underneath the organic cotton sheet and pull everything back over me. "I have no plans of moving to Aston right now." Scooting back, I lean against the pillows resting against the headboard. "It would definitely make things easier, although I feel like it's a drastic change after we've already experienced something big."

"I get that," he agrees. "I do think you have a lot to think about, but maybe just wait and see how things go. Who knows, by the end of summer, you might be Mrs.

Carson Ford." He pauses. "Although, I will need to have a word with him when I come to visit before he even considers doing something like that."

"Please, Vincent," I sigh, rolling my eyes even though he can't see me. "He's the father of my child and that's about it right now. There may be chemistry and we may have kissed, but I honestly don't think it will go any further than—"

"Wait, you guys kissed?"

Shit. I didn't mean to let that slip. "Oops. Uh—love you, bye!"

"Hold up, do not hang up on me, Andalina."

"Talk to you soon!"

My brother lets out a huff. "Goddammit, Andi."

I quickly end the call, a giggle slipping from me as I shake my head at my phone. He can be so damn annoying sometimes, but I'm so glad to have him. Vince and I have been close since I was born, it feels like, and if there's one person who will always have my back, it's him.

He has a huge heart and is a total golden retriever. Vince has always been the one who attempts to see the good in people and the world. I don't know where he gets it from, but he wears his heart on his sleeve and has never been the type of guy to sleep around. He's a total relationship buff and even though he's single right now, I just know there is someone out there who is perfect for him.

A soft knock on my door immediately pulls me back into the moment and slices through the thoughts of my brother. "Come in," I call out softly, adjusting in bed while pulling the covers up over my lap. I'm only wearing an oversized T-shirt and underwear and judging by the weight behind that knock, I know it isn't Matteo.

There's no privacy with him. He would have come bounding through the door without even thinking about knocking.

The door slowly opens and Carson stands on the other side. His eyes meet mine from across the distance. He lifts his hands, gripping the top of the door frame as he stares at me. My gaze immediately begins to take a detour south. He's shirtless, leaving his tattoos on both arms on full display. A thin gold chain rests just beneath the top of his sternum.

My eyes continue to rake over the lean muscles of his chest, tracing and memorizing every curve and plane of his abdomen. There's a small script tattoo just along his ribs on the left and it's red around the writing, as if it's something fresh.

Gray sweatpants hang low along his waist and the *V* shape on the front of his torso disappears beneath the waistband of his black underwear and sweats. My mouth is instantly dry.

"Who was that?" Carson questions me, his voice low, gaining my immediate attention. My gaze flashes to his, but his expression is completely unreadable. His throat bobs as he swallows, the muscle in his jaw tightening as he hovers in the doorway.

I wet my lips as I watch the way his eyes sweep across my face, down my body that's half covered by the blankets before moving back to my face. "My brother."

His pupils dilate, the muscles in his jaw relaxing as relief momentarily floods his expression. He blinks and the action is slow, his nostrils flaring before he opens his eyes again. "Okay . . ." his voice trails off for a beat. "I wasn't sure if I was interrupting something."

Nervous laughter bubbles in my chest and I adjust in bed. "What could you possibly be interrupting?"

"I don't know anything about your life, Andi." He pauses, rolling his lips between his teeth as he swallows hard. "I don't know if you have someone waiting for you when you get back home."

"I told you I'm not dating anyone." My heart skips a beat in my chest. "There's no one there waiting for me."

He releases the top of the doorframe. His arms hang beside his body as he steps into the room. Reaching behind him, he grips the doorknob, softly closing it before he inches closer to the bed.

"I just wanted to make sure." He moves closer and I shift to the side to make room for him to sit along the edge of the bed, but he doesn't lower himself onto the mattress until I pat it with my hand. "I want to know you, Trouble. I want to know what you like or what you don't. I want to know what pricks your skin and what makes your heart sing." He pauses and lets out a soft breath. "I want to know everything."

My breath catches in my throat. "Why?"

A wave of vulnerability washes over him. He stares at me, his gaze unwavering. His expression is unreadable and his throat bobs as he swallows again. "You're under my skin, Andi," he says, his voice barely audible as he tilts his head to the side. "And I don't know what to do about it."

My heart stalls and my eyes widen.

"You have me all fucked up," he breathes, his eyebrows drawing together. "You're just supposed to be the mother of my child . . . but when I look at you, it doesn't feel like that." He directs his attention to his hands in his lap. "It feels like more and honestly, it scares the shit out of me."

"Why does it scare you?"

He turns to look at me, his eyes immediately meeting mine. "Because for the first time, it feels like I might have something to lose."

Rational thoughts cease to exist. I push away the covers, forgetting the fact that I'm only in a T-shirt and underwear. I close the distance between us until I'm against his thighs. Carson doesn't say anything. Instead, he reaches for me, his hands find my waist as he pulls me into his lap. His fingers sweep my hair away from my face, caressing my cheek before sliding back around the nape of my neck.

I settle on his lap, warmth blooming in the pit of my stomach as I feel how hard he is beneath me. There's only a few layers of clothing separating me from the outline of his cock under me. The memory of him stretching me, burrowing himself deep inside of me doesn't feel like such a distant memory right now.

He tilts his head back and drags my face down to his as our mouths collide. My eyelids slam shut and my lips move with his as he kisses me with an intensity that rocks me to my core. What starts out as slow and gentle quickly shifts to something more. Something fueled by lust, with a fervent need to be closer.

His tongue slides along the seam of my lips and I instantly part them, letting him in. His tongue moves against mine, soft like silk. He tastes like the mint from his mouthwash. He kisses me deeply and his fingers tangle in my hair as he pulls me closer. Instinctively, I grind my hips, pressing myself against him as heat builds between my legs.

Carson moans into my mouth and I swallow the sounds, draining the air from his lungs as we kiss each other senseless. Carson Ford is a force to be reckoned with. What started as a one night stand now has me questioning the possibilities of a future.

His hands drift down to my thighs, pushing up the bottom hem of my shirt as he slides his fingers along the inside of my legs. "Fuck, I've imagined touching you again for fucking years," he murmurs against my mouth. I don't stop him as the tips of his fingers graze along the seam of my underwear. "What took you so long, Trouble?"

"Fear," I breathe, nipping at his bottom lip. It's not something I like to admit, but after what happened when I tried to contact him before, I was terrified to see him. Terrified of rejection.

"Of what?" He pushes his fingers beyond the cotton material, groaning as his fingers slide through my arousal.

"You," I moan, my head tipping back as he pushes a finger inside of me.

"There's nothing to be afraid of, babe," he whispers as his lips trail along the column of my throat. "You're changing the game for me. If anyone should be afraid, it should be me." He drags his tongue along the outer shell of my ear as he pushes another finger inside my pussy. "You're not mine to lose, but I'm afraid I will anyway."

"Why would you lose me?" I pant as he fucks me with his fingers. He shifts so he can press his thumb against my clit, rolling it in circles as he continues to move his fingers in and out, stroking my insides.

"Because I can never give you what you deserve." He nips at my earlobe before moving his mouth back to my neck.

A moan escapes me, my body tightens as he continues to work me with his hand. The cast on his right hand is rough against my skin as he slips it under my shirt, moving up to my breast. He pulls my nipple in between his fingers, rolling the pebbled flesh as he presses his thumb harder against my clit.

"Don't stop," I moan as I shift my hips against him, my body quickly coming undone as a wildfire of lust and need spreads through me.

"That's it, baby," he moans, his teeth grazing my neck. He removes his hand from my shirt and grabs the back of my head to pull my face back to his. "Come all over my hand for me."

His tongue pushes through my lips, tangling with mine as he pumps his fingers, applying pressure inside while simultaneously pressing the heel of his hand against my clit. It sends me over the edge, plunging into the abyss of ecstasy as I lose myself on his lap. He swallows my moans, his lips bruise mine and his fingers don't stop until I'm completely spent on his lap.

I break the kiss and rest my forehead against his shoulder. My body sags against him as the aftershocks of my orgasm overrides any logical thought. "You're so good," he murmurs, brushing his fingers through my hair as he drags his other hand away from the apex of my legs. He kisses my temple, breathing in the scent of my hair.

His cock throbs between my legs and I lift my head, my eyes immediately finding his. His pupils dilate, focusing in on me as he stares back at me. My hands move down to the waistband of his pants and just barely push beneath the elastic as I drag my fingers against his skin.

"Andalina," he murmurs. My name sounds like a desperate plea falling from his lips.

"Shh," I whisper, removing my fingers from his waistband as I gently lift myself from his lap. "Let me take care of you," I tell him, pushing his knees apart as I settle onto the floor between them. He drops his chin closer to his chest, his eyes locked on mine as I reach for his waist again.

The red script along his ribs catches my eyes. Emotion washes over me as I see it's Matteo's name written in a beautiful script font. I tenderly touch the skin around it that isn't irritated.

Carson's eyes search mine once more and I drop my hands back to the waistband of his pants. He rises to his feet and I move backwards on my knees, my toes brushing against the wall as he stalks closer. Reaching for his pants, I push them down beneath his ass, his cock springs free and juts out, hard and thick, in front of my face. My eyes drop to the tip and it throbs as I wrap my hand around the base, slowly stroking his length before running my tongue along the bead of pre-cum that forms.

"Jesus Christ, Andi," he moans, his chin touching his chest as he braces himself with his casted hand against the wall behind me. He drops his left hand to my head and grabs a handful of my hair, wrapping it around his hand until his fist is near my skull. "Look at you."

A ghost of a smile dances across my lips and I feel my cunt throbbing, still dripping from the orgasm he gave me. I like seeing him like this, like he can barely control himself. I can't wait to see what he looks like when he's losing himself inside my mouth.

His eyes are glued to mine as I open wide and take as much of his cock inside my mouth as I can. The underside is like silk against my tongue and the corners of my mouth scream in protest from how large he is. I take him in until the tip reaches the back of my throat, even with my hand wrapped around the shaft.

"Fuck," he groans, his eyes rolling back in his head, eyelids fluttering shut. His nostrils flare, and his grip tightens around my hair. He presses his fist against the back of my head, just resting it there as I begin to move, sucking him in and out of my mouth.

I pump my hand in tandem with my mouth, bobbing back and forth as I inhale as much of him as I can. Saliva drips from the corners of my mouth, wetting my hand, but I ignore it as I keep moving, using it as lubricant with my spit already around his cock. A groan rumbles in Carson's chest and he opens his eyes, staring down at me in awe.

His eyes are hooded, darkened with lust. "You look so fucking sexy with my cock shoved down your throat."

It's difficult to smile around his length, but my lips lift and his words fuel me, creating a need inside of me to make him come. He bucks his hips, thrusting into my mouth, knocking against the back of my throat. I gag around him, tears immediately spring to my eyes but I quickly recover.

Carson holds my head, guiding me as he meets me with his own thrusts, although this time, he's gentle, holding back as to not make me gag again. I moan around him, sucking him in deeper, not caring when the tip of his cock hits the back of my throat over and over.

"Goddamn, you take me like you were made to suck my cock," he groans, fucking my face harder. "I'm going to come and I want you to swallow every last drop."

My head bobs, saliva dripping from my mouth, tears drying on my cheeks from choking on him. I cup his balls with my other hand to massage them while fucking him with my mouth. Carson lets out a string of curses and moans, his head falling back as his hips buck again.

His hold tightens on my skull, fire spreading along

my nerves from how tightly he's gripping it. His body tenses, his muscles constricting as his balls draw closer to his body. "Fuck, Andi," he moans, his body immediately relaxing as his orgasm tears through him. His hips buck and my mouth is flooded with his salty release, spurts hitting the back of my throat.

I swallow him down, and continue to suck him, moving my mouth and hand along his length. I don't stop until I'm swallowing the last drop of him. I slowly release him, and wipe the saliva away from the corners of my mouth with the back of my hand as he releases his grip on my hair.

Carson stares down at me, his hands stroke the sides of my face before dragging me back up to my feet. Then he bends back down to pull his boxer briefs and sweatpants up. He lifts his good hand to my face once more, his thumb dragging across my bottom lip before he presses his lips to mine.

His tongue sweeps along the seam of my mouth, my lips hesitantly parting. He kisses me deeply, his tongue tangling with mine. His hands find my waist and he spins me toward the bed, slowly lowering me onto the mattress, although he doesn't follow.

He hovers above me, his mouth just barely grazing mine.

"I should go before I end up crawling into bed with you," he murmurs, dragging the covers up over my body as he presses his lips to my forehead.

"Would that be such a bad thing?"

He stares down at me, tilting his head to the side. He's silent for a moment, conflict dancing in his irises.

"I don't know," he says softly, his eyebrows pulling together. "I don't want either of us getting the wrong idea."

"I'm a big girl, Carson," I tell him as I reach for his arms in an effort to pull him down to me. "I can protect myself."

He doesn't say a word and his brows furrowed as if he's at war with himself. "Fuck it." He climbs over me, crawls beneath the blanket, and pulls me flush against his warm body. "I don't know if I can," he whispers into my hair.

I nuzzle against him, wrapping my arms tighter around his torso. My eyelids are heavy. "You're not the one who will end up getting hurt. You don't do attachments, remember?" The words leave me as little more than a whisper as sleep starts to take hold.

"I don't know about that anymore." The gentle rumble of his deep voice vibrates through his chest and resounds in my head. He falls silent, and the rise and fall of his breathing, the steady thump thump of his heart—together, they lull me to sleep.

I'm safely wrapped in a cocoon of him.

And it's exactly where I want to be.

CHAPTER TWENTY-THREE

CARSON

ndi has been in my bed every night for the past week and the only thing we've been doing is sleeping.

And I'm not complaining one bit.

Okay, that's partially a lie. We've been doing more than sleeping, however, we have yet to have sex. I've been enjoying the steady build up and the anticipation has me feeling like I'm going to come apart at the seams, but I know it will be worth it when we both finally give in.

This isn't a random hookup in a bar in the middle of the night with no promises of ever seeing each other again. This is completely different. It's so much more and I don't want her to feel like it's anything less than it actually is.

I want to take my time with her. I want to memorize her body and the way she moves. The way she smells, the way she looks, and the way she sounds.

Andi rolls out of bed, grabs my T-shirt from the floor

and pulls it over her head. She turns to face me, dragging her long braid out from under the cotton material, her bright hazel eyes finding mine. "Are you sure Matteo is okay with you today?"

I nod, slowly sitting up in bed as I watch her move around the room. "I have to go to the doctor to see about this cast, but he's fine with me." I pause, tilting my head to the side. "Do you need any help with the contractors?"

She shakes her head as she pulls her braid over her shoulder and undoes it. "I'm just meeting with them to see the progress on the mold remediation and what comes next." She flips her long, dark hair back over her shoulder.

"Okay. I was going to go to my appointment and then possibly swing by Cale's house if he's not doing anything."

Andi walks around the end of the bed and bends over to retrieve her sweatpants. I watch her, my cock twitching as she lifts her legs and pulls them on.

"You know, you could come back to bed if you'd like." I pause. A slow smile lifts my lips as I remember her taste on my tongue last night. "I can think of a few different ways to have my way with you before breakfast."

She raises an eyebrow at me. "That depends. Are you going to find another way to give me a mind-blowing orgasm that doesn't involve actually having sex with me?"

"Mind-blowing, eh?"

She huffs, a frustrated breath deflating her lungs. "Can I ask you something?"

"Always."

"Why don't you want to have sex with me?"

Her question renders me speechless for a beat. "Who said I don't want to have sex with you?"

She stares at me, her gaze frosty. "I've been in your bed every night for the past week. We've messed around, but it just always ends with that."

I immediately climb out of bed, my cock hard as I close the distance between us. My hands find the sides of her face, tipping her head back to look up at me. "You have no idea how badly I want to sink my cock deep inside of you, Trouble," my voice low and hoarse. "It's been taking every ounce of self control that I have to not do that every goddamn night."

"Why the self control, though? It's not like we haven't had sex before."

I shake my head at her. "That was different." My tongue darts out to wet my lips and her gaze drops to my mouth before moving back to my eyes. "This is different." I pause, a shallow breath escaping me. "I don't want to fuck this up, Andi."

"And you think having sex with me will?" Her eyebrows pull together.

"I don't know what I'm doing, " I murmur, the honesty deflating my lungs. I don't fully know what I want, but I do know that I want her, and the last thing I'm going to do is ruin this before we even have a chance. "I've never done this before."

"You need to be a little more specific than that."

I close my eyes, inhale deeply and exhale slowly while I figure out what I want to say. When I look back at her, her mouth is set in a straight line, one brow arched. "I've only ever been casual with other women and that's not what I want with you. I don't know what I want exactly, but I know it's not that."

"Are we dating and I didn't know about it?"

My eyes widen. "No, no, I don't date."

"I'm kidding," she says around a soft chuckle. "You know this doesn't have to have a label, Carson." A tender smile lifts her lips. "There's no pressure for you to decide what you want. I told you, I'm a big girl and can protect myself. I know what I'm getting into here. I know you're emotionally unavailable and I'm okay with that."

My forehead creases. "But what if this doesn't go any further than this?"

"Then we had a good time, right?" She questions, her smile not reaching her eyes but her tone is encouraging enough.

It doesn't feel right, but I slowly nod. "Right."

"Stop worrying and overthinking, Ford," she smirks, taking a step away from me as she lets out a quiet laugh. "I'm still planning on going back to Starling Ridge after I get my aunt's house listed. Nothing is changing so there's absolutely no pressure."

Hearing the reassurance from her literally feels like a weight is lifted from my chest, but at the same time, disappointment festers beneath my ribcage. Her nonchalance throws me off and the emotion washing over me has me confused as hell. I'm not supposed to want more with her, but I do.

I'm not sure where this is going with Andi, but I wholeheartedly want to find out. I want to do right by her, but I also have no clue what I am doing here.

She's the mother of my child. I only want her happy, living the life she deserves.

And I know I want to be a part of that—however that may look.

"Hey Andi," I call out to stop her by my bedroom door. She's been making it a habit to get up a little early each morning, that way she can already be awake when Matteo wakes up. She's afraid he might start to ask questions if he finds her in my bed.

She turns her body to look at me. "Yeah?"

"Thank you."

She cocks her head to the side. "For what?"

"For just—" I pause, swallowing roughly as I, once again, resist the urge to drag her back to bed. "For being you."

A tender smile lifts her lips and the gold and green hues in her eyes sparkle in the early morning light creeping through the blinds. "I'll see you later, okay?"

I tip my chin, the corners of my mouth twitching. "Okay."

She disappears into the hallway, pulling the door shut behind her. Matteo isn't awake yet and Andi doesn't disturb him before she leaves the house. After he wakes up, he comes padding into my room and climbs in bed with me to cuddle before we start our day.

Sitting across from Matteo, I look down at my hand, finally free of the cast after six long weeks and I flex my fingers.

"Does it hurt?" Matteo asks me as he shoves a spoonful of Italian ice into his mouth.

Matteo came along to my appointment today and it went better than expected. Since everything looked like it was healing well, they said I no longer needed to wear a cast and they were able to remove the pins from my wrist.

Matteo suggested Italian ice to celebrate and I couldn't deny him of that. I texted Andi when we were leaving the doctor, unsure of what her day looked like, but I didn't want her to worry if she got home and didn't find us there.

"I wouldn't say it hurts," I tell him as I scan the new bandage on my wrist. "It just feels a little weird. A little weak."

"Well, I guess you're not a robot anymore," he says with a frown, his lips purple from his Italian ice.

"I guess not," I agree, chuckling as I fake a look of disappointment. "I guess I'm just a regular human now."

Matteo looks at me, a twinkle in his eye. "I still think you're cool."

My heart swells inside of my chest as I stare back at my son. "Thanks, bud." I smile brightly, my heart pounds strong and steady in my chest. "You're the coolest person I've ever met."

He slowly nods, looking past me as he takes another bite of his lunchtime dessert. "The pillows in your bed smelled like my mom." His eyebrows pull together, like he's trying to piece something together and my stomach quickens as he focuses on me again.

"Oh, well—" I pause, anxiety washing over me. He hasn't caught the two of us together or seen her in my bed. He doesn't know, he can't know. "She was in my room talking to me this morning before she left."

"Oh, okay." He nods again, accepting my response and doesn't question it further. "I know that girls can have cooties, but I think my mom got a shot from the doctor so she doesn't have them." He offers me a smile. "If you like her, I promise I won't tell her."

The words that tumble from his mouth catch me completely off guard. The things that kids say . . . I swear.

"I'm sorry, what?"

"My mom," he says, like he's reminding me who we're talking about. "You guys are always talking and smiling and laughing. Jackson, from my preschool; he really liked Ruby and he would follow her around the playground to talk to her all the time."

A chuckle rumbles in my throat. He's comparing me and his mother to two kids from his preschool class. Honestly, I'm not sure we're so different, really. I do like his mom and definitely more than just as a friend.

"Did Jackson have a crush on Ruby?"

"Yep." Matteo takes another bite. "He said she got the cootie shot from the doctor so she didn't have it anymore, just like my mom."

I roll my lips between my teeth, biting back my smile. "Well, that's good to know. About your mom, I mean."

"Yeah," he says, his voice trailing off for a second. "It would be cool if you did like her. Then we would be like a family with my mom and my dad like the other kids."

My heart splinters and the smile on my face shrinks. Since the two of them have been in my house, it's become a home. It's filled with warmth and laughter. It's my safe place, it's where I feel comfortable and content.

With the two of them. With my family.

"We are a family, Matteo." My voice is soft as I stare across the table at my son. "I know ours might look a little different than other peoples', but that's okay. Whether your mother and I are together or not, we will always all be a family. I promise."

He stares at me for a second then shrugs and focuses on scooping more Italian ice. "Okay."

This was all completely unexpected and my heart aches. I wish Andi were here with us right now. I can't help but feel like she would know the right things to say to ease his mind.

I meant everything I said to him. We are a family. They are mine.

The more time I spend with Andi and Matteo, the less time I want to be away from both of them. I'm fairly certain this is what a growing attachment feels like . . . and I'm afraid it might be too late for me to do anything about it.

I'm officially and irrevocably fucked.

CHAPTER TWENTY-FOUR

ANDI

When I get back to Carson's, it's already later in the afternoon and the house is quiet as I step inside. The front door clicks shut behind me as I kick off my shoes and pad through the foyer, my ears straining to hear any sounds of Carson or Matteo, but there's nothing for me to hear.

Last I had heard from Carson was that they had finished their Italian ice, were grabbing something for lunch since they decided to do things a little backwards and then they were stopping by Caleb's house.

That was almost two hours ago now.

I walk into the kitchen, noticing that there's no one to be found, but the backdoor is open, with the screen door pulled shut in its place. My heart races in my chest, my body on high alert. I should have checked for Carson's car in the garage.

I don't hear Matteo playing in the yard. Did Carson forget to shut the door or is there an unexpected intruder in his house?

Pausing by the backdoor, I don't open the screen door. Instead, I get as close as I can to look outside without catching any unwanted attention hopefully, if the latter is what is going on here.

Relief floods me as soon as I see Carson walking across the backyard. Confusion follows close behind when I realize he's alone.

I step out onto the patio, immediately gaining Carson's attention. "Hey. Where's Matteo?"

Carson walks onto the patio, stopping when he reaches me. "Hey, you." He flashes his bright smile at me, the same one that caught my attention that first night six years ago. "He wanted to play with Tella, so I left him at Caleb's." His eyebrows shift downward. "I hope that's okay."

"Oh, yes." My own smile crests my lips. I'm instantly relieved and it brings me a sense of peace to know that Matteo is connecting with his family. "I just got a little worried when I didn't see him. It's a thing I do sometimes."

Carson's head bobs and he gives me a look of understanding. "It's okay. He's safe," he assures me, his eyes slowly searching mine. "He'll always be safe with me and my family." His gaze stays focused on mine, his expression relaxed and soft. "Do you want to go get a late lunch? I know it's already the middle of the afternoon, so maybe we can call it an early dinner instead."

"I would love that."

Carson takes me to a small, quaint place in town. It's on the outskirts of Aston, along a lake. It's a beautiful day outside, so we opt to sit out on the back deck that over-looks the water.

"This is beautiful," I tell him, my eyes surveying the scenery. We're quickly approaching summer, so all the flowers are blooming, trees are covered in leaves and the sun hangs brightly in the sky above.

"It is," Carson murmurs. His eyes immediately meet mine as I turn back to look at him. He slowly lifts his glass, his lips brushing the outer rim before he takes a sip of the lemonade. "I love coming here during the summer."

"Well, thank you for bringing me."

Carson smiles back at me. "Of course. How did it go with the contractors today? What's going on with the mold remediation?"

I take a sip of my own drink, gently setting it down on the table top. "It went well. They're almost finished and it should be safe for us to go back within the next week. The contractors are ready to get back to working and based on the current timeline of things, they're anticipating another month or so before the house is completely finished."

He drops his gaze down to the table, his fingers toy with the napkin in front of him as he slowly nods. "That's good," he says quietly, his voice semi detached and void of any emotion. "So, I guess that means the two of you will be heading back to Starling Ridge sooner than later."

Before I realize what I'm doing, I reach across the

table and cover his hand with mine. He wraps his long fingers around mine, eyes closing as he sucks in a deep breath. "Hey." He opens his eyes, lifting his head to look at me. "We're not leaving yet and even after we do, you're still going to see him."

Carson's eyebrows tug together, his lips parting as he cocks his head to the side. "That's—"

He's cut off by our server arriving with our food. I pull away, releasing his hands as I drop my own into my lap for a moment. The server smiles at both of us, setting the plates down, and asks if we need anything else, and then she turns around and begins to walk away.

Carson glares at his plate with irritation woven into his expression.

"What were you saying?"

The irritation washes away as soon as he lifts his focus to me. "What?"

"When she brought our food, you were saying something but got interrupted."

Like a switch has been flipped, the conflict contorts his handsome features again. He stares at me for a beat before shaking his head, like he's shaking away a bad thought. "I don't remember," he says, his voice low. "It wasn't important."

The air between us has shifted, almost as if there's a tension that wasn't there before. Carson picks up his sandwich and takes a bite as he looks past me, out at the rippling surface of the lake. I want to know what he was going to say, I want to tell him that everything is important . . . but I don't.

I don't want to push him and I certainly don't want to prod. Carson Ford is the epitome of a man with golden retriever energy. He's pleasant and normally happy, so even this little shift in his mood is a stark contrast to how he normally is.

And I don't want to cause any more tension than there already is.

"How did your appointment go?" I motion to his hand with my fork. He has it beneath the table, resting on his lap.

Carson lifts it in the air, showing me the bandage covering a small section of his wrist. "It went great. I have to start physical therapy, but they said it's healing faster than they expected. They removed the cast and took out the pins and I should be good to go in a month or two."

"That's amazing." I smile at him, lifting a forkful of my salad toward my lips. "I'm so glad that your recovery isn't going to take too long."

He nods, smiling back at me, although it doesn't quite reach his eyes. "Me too. It still sucks that this happened during the playoffs. If it would have happened in the regular season, I could have still played with them probably. I wouldn't have left them short."

I tilt my head to the side, swallowing my mouthful of lettuce before speaking. "They didn't lose because you weren't there."

"Well, they didn't win either," Carson counters, a subtle bite in his tone. "I'm sorry, I'm projecting. This has all been a very frustrating and defeating situation.

Surprisingly, this is the first time I've ever had to experience something like this."

"It's not your fault and there's nothing you could have done to prevent this from happening. It was a freak injury and you're lucky. It could have been much worse."

His shoulders sag, just a touch. "I know," he agrees, his voice softer. "I've been trying to be kinder to myself and not beat myself up over it. All that matters now is healing properly and getting back into it."

"Do you plan on working on the ice at all during the off season?"

Carson nods. "I'm going to try to get as much ice time as I possibly can. I'm going to meet with our athletic trainer after I get situated with PT and see if we can come up with a routine for me for the off season." He pauses, taking another sip of his drink. "You can always tell during training camp who wasted their summer doing nothing and who worked their ass off. I don't want to show up out of shape."

"That makes total sense." I give him a gentle smile. "You're going to come back stronger than ever."

"I hope so," he says, his voice quiet, eyes slowly searching mine. "Before, I only had to worry about disappointing myself or my team. Things are different now with Matteo. I want to set an example. I want to be the person he looks up to and someone he wants to be like."

Something in his tone hits me directly in his chest. That and the way he's looking at me right now—like he's afraid of being a failure. And that is the last thing he will ever be in our son's eyes. "Carson . . . whether you play hockey or not, that little boy will look up to you. I see the way he is with you and it's different from how he's ever been with anyone before. You're his father. Set an example by continuing to be the amazing person you are. Fuck hockey. It won't always be there."

Carson falls silent, his eyes burning holes through mine. His lips part for a second, then he closes them and his jaw clenches. His eyebrows tug closer together, his eyes growing unfocused before something inside him clicks and he relaxes once more. "You're right. Hockey has always been the most important thing to me. It's been my entire personality for as long as I can remember, but you are so right. One day, I will have to move on from the sport and I'm beginning to see there's so much more to life outside of the arena." He pauses, the rest of the tension leaving his shoulders as he huffs out a breath. "Hockey doesn't define me as a person or as a father."

"No, it doesn't," I agree, smiling at the revelation he seems to be having. "You're Carson Ford—amazing father, exceptional friend and dare I say one of the best people I've ever had the pleasure of getting to know." I roll my lips between my teeth, anxiety welling inside of me as the words swirl in my brain. Fuck it. "I'd be lying if I didn't say that you're quickly becoming one of my favorite people on this stupid spinning rock in space."

His lips quirk and eyes light up. "Is that so?"

"It is."

"Well, Trouble," he starts, lifting his glass up to take another gulp of lemonade. He sets it down and runs his tongue along his top lip to swipe up every drop of lemonade before he smiles. "The feeling is one hundred percent mutual."

"I like that."

His eyes don't leave mine as he winks. "I like you."

CHAPTER TWENTY-FIVE

CARSON

"Great work today, Ford."

I glance over at Gerald, the physical therapist I started seeing. I've been seeing him every other day for the past week, in an effort to get my arm as strong as possible and back into working ability. Shooting shouldn't be an issue, but it's more so about protecting my wrist so this doesn't happen again.

In a way, I'm grateful that this injury happened when it did. I have the entire offseason to get stronger and to rehabilitate my wrist. If this would have happened in the middle of the regular season, it would have been more of a race to get back on the ice and back into the game.

"Thanks."

"At the pace that you're healing and the way rehabbing is going, I imagine we'll probably be able to discharge you earlier than we expected." He rises to his feet the same time I do. "Have your trainer contact me and I'll touch base with him again since we're one week in already."

"Okay, perfect," I nod, holding my hand out to shake his. "Thanks again, Gerald."

"Of course," he shakes my hand, giving me a pat on the shoulder with his free hand. "See you next week."

I leave his office feeling refreshed and stronger. My muscles are definitely tired with all the work I've been putting in, but I can feel that my body is healing and for that, I'm eternally grateful.

This career is so demanding and it's something that can vanish in the blink of an eye. One injury is all it takes to not have the same stability in your body and to no longer be able to continue playing. I'm thankful that isn't the case for me right now and I can only hope it's many years yet before I am forced to retire.

Fingers crossed that I get to have a choice when it happens and not have the choice made for me.

When I get back home, I pull my car into the garage and walk into the house through the door that leads into the mudroom—the side entryway from the garage into the kitchen. I kick off my shoes and find Matteo in the kitchen waiting for me. He greets me as he hops off the counter with a sheepish grin on his face.

He's holding a banana and starts to peel it. "Hey, Dad. How was therapy?"

"It was good." I walk over to him, ruffle his hair, and plant a kiss on top of his head. "Where's your mother and does she know you were climbing on the counters?"

Matteo smirks and shrugs. "I couldn't reach the

bananas." He walks over to the island, pulling open the drawer with the trash can and drops the peel into it. "She's upstairs packing."

I lift an eyebrow at him. "For what?"

"To go back to Great-Aunt Bella's." Matteo chews a bite of the ripe fruit and swallows it. "She said we can go back there now."

My heart picks up the pace inside my chest, dread rolling in the pit of my stomach. "Oh, okay."

"I don't want to go," Matteo tells me, his voice quiet as he glances around to make sure Andi doesn't hear him. "I don't like that house very much and I wish we could just stay here with you instead."

I roll my lips between my teeth. "Let me go talk to your mom. Maybe I can talk her into you guys staying here."

"Can you see if we can just stay here forever?"

My eyes widen. "You don't want to go back home?"

"I like it here," Matteo tells me with nothing but pure honesty. He takes another bite of his banana. "If we stay here, then I get to see you and mom all the time."

My heart splinters as his words seep into my soul. Over the past few weeks, we've really had an amazing opportunity to bond. Feeling this connection between us growing has filled my cup in ways I never knew were possible. To feel the love from your child is unlike anything else.

Given the circumstances, it feels like there has never been any missed time between us. Matteo immediately became attached to me and I to him. The thought of him not being here every single day had already been weighing heavily on me, and hearing this admission from him is only compounding the weight.

"I'll talk to her, at least to see if you can stay here instead of Bella's, okay?"

That sweet smile spreads across his face again as he nods eagerly. "Okay, Dad. Thanks."

"And no more climbing on the counter. I don't want you to fall and get hurt."

He tips his chin. "Yes, sir."

I follow Matteo as he walks into the living room and make sure he's situated before I head upstairs to find Andi. I take the stairs two at a time up to the second floor, breeze past Matteo's room first, then reach Andi's. Although, I'm not sure I would even call this her room anymore. Her things may occupy the space, but she's been occupying mine instead.

She doesn't hear me or see me at first and I take a moment to stand in the doorway, completely unnoticed. I drink her in, my eyes trailing over the side of her face, down her straight nose, over the curves of her lips. I let them continue to roam, memorizing the planes of her body. She's wearing a yellow dress that hugs her torso and flares out around her hips.

I watch her fold a pair of pants, laying them on the bed before turning back around to reach for something in one of her drawers. Her body falls rigid, head whipping to the side as she catches sight of me from the corner of her eye.

"Oh, you startled me," she laughs quietly, lifting her hand to her chest. "Hi."

I smile at her, leaning against the door jamb. "Hi." My eyes scan the room before resting on hers once more. "Whatcha doin'?"

"Packing." She gives me a small smile. "They called and said the house is safe for us to move back in now."

"Oh." I run my tongue over my top teeth. "Seems like you're in a rush to get out of here."

She purses her lips, blowing out a soft breath. "I figured you would want us out of your space."

"Quite the opposite, actually." I step closer, the distance between us vanishing as I lift my hand to cup the side of her face. "You're already everywhere and I want to keep it that way."

Her lips part, a breath escaping her. She stares up at me, her eyes searching mine as if she's looking for the answer to the question she hasn't asked.

"I want you and Matteo to stay." I pause, my thumb running along the soft skin on her cheek. I wet my lips and swallow back the emotion that wells in my throat at the thought of everything Matteo said in the kitchen. I want to ask her to move here, but that feels like too much too soon.

I have to start slow, because I'm treading in unknown territory. I don't know what the hell I'm doing here. I don't want to ask her to upend her entire life to move here and then what. What if things don't work out with us? Not that we're together or have even talked about anything like that.

But what happens if I can't be enough for her? What happens if I can't give her what she deserves? I'm not sure I can take the pressure of being held to an expectation and then not meeting it.

I know what Andi deserves and I don't think she will settle for anything less. If they were to move here and she were to move onto someone else, I would have that constantly in my face.

And I can't predict how I would handle something like that.

"You want us to stay here with you?"

"Yes." I nod at her, lifting my other hand to her waist as I pull her flush against my body. She tips her head back farther, her eyes still fixated on mine. "I want you in my space. I want you and Matteo here when I wake up in the morning and I want you both here when I go to sleep at night." I pause, a smirk pulling on my lips. "And I want you in my fucking bed, not in the room across the hall."

"But only until we get the house listed, right?"

I tilt my head to the side. "What would it take to get you to stay longer than that?"

"We're not together, Carson. I can't live here forever. I have a life in Starling Ridge."

Fuck. There it is. The cold glaring truth that I find myself wanting to change. "I know, but what if you didn't have to? You can stay here and you wouldn't have to work. We can enroll Matteo in school here."

Her eyes widen before she narrows them. "And what about us? It doesn't feel right to just move in with you like that when we aren't together."

"I know," I murmur, my eyelids falling shut as I lean

forward, resting my forehead on hers. "I—we can figure it all out."

"We're doing things a little backwards, don't you think?" The corners of her lips lift into a devastating grin. "We slept together, had a kid and now I'm staying in your house?"

A chuckle escapes me and I lift my other hand to the opposite side of her face. "I think that's just us, Trouble. Unconventional, but it works."

"Hmm, it does, doesn't it?" She lifts her arms, wrapping them around the back of my neck before pulling my face down to hers. My mouth crashes into hers, the taste of lemon and sugar on her tongue as mine immediately sweeps against hers.

Her lips are soft, moving and melting with mine. Her warm body presses against me and I breathe her in. Tongues tangling with an electrical current sizzling between us. My hands begin to drift, sliding down the sides of her neck, along her collarbones. My fingers catch the straps of her dress and I slip them over her shoulders, feeling her skin beneath mine.

"Carson," Andi murmurs against my mouth, a soft giggle escaping her. "Matteo's awake downstairs."

"Shit," I mumble, nipping at her bottom lip. "He's too old to take a nap, isn't he?"

She laughs again, pressing her lips to mine before pulling back. "Yes, he would not be okay with either of us telling him he needs to take a nap." She untangles her arms from behind my neck, taking a step away as she adjusts her dress. My cock is already throbbing in my pants, but I ignore it for the moment. "I'm not busy later. You know, if you want to pick up where we left off."

"Done. Sold."

"Your room or mine?" She questions, turning away as she grabs her things from her small suitcase and begins to put them back on top of the bed.

"Mine," I tell her, walking up behind her to press my lips against the side of her neck. "This is just a guest room. You belong in my bedroom with me."

This is exactly where she belongs—I just need to figure out how I can make her see it too.

And somehow work past my own reluctance of being in a real relationship.

CHAPTER TWENTY-SIX

ANDI

Matteo's bedroom door is ajar and the soft sound of Carson's voice drifts through the gap. I can't make out the words he's saying, but the melody of his tone slides like a calming breeze, immediately tangling in my soul. A smile lifts the corners of my lips and I idle outside of the door.

Through the space between the door and the jamb, I watch Carson and Matteo together. Carson sits on the edge of Matteo's bed, Matteo's head resting on his lap as Carson reads a book to him.

We've been doing the whole bedtime routine together most nights, but I said goodnight to Matteo a bit ago so they could have this time together. I love these candid moments, seeing the two of them like this.

The growing bond between them lights my heart on fire.

The easy rise and fall of Matteo's chest tells me he drifted to sleep, yet Carson doesn't bother to move. After a minute, he must notice that he's asleep as well.

He gently closes the book, laying it on the bed beside them as his hand smooths Matteo's tousled hair along his head.

My heart crawls into my throat and I linger for another moment, watching the two of them before turning away. I pause in the hallway outside of the door to Carson's room, unsure of what I'm supposed to do. I've been sleeping in his room, but all of my things are still in the room that was designated as mine.

"You look lost."

His voice knocks my heart into overdrive. Inhaling deeply, I slowly turn around to face him. My gaze meets his and there's an inquisitive look in his eyes as a ghost of a smile dances across his lips.

His footsteps are slow, yet his strides are long as he walks across the hallway, closing the distance between us. "Do you need help getting to where you're going?"

I swallow. "I think I might."

His hands fall to my hips, pulling me flush against his body. I tip my head back, lifting my chin to look up at him. *God, he's so tall.* His legs press against mine, inching me backwards until we're stepping into his bedroom. He lifts one hand and slides it through my hair as he cups the back of my skull.

"Fuck," he groans, the sound rumbling in his chest as his face dips down to mine. "I've missed you."

His mouth crashes into mine, his lips claiming mine. I lift my arms to link them around the back of his neck and kiss him back. His lips are soft and tender, kissing me with a sweetness that has me ready to come undone.

His tongue is urgent, sweeping along the seam of my mouth, but when I let him in, it's like he holds back.

It's slow and torturous, and he takes his time, touching and tasting, teasing me with his tongue as he explores my mouth. My toes curl, back arches, and I'm swept up in him. My fingers slide through his silky hair as I grip the back of his head, needing and wanting more.

"Six years," Carson murmurs, his breath soft against my lips. "Six fucking years that I've been dreaming of feeling you again." He pauses, pulling back as his eyes search mine. "I want you, Trouble. Fuck," he groans while he presses his hips against me, letting me feel his erection. "I need you."

Untangling my hands from his hair, I drop them down to the bottom hem of his shirt. As I push it up his torso, he breaks away, just long enough for me to strip him of his shirt. He reaches for mine, doing the same before wrapping his arm around my waist and pulling me back to him.

He nips at my bottom lip. We're panting and pulling at whatever piece of clothing our hands could find. We crash back into each other, stealing the air from each other's lungs before breaking away again. We repeat, stripping and kissing until there's nothing left to strip away.

He doesn't take his eyes off mine as he pushes me closer to the bed and lowers me down onto the mattress. I scoot back, my legs splayed as I lie in the center of his bed. Heat spreads through my body, lighting my nerve endings on fire as his gaze rakes over every inch of my flesh.

"Goddamn," he says on an exhale, his breath catching in his throat. "You're fucking beautiful. So fucking perfect." He leans forward and his hands find my knees as he presses them open. "I need to grab a condom." A mischievous grin appears on his lips. "The last time we did this, you ended up pregnant."

I let out a soft breath, my lips twitching as I reach for his wrists. "I have an IUD, so unless you feel the need for added protection, we don't need one."

His eyes slowly search mine and he shakes his head. "I don't. I've been tested recently."

"Good," I murmur, rolling my lips between my teeth before wetting them with my tongue. "Now, stop wasting time," I say as I slide my hands up his fore-arms. He lets out a soft chuckle, settling on his knees between my legs.

"My apologies." He winks as he draws spit into his mouth. He spits into his hand then wraps his fingers around the girth of his cock. He drags his saliva up and down his length, from base to tip and back again. "I feel like we've both waited too long for this."

He inches closer and plants his hands on the bed beside me as he lowers his face down to mine. Not waiting a second longer, his lips crash into mine, his tongue invades my mouth and I give it a gentle suck. I'm so distracted by his mouth, I don't even realize he's lined himself up until he plunges his cock into me.

A moan escapes me and he swallows the sound, lowering his body to mine as he rocks into me. My legs instinctively wrap around his waist and my arms circle around his back to keep our bodies locked together at all points. I forgot how big he was and he stretches me wide as he starts to fuck me with long, languid strokes.

His cock slides in and out with each thrust of his hips as he strokes the walls of my pussy. His tongue tangles with mine, hands sliding into my hair as he pins me on the bed with his full weight. My nails dig into his back, scratching at his flesh as he rocks in and out of me.

"You feel like fucking heaven," he moans against my lips, nipping at them with his teeth. "Just like I remembered, only better."

"And why is it better?" I ask, my tongue darting out to trace the outline of his lips.

He grabs it with his teeth and sucks it into his mouth before releasing me. "Because this time I know it isn't just for tonight."

His mouth captures mine once more, one hand slides down under my ass as he lifts my hips for better access. He nestles himself in deeper, fucking me so deep that my eyes rolling back in my head. Our surroundings fade away and it's just the two of us. Everything else melts away. Time ceases to exist.

It's just us . . . and my god, it's everything.

He consumes me. He invades my senses and penetrates my thoughts. I can't think or see straight. Everything circles back to him. Him and those misty grey eyes. He shifts his hips, each thrust like a piston, driving me into the mattress, fucking me harder.

On Carson's next thrust deep inside me, I cry out

from the force, a mixture of pleasure and pain. I lift my hips instinctively, meeting every movement, taking every stroke of his cock. He fucks me deeper and deeper until he has nothing left to give.

With each thrust, his pelvis grinds against my clit. "Harder," I plead, my teeth sinking into his bottom lip, warmth building in the pit of my stomach as my orgasm creeps closer. I need more of him. "You feel so good. Please, Carson."

I need the release. I need *his* release.

"Fuck," he groans. He pulls out until just the tip is inside of me. His eyes search mine, a devious and feral look filling them as he sucks in a breath, like he's trying to collect himself. Without another word, he slams into me, filling me to the hilt. I let out a cry, my nails scraping at his flesh. He slams into me, again and again, unrelenting.

It isn't long before his movements become frantic, driven by a primal need and urgency. We're a mess of moans, the sounds of our bodies fill the bedroom as he drives himself into me. He rocks into me once more, his body grinding against my clit nearly sends me over the edge.

He starts rocking again, his movements are rushed as his instincts take over. "Oh fuck, Carson. Please don't stop. Make me come." He doesn't stop until I'm coming apart at the seams, splitting in two with his name nothing more than a hopeless prayer falling from my lips. I lose myself around him, my organs sucking me into a vortex of ecstasy.

Carson's thrusts become jerks as he murmurs my

name, his teeth nip at my neck as his body bucks one last time and then stills. He spills himself deep inside of me, his cum filling my pussy. He doesn't stop until he has nothing left to give, until we're both fully satiated and on the brink of an orgasm induced coma.

Locked together, we ride out the waves of euphoria, my head swims in the clouds as every nerve ending in my body tingles. He slowly pulls out of me and I immediately feel his absence, wishing he was still deep inside of me. He rolls over onto his back, pausing for a moment as he catches his breath and then lifts off the mattress.

My head rolls to the side and I watch him through a daze as he disappears into the bathroom. He isn't gone for long and I feel the bed dip on his side when he lowers himself back onto it. He's silent as he presses a warm washcloth between my legs, taking a moment to clean me up.

"Thank you," I murmur, my eyes searching his as he pulls the washcloth away from between my legs. Blood rushes from my head as I rise into a seated position and my pussy throbs from him. "I'll take that," I tell him, taking the washcloth as I get up off the bed. His gaze follows me as I slip into the bathroom to use the toilet before washing up.

I find him lying in the center of the bed, still naked, arms spread wide. "Come here, Trouble," he murmurs, scooting to the side to make room for me. I crawl across the mattress to him before dropping onto my side. He slides his arm under my neck and pulls me flush against him. His arm is a strong presence against my back.

His touch is like a feather dancing across my flesh. His fingertips roam over my shoulder, down my back, and along my hip, tracing invisible patterns on my skin. He buries his face in my hair as I nuzzle my head against his chest, breathing in the scent of him, reveling in the way he feels under me.

"I emptied out the dresser beneath the TV," he whispers. "There's no pressure, but if you want to move your things in there, you can."

My heart stumbles over itself in my chest. "I—" I pause and wet my lips. If there's one thing I've learned about Carson Ford, it's that he does things intentionally and he means the things he says. He wouldn't have made that space if he didn't want me to occupy it. "Thank you."

"Anything for you, Trouble," he murmurs, pressing his lips against the top of my head. "Always for you."

CHAPTER TWENTY-SEVEN

ANDI

These last two weeks have felt like a dream, but it's one I don't want to wake up from. Life with Carson is so damn easy. He's been nothing short of attentive to both Matteo and me. He's been working his ass off between being in the gym and trying to get as much ice time as he possibly can to work towards being in his best shape for the next season.

By the time he gets home each day, he's exhausted and usually ends up taking an afternoon nap while I finish up any work I'm doing remotely. After he gets some rest, he's been keeping Matteo and me busy before we settle in for dinner and time together in the evening.

Most nights, I cook, but he's right there, trying to figure out how the hell he can make an edible meal. He tries, but goddamn, he truly shouldn't give up his day job.

We finish out the day with him buried deep inside of

me until we're both spent and satiated, falling asleep wrapped up in one another.

Our time together is wearing thinner each day. It won't be long before Matteo and I will be going back to Starling Ridge. As much as I don't want to leave, I know I have to.

My feelings for Carson continue to grow the more time we spend together and I know he can feel it too. But I also know I can't stay if he can't be honest with himself and with me. He keeps his feelings guarded close to his chest. If he can't admit the way he feels for me, then I know there's really no chance here.

I watch Carson and Matteo out on the ice together, weaving through people as they pretend to race around the rink. We've been coming to public skates together, just so they can both get some extra time on the ice. It's an amazing bonding experience for them and I'm so glad I get to be a part of it all.

The relationship between them is truly amazing and after watching it blossom, I don't want to interfere.

I throw out my drink, making sure it lands in the trash can, then prepare to head back onto the ice with my guys.

"Excuse me, ma'am."

I slowly turn around at the sound of the unfamiliar voice. A woman standing behind me offers me a smile. "Hi. I'm sorry, was I in your way?"

"Oh, absolutely not." She points down at her feet that are covered by boots. "I'm not skating tonight." She holds out her hand for me to shake it. I remove my glove, reaching for her hand. "I'm Ellen, I run the learn to skate program here."

"It's nice to meet you. I'm Andi. My son plays hockey here."

"Yes, I've seen him here a few times." She pauses, tilting her head to the side. "I remember you from your figure skating days. My daughter competed against you often." She purses her lips. "You were an exceptional skater."

"Oh, thank you," I tell her, smiling. "I spent a lot of time skating, but when I got to college, I wanted to see and do other things. It felt like I had sacrificed so much for it growing up that I was just burnt out."

She nods. "I completely understand that. Have you considered doing anything with your abilities now?"

I shake my head at her, letting out a nervous laugh. "Oh, no. I just do it for pleasure now. I don't have it like I once did."

"Well, if you're ever interested, we are always looking to add skilled coaches to our skating program." She reaches into her pocket, pulling out a small business card before handing it to me. "We would love to have you come join us. The kids could really benefit from lessons with someone who knows the ins and outs of skating like you do."

I stare down at her card, my heart pounding erratically inside my chest. I look up at her, catching that hopeful look in her eyes. "I'm not sure how good I would be at teaching."

"And I completely understand that too." She gives

me a warm smile. "No pressure or obligation, just think about it."

"Okay, I will," I tell her, tucking the card into the side pocket of my pants. I've helped with camps when I was younger, but that was years ago. I'm not sure how great I would be at teaching and committing to something like that wouldn't be possible when it's time for Matteo and me to return home.

"Have a great night, Andi."

"Thanks, you too," I tell her, offering her one last parting smile before turning back around to the rink. I make my way around the boards, back over to the door where Matteo and Carson end up meeting me at the same exact time.

"Mommy, look!" Matteo spins around to face me, skating backwards at a slow and steady pace. I watch him as he transitions forward again before moving to face me once more.

"Wow, *caro*! Your transitions are getting so much smoother!"

"I know!" He exclaims, his body bouncing up and down. "Dad was showing me how to use different edges to make it easier."

I glance over at Carson, who's skating slowly beside me with a tender smile on his face. "Well, it's a great thing you have such an amazing dad to show you all the tricks."

"I know," Matteo smiles, looking up at Carson. "He's really great."

"He is, isn't he?"

Carson reaches out his hand, threading his fingers

through mine as he winks at me. We both look at Matteo, who's looking back and forth between the two of us with his eyebrows scrunched. He knows I've been staying in Carson's room and thankfully he hasn't questioned me on it. He's too young to really understand what's going on, but at the same time, I think he knows enough.

"Are you guys boyfriend and girlfriend?"

I glance at Carson whose eyes grow wide, as if he doesn't know how the hell to answer that. "We're friends."

Matteo narrows his eyes on me. "Boyfriends and girlfriends hold hands and kiss and do gross stuff."

"What kind of gross stuff?" Carson questions him with hesitant curiosity.

Matteo shivers. "Snuggle." He shakes it off as Carson and I laugh at his distaste for the thought of couples snuggling. He spins back around to face the same way we are. "Can you time me?"

"Absolutely, bud," Carson chuckles, pulling his phone out with his free hand. He unlocks the screen and taps on the clock app. "Ready?" Matteo gets lower, nodding as he looks straight ahead. "Set. Go!"

He takes off, his little legs working hard as his skates move across the ice. An overwhelming amount of pride fills me and I can't help the smile that pulls across my lips as I watch him making his way around the end of the rink.

Carson glances down at me, raising an eyebrow. "Friends, huh?"

"That seemed like the most appropriate response."

A low chuckle escapes him and he skates closer, his hand dropping from mine as he wraps his arm around my waist. His body presses against mine, lips brushing against my ear. "Do friends fuck the same way we do?"

My entire body is on fire, my breath catching in my throat as my fingers dig into his shoulders as I hold onto him for support. Our legs continue moving, skating together as he keeps his body flush with mine.

"I'll show you how good of a friend I am later tonight," he murmurs, nipping at my earlobe, mischief dancing in his irises as he pulls away.

Matteo comes to a screeching halt in front of us, abruptly severing the moment, although it doesn't extinguish the tingling sensation rippling in my body. "How did I do? What was my time?"

Carson glances down at his phone and tells him the time. "Want to see if you can beat it?"

"Yep!"

Carson sets his timer again and Matteo takes off once more. I glance over at Carson, feeling the excitement racing through my veins. "Meet me in my bedroom after Matteo goes to bed. I want you naked, face down with your ass in the air waiting for me." He raises an eyebrow. "Think you can do that for me?"

My mouth is immediately dry and I clench my thighs together. "Yes."

He smirks, sliding his hand into mine once more as he threads his fingers through mine again. "Good girl."

CHAPTER TWENTY-EIGHT

CARSON

My footsteps are light as I push open Matteo's door. His little form is curled up on the bed and a bigger body is lying next to him. She must have fallen asleep while reading to him. A smile lifts my lips and I hover in the doorway for a moment, watching Andi as she holds our son close to her.

I had other plans for her tonight, but seeing her like this with him, I can't bring myself to disturb her. Time moves too quickly and one day, Matteo won't be small like this and he won't want Andi to fall asleep in his bed with him.

My heart swells and I linger for another moment before leaving the two of them undisturbed. I pull the door nearly closed before I head back downstairs. I make my way to the sink still full of dishes from dinner. I arrange the dishes that will fit into the dishwasher, and the ones that won't, I decide to hand-wash just so there isn't anything left to do.

It's quiet, peaceful in the house. Too quiet. So I open a music app on my phone, connect to the sound system in the kitchen, making sure to turn it down low. Then I roll up my sleeves and fill the sink with soapy water.

I don't keep track of the time as it passes. I just hum along to the music as I wash all the dishes. In no time at all, the sink is drained and I grab a towel from the cabinet to dry the dishes. I'm not exactly tired so I might as well dry them all.

"I didn't plan on falling asleep in there with him."

Her voice startles me, sending a jolt of electricity through my body. My lips twitch trying to hide a smirk as I dry my hands and toss the towel onto the counter next to the dishes. I slowly turn around, my eyes finding hers as she steps into the kitchen. My eyes rake over her body. She must have gone and changed, because she's no longer wearing the sweatpants and shirt she had on earlier. Instead she's in nothing but a pink satin nightgown that stops just along the middles of her thighs.

My cock twitches as she lifts her arms above her head, stretching as she yawns. The slip dress shifts farther up her thighs and I resist the urge to fall to my knees by her feet.

"You looked too peaceful for me to wake up."

She tips her chin down and raises an eyebrow. "You should have woken me anyways." She pauses, closing the distance between us as she drags her top teeth over her bottom lip. "What are you doing down here?"

"I was just finishing up washing the dishes." I reach for her hips and spin her around to face me. A soft gasp escapes her as I wrap my arms under her ass and set her down on the countertop. The weight of my body pushes her knees apart as I step between them.

"What are you doing, Carson?" She lets out a shallow breath, and her soft hands run along my bare arms, up over my shoulders. Her fingers meet at the nape of my neck, sending a shiver down my spine. She locks her arms around the back of my neck and stares up at me through her dark eyelashes. "You were very specific about how you wanted me earlier."

A chuckle escapes me and I duck my head, burying my face in her neck as I press my lips to her skin. I breathe in the scent of her, a groan rumbling in my throat as I move my mouth along the column of her throat. "I changed my mind."

"Okay," she says breathlessly, her fingers drifting through my hair as I shift in front of her. Reaching up to grab her wrists, I pull them away from my neck and move her hands down to the counter to pin her in place. My hips have her legs pinned open and her hands are trapped beneath mine.

My face shifts and I stare down at her for a single breath before capturing her mouth with my own. She kisses me back with a reverent need. There's nothing gentle or tender about the way I kiss her. It's torturous and teasing, but it's filled with urgency and need. I nip at her lips, my tongue sliding against hers, tasting the mint from her toothpaste.

Abandoning her mouth, I begin my descent, trailing my lips down her neck, across her collarbones. The straps of her lingerie fall down along the sides of her arms and I move my lips over her shoulders.

A soft moan escapes her as I move down to her chest. She's not wearing a bra and her tender nipples are hard, poking through the satin material. My teeth bite at her pebbled flesh through her dress and my hands still hold hers down, keeping her from touching me.

She moves against me, the heat from her cunt pressing against my groin. A groan rumbles in my chest once more as I slowly move down her body, lowering myself down onto my knees in front of her. Her eyes flash to mine as I release her hands and move my hands to her hips.

"What are you doing?"

A grin dances across my lips. "Making you come with my tongue." My fingers slip beneath the waist-band of her panties. "Lift your hips for me, Trouble."

She complies, her lips parting as she plants her hands on the counter, lifting her hips for me to slide her panties under her ass. "Now put your feet on the counter." Her eyes are glued to mine as she repositions her. My hands press against her knees, parting them wider. I inch closer, splaying my fingers along the insides of her thighs. She lifts her feet and positions her legs over my shoulders as I lower my face to the apex of her thighs.

Her eyes don't leave mine as she lifts her hands to slide her fingers through my hair, tangling them in the locks. My lips brush against her center and her body jerks in reaction. I flatten my tongue and lick up her entire pussy, applying gentle pressure to her clit as I move past it.

"Oh, fuck," she moans, her eyes rolling back into her head. I smile against her cunt, reveling in her moans and whimpers. She tips her head back as I move my tongue again, continuing the same repetitive motions over and over until she's coming apart at the seams.

Her fingers dig into my skull, her hips lifting again as I stop licking and slide my tongue inside of her. She lets out a low moan followed by a shallow breath that has me about to explode in my pants. I thrust my tongue in and out of her, slowly pulling it out before moving back to her clit once more.

"Goddamn, I love how you taste," I murmur against her flesh, flicking her clit with my tongue once more. "I want to eat your cunt for every fucking meal."

"Don't stop," she urges, her hands pressing my head closer to her. "I'm so close."

I roll my tongue over her clit once more and she rewards me with another whimper. "Do you want to come, Trouble?" I question her, lifting my gaze to hers as she lifts her head to look at me.

She pulls her bottom lip in between her teeth, biting down as she nods while I swirl my tongue in a slow circle around her clit. Sliding one hand between her thighs, I run two fingers through her lips. "You're dripping for me, baby," I growl against her, then push them inch by inch into her tight pussy, lazily stroking her insides as I nip at her clit.

"I can't hear you nodding, Trouble." My teeth

connect with the bundle of nerves and her hips buck. "Give me your words."

"Yes," she breathes, nodding as desperation washes over her lust filled eyes. "Please make me come, Carson."

My groans rumble in my throat and vibrate against her cunt. "You beg so well." I slide another finger into her, my movements becoming more intentional as I start to fuck her with my hand. "Let me reward you. Let me fucking worship you."

My mouth suctions around her clit once more and she's a mess of moans as her head tips back. I press my arm against her thigh, pinning her down as I curl my fingers inside of her and massage the spot I know will drive her wild. Her body writhes beneath my touch, beneath my mouth as I devour her.

Showing no mercy, I take everything I want from her. I draw her orgasm from her, her body shakes as she starts to come apart. Her pussy tightens around my fingers, her nails digging into my scalp as she claws at me.

"Oh my god, Carson," she moans as she crashes over the edge. I lap at her, drinking her up, working my tongue against her cunt until there's nothing left for her to give. Her legs shake, her hips buck, chasing every last ripple of pleasure, and I continue to feast on her through every wave of euphoria.

When her body finally goes limp and she looks like she's about to drift into a lust induced coma, I slowly lift myself from my knees, holding her legs apart with one hand while the other wipes her arousal away from my lips. She lifts her head, an inferno burning brightly in her irises as she stares back at me.

She's wordless as she moves closer, reaching for the waistband of my sweatpants. I don't bother to stop her as she pushes them down, dragging my boxer briefs with them. "I want you to fuck me, Carson. I want you deep inside of me."

My tongue darts out to wet my lips and I taste her on my tongue. A groan vibrates in my chest as pull her closer to the edge of the counter. I position my cock against her cunt, not bothering to take a breath as I push into her, sinking deep. She lets out a soft sigh, taking every inch of my cock.

My hips shift and I begin to pump them, sliding my cock in and out of her. "Look at you, Andi," I moan, the sound leaving me in a rush. My hands grip her hips. "You take my cock like you were made for it."

She stares at me as she wraps her arms around my neck. Her lips part slightly and I lean forward, immediately capturing them with my own. My tongue sweeps over hers, tangling together as I sink into her over and over.

Her legs wrap around my waist and she uses them to rock me in and out of her as her soaked pussy starts to constrict. Our mouths break apart, our breath mingling as we pant, my face still so close to hers as she nips at my bottom lip. "I love how your cock feels inside of me."

"Mmm, good," I groan. Working my hips in a steady rhythm, I fuck her harder. "You're so fucking good. So fucking perfect." Warmth floods the pit of my stomach and my balls draw in tight to my body.

I slide my hand from her hip to between us, my thumb finding her clit as I rock into her hard. Her pussy is stretched tight around my cock as my fingers work over the bundle of nerves, working her into a mess of moans again.

Her back arches, her head tips back as her nails dig into my shoulders. "Oh my god, Carson. Please don't stop. Please." The words fall from her lips in a desperate plea and it only has me fucking her faster.

"You're so fucking beautiful," I murmur, my lips stealing hers once more in a breathless kiss. "I love you like this, spread out, soaking wet while taking every inch of me inside of you."

"I'm going to come," she moans, her voice completely breathless as her hips buck again, pushing herself closer to me.

"That's it, baby," I sigh, thrusting into her harder and faster while my fingers roll over her clit. "Let go. Come all over my cock."

My hips shift and when I thrust into her once more, her pussy squeezes me even tighter. She pinches her eyes closed and inhales, the sound sharp before it's chased away by her crying out her orgasm. My lips find hers, swallowing her whimpers as she loses herself, her pussy pulsing around my length. I'm right there with her, falling over the edge as I rock into her. I spill deep inside of her, her name falling from my lips in a breathless chant.

I'm with her, free falling into the abyss of ecstasy

together. I want to be lost with her like this for the rest of eternity, balls deep inside of her perfect pussy. She's mine. And I'm hers.

My hips don't slow down until she's filled with my cum. I drag out of her, not wanting to leave her warmth until the last possible second. My gaze drops down to her still slick cunt. I drag a finger through her wetness as my cum begins to drip from her. I collect it on the tip of my finger and push it back inside of her.

She's breathless, her cheeks flush, chest heaving with every shallow breath. I reach down to push my cock back into my pants that didn't even make it all the way to the floor. Once I'm tucked away, I reach for her. My hands lock around her waist and I haul her off the counter, holding her in my arms as I spin around on my heel and carry her to my bathroom.

Andi's eyes are locked on me, dazed and content as I set her on her feet and start filling the tub with hot water. My fingers hook under the straps of her lingerie and I push the material down the length of her body. It pools around her feet and she stands completely naked in front of me.

"You're a fucking goddess," I murmur, my fingers skate up her hip, over the curve of her waist, along the outer edge of her breast, causing her skin to pebble and nipple to peak, then up over her collarbone. "I want to worship you for the rest of my life."

She lets out a soft breath as I guide her over to the bath. She lifts her feet, another sigh escaping her as she sinks down into the water. As she situates herself beneath the surface, her face turns up to mine. She shifts forward, making space behind her. "Get in with me."

There's no hesitation as I push my pants and boxer briefs down to the floor and climb into the bath with her. The water is hot on my flesh as I sink under the rippling surface. When I get settled, she leans back against me between the cradle of my thighs.

She rests her head against my shoulder as I wrap my arms around her torso, holding her close to me. The silence settles around us and I let my eyelids flutter shut, burying my face into her neck to breathe her in.

This is exactly where we're both supposed to be.

Wrapped up in each other, souls tangling, flesh melting together.

Andalina Rossi is lodged in my chest, nestled beneath my ribcage.

She has planted herself in my heart and I know now that I'll never be able to let her go.

CHAPTER TWENTY-NINE

ANDI

Matteo scoots farther forward in his seat, his arm extending as he points out to the glass along the perimeter of the rink. "Look, look! There he is!"

A smile lifts my lips and I stare out onto the ice, watching Carson as he skates around to warm up. He was able to get a group of guys together to rent the local rink for a few hours so they could have a small pick up game.

He looks up over to where Tella, Matteo, and I are, raising his hand to wave as his eyes shine back at us. The guys all agreed to have it be a low contact game, in an effort to curb any potential injuries to the guys. No one else needs anything bad happening to them, but getting together for some healthy competition is great for them all right now.

Since they rented the rink, the only people in the stands are friends and family who came along to watch. The public doesn't need to know about it—it's just a group of guys who play professional hockey getting together to play a non league game.

"I see him, *caro*," I smile at my son, lifting my gaze back out to the ice as they get into position in the center of the rink. Caleb waits until everyone is in place and ready to go before he moves toward the dot for the face-off.

The puck drops and Caleb wins the face-off, sending it back to Carson before they begin to skate towards their offensive zone. It's exciting to get to see him play in person for the first time, even if it's a game that means nothing.

Tella came with us to watch the guys play. Caleb's nanny is getting ready to retire and he gave her the off-season off, in the hopes that he can find someone before the season starts again.

I sit with both kids, watching the game as the guys have the best time on the ice. It's almost like watching an All Star game. There isn't the aggression and competitiveness that comes with a normal professional game, but none of them like to lose, so they aren't slacking off either.

They're just being more careful, avoiding any hard hits and genuinely just enjoying their time without the pressure of needing to win.

My phone vibrates in my pocket and I lean to the side, pulling it out. It's just a notification for an email, but it strikes me as weird that it was one that triggered a notification. I unlock my screen and tap on the app only to find that it's just an email about youth hockey. But my eyes scan the other items visible in the inbox and my stomach immediately sinks when I see an email from earlier in the day.

It's from the director of the historical foundation that I work for.

My stomach sinks even further when I open up the message and begin to read the text. I inhale deeply, my lungs expanding to capacity as disappointment washes over me. None of this is good and it completely derails all of my plans.

They're removing all remote positions and if I want to keep my job, I will have to start working in the office. Per the email, the new changes will go into effect at the start of next week and I'm to reach out if that is any issue or if I would like to decline the position.

Today is Wednesday.

That means I have five days.

"Shit," I mumble to myself, not realizing I spoke the word out loud.

"Why did you say shit?"

I whip my head to the side, eyes widening as I look at Tella. "Tella, that's a bad word."

"But you said it." She gives me a pointed look. "Daddy puts a dollar in the jar at home every time he says a bad word. You can give the dollar to Daddy to put in with all his dollars."

"We don't have a jar," Matteo tells Tella before glancing at me. "Do I get a dollar too?"

A sigh escapes me. "I don't have any cash on me right now, but I will give you each a dollar then." I look back at Tella. "And do not say any more bad words, okay?"

Tella nods and leans closer to Matteo, whispering something that has him giggling. She's a sweet little girl, but goddamn, she's a bit of a menace. Caleb certainly has his hands full with her.

My gaze travels back to the ice and I watch as the puck gets passed to Carson. He doesn't even look like he's trying when he receives it and skates around another guy before shooting it. It soars toward Rowan and he doesn't move fast enough. It flies over his shoulder, sinking into the net behind him.

"Yes!" Matteo yells, jumping up and down. Tella is right there with him, both of them doing a celebratory dance. I lift my phone, taking a video of the two of them before moving it down to the ice.

Carson skates past, his feet moving slower as he looks right out to me, pointing at me with his gloved hand. A smile lifts my lips and he winks, tapping his stick against the glass in front of me before making his way back to the face-off circle in the center of the ice.

I love seeing him like this. Happy and carefree—doing the exact thing he loves to do. And I hate the thought of ruining his buzz later tonight when I tell him the news.

That Matteo and I have to go back to Starling Ridge this weekend.

———

"Thanks for coming and watching tonight," Carson says softly as he walks into the kitchen after getting Matteo in bed.

I turn off the faucet and spin around to face him as I dry my hands on the towel. He walks over to me, hair damp from his shower as he spins me around to the other side of the counter. His hands find my hips, lifting me into the air before setting me down on top of the counter.

"I enjoyed watching you play."

Carson leans forward, his lips connecting with the side of the throat. He peppers kisses along my flesh, nipping and sucking his way up to my jaw. "I'm going to see what I can do to get you and Matteo good seats for next season."

The words prick my skin, reminding me of that stupid email from earlier. "Carson," I say softly, my hands finding his shoulders. He murmurs against my skin, continuing to kiss my neck as he slides his hand up to cup the side of my face. "Carson, stop."

He immediately freezes and pulls back, just enough to look at me. "Is everything okay? Did I hurt you?"

"No, I'm fine," I tell him, a sigh following my last word. "It's about next season. I have to tell you something."

His eyebrows tug together and concern knits his brows. "Okay."

"I got an email from work earlier and they're getting rid of the remote positions. Everyone will be required to come into the office as of next week."

He stares at me, his shoulders sagging in defeat. "So, you're leaving."

I swallow the lump in my throat, nodding. "I have

to meet with the realtor tomorrow, but Matteo and I will have to leave by Sunday at the latest."

He's silent, his eyes slowly searching mine. "Quit your job, Andi."

"What? No, I can't do that."

"Why not?" His voice is hoarse and his tone is off. There's a desperation lingering in his tone, but he doesn't dare speak on it.

"Because it's my job. It's how I pay my bills." I pause, snorting as I shake my head. "What would I do if I quit my job?"

"Stay here with me." His throat bobs as he swallows. "You could find a job here or do whatever you want to do."

My breath catches in my throat, my heart stalling in my chest. When Carson said Matteo and I should stay indefinitely, I thought he was saying it from a place of emotion. Like he was caught up in the moment, but that it wasn't something he truly felt or meant.

"I don't know, Carson." I let out the breath I didn't realize I had been holding. "That's a really drastic thing to do on a whim."

"It's not a whim," he presses, lifting both hands to cup the sides of my face. "I want you here. I want you both here with me. We can figure it all out."

My heart stumbles over itself. It's a nice thought and honestly, it's exactly what I want to hear from him, but I can't blindly trust a nice thought. "What happens when you decide you don't want a relationship? What happens when things don't work out between us and then I have to start over for a second time in Aston?"

He wets his lips. "What if I do want a relationship? What if I want more with you?"

"Is that really what you want?"

He hesitates and my stomach fucking drops to the floor. "I think it is."

I shake my head at him, gently pushing him away as I slide off the counter, my feet hit the floor with a thud. "I can't uproot our lives because you think you *might* want a relationship with me." I give him a small, sad smile. "I need you to know that you want us, that you want me, Carson. I can't accept anything less than that and this bullshit of you thinking you can't give me what I deserve is exactly that—bullshit."

"Andi, wait," he says, reaching for me as I breeze past him. "I do want you, I want more with you. The thought of having to balance you and Matteo and hockey is fucking intimidating as hell, but I want to do it. I'll do whatever I have to do to make this work."

Rolling my lips between my teeth, I bite down and shake my head. I take a chance, closing the distance between us, and reach up to cup the sides of his face. "I need you to take some time and think about what you really want. I won't be mad at you if you decide it isn't me, but I need you to be honest with yourself and with me."

I let my hands fall away from the sides of his face. My arms hang heavy at my sides.

"Andi," he says softly, longing in his tone, eyes desperately searching mine.

I press two fingers to his lips. "Not now," I tell him,

my heart breaking as I force a smile. "I don't want you to make a rash decision in the moment."

"I don't need time to think."

"Well, I need you to take the time."

Conflict washes over his expression, but he reluctantly nods. "Okay."

He's silent as I leave him in the kitchen, but he isn't far behind me. I head to his bathroom, brush my teeth and slip into his room to get ready for bed. Carson comes in a few minutes later and he's quiet as he follows suit and climbs into bed with me.

He doesn't ask and I don't push him away as he moves close to me until our bodies are flush together. The front of him pressed against the back of mine. He circles his arms around me, holding me tightly as he buries his face into my hair, waiting for sleep to pull us under.

And when it finally does, the only thing I dream of is him.

CHAPTER THIRTY

CARSON

"So, what did she say?"

I glance over at Matteo, standing on a chair beside me, holding onto a spatula as he tries to flip a pancake. Pancakes are one thing that I've found to be easy after helping Andi a few times, so Matteo and I decided on breakfast for dinner while Andi is meeting with the realtor.

I raise an eyebrow at him. "About what?"

"About us staying." He plucks a small chocolate chip from where it fell from the bag onto the counter and pops it into his mouth. "You said you were going to ask her if we could just stay here instead of going home."

My stomach sinks. "I did talk to her." I roll my lips between my teeth. How do I tell him about our conversation in a way he might understand? I don't want to tell him that I'm fucking afraid of letting his mother down, so I'm considering letting her walk away instead of dealing with that disappointment. "She has to go back because of work, but we're going to figure it all out, okay?"

He frowns, disappointment washing over his expression. "Well, that's fucking stupid."

My eyes widen. "Matteo, no. That's an adult word that you can only use when you're older."

He purses his lips. "Sorry," he huffs, struggling with the pancake again.

"Here, let me." He hands me the spatula and I flip it over. There's a weird shift between us and I don't know what the hell I'm supposed to do to make it better. I don't know how he feels about everything that has already happened in his life, but the last thing I want is for him to feel like he's being abandoned by me. "I want you and your mother to stay."

"So she doesn't want to stay?"

I shake my head, removing one of the finished pancakes from the pan and setting it on a plate. "No, she wants to. It's just a little bit more complicated than that, but I promise that we will figure it out. I want to see you as much as I can."

"Okay," he says after a beat, nodding at me in understanding, although I'm not sure he fully gets it. Thankfully for him, he's only five. He doesn't have to deal with all the bullshit that comes along with being an adult.

He climbs down from the chair and I hand him his plate. I finish another pancake, setting it on a different plate before dropping batter for two more into the pan. Matteo settles at the island in the kitchen and I grab the maple syrup from the fridge. He attempts to butter his pancake and while he's making a valiant effort, I end up taking over, cutting it into small pieces and drizzling syrup over it.

He grabs his fork, pierces a piece and shoves it into his mouth. I watch him for a moment, his face contorting as he starts to chew. "It kind of tastes like cardboard."

I snort, a laugh escaping me. "Let me try it," I say as I stab a piece doused in syrup from his plate with my fork. I put it in my mouth and chew, the same flavor and texture definitely off. "It really does taste like maple cardboard."

Matteo giggles. "My mom's don't taste like that."

"No, they don't," I chuckle, shaking my head as I grab the plate from the table and he drops his fork onto it. "Should we order take-out from somewhere?"

He nods eagerly. His smile is bright with laughter lingering in the air around us. "I think we should."

He's so right. The pancakes taste nothing like the ones Andi makes.

"Good idea." I grab my phone, unlocking the screen and opening the web browser. "Should we just get pizza instead?"

"Can we get pineapple and ham on it?"

I raise an eyebrow at him. "You're one of those people?"

"Yep. My mom said that pineapple and ham belong on pizza and not to let anyone ever tell me anything different."

Laughter rumbles in my chest and I shake my head

at him. "Fair enough. I've never actually tried it, but if you two both like it, then I want to try it too."

At this point, Matteo and Andi could probably convince me that the sky is green and the grass is blue. They both crashed into my life unexpectedly and I can't imagine not having either of them here now. I love this little guy with my whole damn heart and I'd put my life on the line for him.

And not just him . . . Andi too.

Goddammit it. The realization hits me in the chest like a ton of bricks.

I'm hopelessly in love with Andalina Rossi.

———

"Okay, since Matteo is in bed, I want the truth about the pineapple and ham on the pizza."

I glance over my shoulder at Andi as she walks into the bedroom, moving over to the dresser with her clothing. I turn around just as she bends over, my eyes trailing over her perfectly shaped ass. She got home just before bedtime because her meeting with the realtor ran a little late and this is the first time I'm getting her alone since.

A chuckle escapes me and I reach down to adjust my hard cock in my shorts as she turns back around to face me. "It wasn't terrible." I pause, snorting. "It was definitely better than the cardboard pancakes I made."

A smile cracks her face and her soft laughter vibrates through my soul. "Matteo asked me in private if I can make sure you never cook again."

I smile back at her, shaking my head. "I agree. I would like to never cook again if it's going to taste like that shit."

"I'm sure it wasn't that bad."

I laugh. "I can promise you, it was."

"Well, in that case, I'll handle the cooking." She bites her lip and tips her head down, her hair swinging over her shoulder, almost like she's nervous to say what's on her mind. "Did you already shower?"

I run a hand through my now dry hair. "I got one after we ate."

"Okay. Do you mind if I get one?"

My eyebrows pull downward and I tilt my head to the side. "You don't have to ask, Andi. My home is your home."

Her throat bobs as she swallows hard. Her lips part as if she's going to say something, but she abruptly shuts them and nods. "I won't be long."

"Okay," I say softly, watching her as she turns around and heads in the direction of the bathroom. She steps inside and pushes the door shut, although she doesn't shut it completely. She leaves it ajar, almost as if it's an invitation.

I hesitate . . . I don't want to overstep, but I want to be close to her.

The water in the shower turns on and I listen for a moment, hearing the glass door open and then close. My footsteps are light and I gently push open the bathroom door, lingering in the doorway as I watch her through the mirror.

The doors are designed to be foggy and I watch the

way her body bends backwards, back arching as she tips her head back. Her dark hair hangs in the water and she runs her hands over it, drawing her fingers through her long locks. My cock is hard, throbbing inside of my pants as I step all the way into the bathroom, gently pushing the door closed behind me.

Her head turns to the side, her body motionless under the water. I hear the sharp intake of her breath, but she doesn't say anything else as she straightens her spine, turning to face me. My hands reach the bottom hem of my shirt and I lift it up over my head, tossing it onto the counter behind me without saying a word.

She's watching me through the glass door as I slowly remove the rest of my clothing, leaving them on the floor. I reach for a towel, moving it to the hook near the shower and I reach for the glass door. Andi lets out a ragged breath, her eyes raking over me as I step into the shower and pull the door shut.

She steps towards me, her arms immediately snaking around the back of my neck as she pulls my face down to hers. My mouth crashes into hers, her wet body pressing against mine as I back her into the hot water, devouring her mouth. My eyelids flutter shut, the water pelting down on our skin.

My hands find her hair, smoothing it out beneath the stream as my tongue slides into her mouth. Her tongue is like silk, tangling with my own as she knots her fingers in my hair. Our bodies are wet and slick from the water in the shower. My fist wraps around her long locks before I grip the back of her neck.

She moans into my mouth, pushing her hips

forward against me. My cock is rock hard between us, pressing into her stomach. Her breasts crush against my chest and I grin against her mouth, earning another moan from her.

Her hand slides away from my neck, trailing down my tattooed arm before making its way down my torso. She reaches between us, wrapping her delicate fingers around my length. My lips bruise hers, nipping at her flesh, kissing her deeper as she begins to stroke me in long, drawn out, fluid movements.

I moan against her mouth, hungry for her in a way I can't explain. "I need to be inside you, Andi," I groan, sucking her bottom lip into my mouth and sinking my teeth into the soft flesh. I release her, running my tongue along the indents I leave behind.

"I want you to fuck me in here."

Pulling away from her face, I slide my hands down and grab a handful of her sweet ass. "Turn around for me, Trouble. Show me where you want me to fuck you."

Holding onto her, I spin us around so the water is beating down on my back. She turns in my grip, shifting to face the tile wall as she presses her ass against my crotch. She bends at the waist, plants her hands on the wall, and lifts up onto her tiptoes, granting me better access.

"Fuck," I practically growl. I cup her cunt and slide a finger through her lips. There's zero resistance. "You're soaked, baby. So needy for my cock." Eager to sink inside her, I take myself in hand and rub the tip against her pussy, coating the head in her arousal. She moans and her hips start to rock back and forth. She's showing me what she wants. I press the tip against her center, and when she pushes back against me as I step forward, my cock sinks into her heat. I fill her to the brim in one swift movement, filling her completely.

She lets out a breathy moan, pressing harder into me. I'm so deep inside of her and she clenches around my length. *God, she feels like heaven.* I begin to move my hips, pulling out before pushing back into her, filling her over and over. She's so tight around me, taking every inch as I begin to fuck her harder and deeper.

"I want all of you, Andi. Every fucking piece of you."

She meets every one of my thrusts with a press back of her hips, panting as she turns to look at me over her shoulder. I lift a hand to her hair, wrapping it around my fist and giving it a gentle tug, forcing her back to arch. "Then take it all."

My movements become frantic and I pound into her harder. She lets out a cry of pleasure and my hand slips out of her hair, snaking around the front of her throat. I wrap my fingers around her, my other hand digging into her hip and I give her a gentle squeeze.

Her body rocks forward with the force of my thrusts and she braces against the wall, using the strength in her legs to hold herself steady. The sound of our wet skin slapping together with each thrust echoes off the shower walls.

Warmth builds in the pit of my stomach in rapid succession as my orgasm approaches. I slam into her, my balls constricting as they slap against her clit. I fucking love her like this. I look down at her ass and take in the sight of my cock disappearing inside her cunt.

"Fuck, I love watching the way your pussy sucks my cock in."

Andi moans, pressing harder into me. "You feel so good, Carson."

"Come with me, baby," I murmur, my hand releasing her throat to run it through her hair and trail it down her spine. "Come for me."

I pump into her, fucking her harder and faster until we're both calling out each others names. Her body shakes as she comes, pussy quaking around me as I slam into her, milking my cock with her tight cunt. My cock pulses, filling her with my cum with jerky thrusts until I stop completely. We stay like that, my cock buried deep in her, as the final waves of ecstasy crash over us.

Slowly releasing her, I pull out, my hands trailing over her back and to her waist to pull her upright. I spin her around to face me. She's breathless, her chest rising and falling with every shallow breath that escapes her.

I turn both of us around, pushing her back into the water. She tips her head back, her eyelids fluttering shut as it rains down upon her hair. Reaching past her, I grab the shampoo, pumping some into my hands before sliding it against her scalp. When I step back, she steps forward, her hair out of the water as I work it into a lather.

"You know, I can wash myself," she murmurs but her words are followed by a groan of satisfaction as I lather up her hair, massaging her scalp, and then rinse it.

"I know you can, but I want to," I breathe, pulling her back out of the water to put conditioner in her long locks. She stands silently, watching me as I finish her hair and move on to her body. She waits until I'm completely done and she's rinsed off before reaching for my shampoo.

"Let me wash you," she murmurs, her eyes slowly searching mine. Emotion catches in my throat and I nod. A groan rumbles in my chest as she pushes her fingers through my hair, working the soap into a lather along my scalp.

She washes my hair and my body and I let her, reveling in the way her hands feel rubbing every inch of my skin. Only when she's done do I pull her back into the water with me again. My lips sweep across hers, stealing the air from her lungs as my tongue explores her mouth.

Andi breathes me in, her hands roaming across my body, the same time her heart infiltrates mine. She's in my veins, running rampant like a drug and I'm a hopeless addict.

I know I can't let her go, I can't let her leave me. I don't know how I'm going to convince her to stay, when she's already planning on leaving this weekend.

I don't know what I'm going to do, but there has to be a way.

There has to be a way to get her to stay.

CHAPTER THIRTY-ONE

CALEB

A frustrated sigh leaves me as I rake my hand through my hair. I don't know what I'm going to do with Gloria retiring. She's an old friend of my mother's and after Amelia passed, she stepped in with my mother to help out. My parents have been traveling the past year and since they've been gone, Gloria became my full-time nanny.

I don't fault her for wanting to retire, but fuck. This leaves me in a fucking weird situation. Trust has always been an issue for me and especially once I was left to care for Tella by myself.

I will not put my daughter in any form of danger. And if danger should find her anyways, I'll put whoever is behind it in a grave.

There's a soft knock on the front door, drawing my attention away from the list of scratched out names I have. I decided to sit down this morning to try and plan better, but after writing down a list of competent women that I know and trust, I ended up scratching off every single name for one reason or another.

Mainly because I don't want to burden them when I know they have their own families to be worrying about.

My footsteps are hurried as I stride toward the front door, confusion washing over me when I flick on the porch light and see it's my brother standing on the other side. "Cars?" I question him, pushing open the screen door.

He glances over at the two white rocking chairs on the front porch. "Can we talk?"

I swallow roughly over the emotion that immediately floods me. This is the same place Carson found me night after night when I moved here. After I lost Amelia. It was the place I went when I didn't know what else to do—and my brother seems to have adopted the same connection to those two white wooden chairs.

The screen door creaks as I step onto the porch, letting it fall shut with a loud snap behind me. Carson walks over to the farthest chair, lowering himself as he folds his hands into his lap. The silence stretches between us and I just observe him for a moment, the way he stares out into the night, like it's going to give him whatever it is that he's looking for.

I sit down in the chair next to him, letting the hush hang between us. The smell of fresh cut grass fills the air as we inch closer to the summer months. It's the same kind of night Amelia used to sit next to me on our old porch with her bare feet on the railing and glass of wine in her hand.

"What's going on, Cars?" I finally ask, my voice gentle.

Carson doesn't look at me. He picks at the cuticle around his thumb, his fingers twitchy and restless.

"Andi's leaving tomorrow," he mutters, his shoulders sagging in defeat. "She's taking Matteo and they're going back home."

My stomach sinks. "Did she say why?"

"Her job at the historical foundation requires her to come into the office now. They're getting rid of their remote positions." He purses his lips, shaking his head. "I knew she planned on leaving eventually, I just thought maybe she'd change her mind. I can't help but feel like she's leaving me behind."

"I doubt that's what she's thinking."

He falls silent again and the crickets chirp along the fence line. The night is still and so quiet that it feels like something might break if either of us speak too loudly.

He looks at me, his eyes glassy. "You ever feel like you're standing in your own life, and somehow you're still too far away to touch it?"

"Every day since Amelia died."

He closes his eyes. Her name always landed like a lead weight between us.

"I'd give anything to have one more night," I admit, barely louder than a whisper. "One more fight. One more stupid fucking conversation about what we're going to have for dinner. But I don't get that." I pause, swallowing over the lump of emotion lodged in my throat. "You do."

He opens his mouth, immediately closing it as he drops his face into his hands, stroking his eyebrows with his fingers and thumb. He lifts his head to look at me, his foot tapping with the restrained guilt swimming in his eyes. He turns toward the yard, tipping his head back to look up at the night sky.

"I didn't realize I was falling in love with her ," he says, his voice trailing off for a moment as he lets out a breath. "One day we were just two people trying to navigate raising a kid together, but then she went and turned my house into a home. I just didn't realize it until she told me that she's leaving."

"She's not gone yet."

He turns his head to look at me. "She's got one foot out the door."

"Then grab her hand," I insist, my brow furrowing. "Before the other foot follows."

He runs a tired hand through his hair, letting out a frustrated breath. I study him for a moment, my eyes scanning his tired face. My younger brother. The one I've always tried to protect. The one who's always been there for me.

"Did you tell her that you're in love with her?"

Carson diverts his gaze from mine, glancing down at his hands in his lap again. "No." He lets out a shallow breath. "Not in a real way."

My eyebrows pull together but I don't ask him to elaborate. "Then you still can."

Caron purses his lips. "I don't think I can. She's already decided that she's going back."

"Then give her a reason to question it."

Carson turns back to me, the muscle in his jaw tightening. "You don't get it—"

"I *do*," I tell him, my tone sharper than I mean for it to be. "You think you've got more time. You think you can just wait until you're ready, but that's not how this works."

Shock washes over his expression, like he's too stunned to speak for a moment. Like he forgot I was the one who packed up Amelia's things to donate. Who moved to a new house because I kept seeing her everywhere I looked. Who still can't drive down the road where she was killed.

"I waited too long to say the right things," I admit, my voice softer. Carson is the only one who knows what happened that night before a drunk driver killed her. The stupid argument we had. "I thought there would always be another morning. Another Sunday. Hell, another fight, even. But one day it was just gone. No warning, no do-over."

Carson's face goes still.

I swallow roughly, shoving the emotion back into the small box I keep it tucked away in. "You've still got time," I tell him, giving him a nod of assurance. "Don't waste it being scared."

He lets out a ragged breath, then stands up like the chair beneath him is burning. He turns to face me, running a hand through his hair. He paces a few steps past me and then back again before facing me once more.

"What if I tell her and it changes nothing?" His eyes are filled with worry. "What if she leaves anyway?"

"Then at least you know you told her how you felt," I say, wishing I would have had the same opportunity. What I would give to go back in time just to tell her I love her once more. "You can live with that. Trust me— it's the things you *don't* say that'll eat you alive."

Carson stands in place, the silence settling around us as time stretches. He wrestles with the thought, at war with himself. His chest rises as he closes his eyes, taking a deep breath. I watch him carefully as his eyes open once more, releasing a long exhale.

"I'll tell her in the morning before she leaves."

"No." I shake my head. "Tell her tonight."

"I don't even know what to say," he murmurs.

"The truth," I say. "Say exactly how you feel. She's still here," I remind him. "That's the whole point. She's *still here*."

He stares at me for a moment, eyes slowly searching mine. "Okay." He nods in agreement. "I'll tell her tonight." He reaches for me, hand clasping my shoulder. "Thank you, Cale."

He gives my shoulder a gentle squeeze and then releases me. We share one last knowing look and then he moves down the steps and into the dark. I linger on the chair, my body slowly rocking it back and forth. The porch light hums above and the night presses in, quiet and thick around me.

I look out across the yard and the hedges along the

front of the property. The world has a funny way of feeling so much bigger, yet so much simpler than the pain we carry around deep rooted inside of our chests.

My mind drifts to Amelia and the warm nights we spent rocking on these chairs together. To all the things that were left unsaid and the ones I whispered into the empty house after she was gone. You think you'll have time to say it all, but you never do.

And I would never wish that on anyone—especially not my brother.

As the night wears on, my thoughts drift as the loneliness that settles over me, the longing for my dead wife and my single hope for my brother.

I hope that he shoves his fear into the backseat, walks into that house, and tells Andi everything that he needs to say.

And I hope—with the quiet, aching hope that only the broken carry—that he will never end up sitting where I am right now.

Wishing he could go back and love her louder.

CHAPTER THIRTY-TWO

CARSON

The house is silent as I let myself in through the door from the garage. If I hadn't seen Andi's car in the driveway, I would have thought she left already. I kick my shoes off, discarding them near hers and Matteo's before stepping into the kitchen.

The air leaves my lungs in a rush as I find her sitting at the island. She lifts her head, her gaze finding mine. I pause, freezing in place as my breath catches in my throat. Behind her, sitting just outside of the foyer, is Matteo's small suitcase, along with hers.

Fuck.

"Hey," she says softly, tucking her hair behind her ears. "Is everything okay with your brother?"

After Matteo went to bed, I told her I was going to go over to Caleb's for a bit, but I didn't give her any more explanation than that. I wasn't about to tell her that I was going over to ask him for advice—advice on what the hell I'm supposed to do with her leaving.

"Yeah," I tell her, letting out a sigh as I finally walk into the kitchen. "He's fine."

Andi lifts the mug from in front of her, bringing it to kiss her lips as she takes a sip of what looks like a cup of hot chocolate. She slowly sets it back on the counter in front of her. "Are you okay?"

Emotion lodges in my throat. "No," I admit, shaking my head as I step up to the island, planting my hands on the quartz countertop as I stare back at her. "I'm not okay."

Her eyebrows scrunch together, head tilting to the side as her eyes search mine. "What's going on?"

"I can't let you go," I tell her in a rush, my voice sounding breathless. My throat bobs as I swallow roughly, choosing to rephrase my sentence. "I don't want you to leave."

"Carson . . ."

I inhale deeply, lifting my hands from the counter as I close the distance between us. Andi turns to face me in her seat, but I lower myself onto the floor, kneeling in front of her. Her chin dips, eyes laser focused on mine. "I'm in love with you." I let out a ragged breath.

Her eyes widen and she sucks in a sharp breath. My hands find her knees, careful not to grip her too tightly, but it's nearly impossible. She's like sand drifting through the spaces between my fingers and I can't let her get away.

I let her walk away once before, under different circumstances, and fuck that. I'm not letting her walk away again.

"I love you, Andi."

Her mouth hangs slightly open, her hands lifting to cup the sides of my face. Instinctively, I sigh, resting my cheek against her warm palm. My eyelids flutter shut and I revel in how soft her touch is. "You know, I never thought you would actually say it."

My eyelids lift. "What?"

A soft chuckle escapes her and she shakes her head at me. "I love you."

"Wait, are you saying it back or are you answering my question?"

Andi gives me a look, letting out a soft breath. "I'm saying it back, dummy."

"Oh, thank god," I let out a sigh of relief, a chuckle vibrating in my chest. "I'm sorry I didn't say it sooner. You know this is all new to me. Feelings aren't exactly my thing, but I'm trying. I'm learning how to be more in touch with them and honest with myself and everyone around me."

She slowly nods, her hands moving down to my shoulders. "I know. We're all a work in progress, constantly changing and learning." The smile that lifts her lips has my heart melting inside my chest. "I'm proud of you. And I'm glad you decided to take a chance and tell me the truth."

"The thought of you and Matteo leaving has been eating me inside." I roll my lips between my teeth, my chest expanding as I inhale deeply. "I understand if the two of you can't stay here, but I really wish you'd reconsider."

Her eyebrows pull together once more. "What about my job?"

"I know that working is important to you," I tell her, nodding slowly. "I would never ask you to give up your life or any part of yourself for me." My throat bobs. "I know exactly what that feels like, but since you and Matteo have been here, I've realized that the things I thought were important really aren't. I've devoted my entire life to my career, but at the end of the day, it's just that. It's just a job. One day I'll retire and then it will be time to turn the page."

She tilts her head to the side. "What are you saying?"

"You and Matteo are more important to me than hockey."

She searches my face before settling on my eyes once more. "Stand up."

My forehead creases, but I don't object. I do exactly as she says, rising to my feet, taking a step back so I can look at her. She gets out of her seat, standing upright as she inches closer. She lifts her hands to circle them around the back of my neck, her head tilting back to look at me.

My hands find her hips and I slide them around her lower back, pulling her flush to me.

"I'm still going to go back to Starling Ridge tomorrow," she says, her voice soft as her eyes burn through mine. My stomach sinks. "But I don't plan on staying there." She breathes out a gentle chuckle and my heart pounds with a hopefulness inside of my chest. "I want you to come with me and then we will all come back here. Back home."

"You don't want to stay there?"

She shakes her head, a smile lifting her lips. "You're right. It's just a job and I can find a new one here." Her eyes shine back at me. "This is where we need to be. Here, with you." She pauses for a beat. "I want you to come with me and meet my family. I'd like to quit my job in person and then Matteo and I can pack the rest of our things."

"You want to live here with me?" My heart crawls into my throat. "Like officially live here, permanently?"

"Yes," she lets out a soft laugh. "You're the one, Carson."

"Fuck, I love you," I say in a rush, lifting a hand to cup her chin. I drag my thumb over her bottom lip before sliding my hand along her jaw. My face drops down to hers, lips crashing like the waves along the shore. "I want to be the man you deserve," I murmur against her mouth. Goddamn, she's everything to me. "I want to give you the world."

She slowly pulls back, eyes gazing directly into my soul. "You already have." A smile lifts her lips, happiness dancing across her expression. "You gave me Matteo and now I have you too."

"You'll always have me," I promise, inching closer as my lips connect with her forehead. My eyelids flutter shut, breathing in her intoxicating scent. I don't mean always in a way that implies that I'm invincible. I mean it in the way that I'll be here with her, every damn day, fighting for us. "I promise you that."

"I hope so," she breathes, wrapping her arms tightly around my body as she buries her face against my chest. "That's everything I could ever want."

I hold her tightly, our bodies fuzing together as I hold her in the silence. My mind drifts to my brother, to the way he used to look at Amelia. To how he'll never get to hold her like this again.

Love is never a guarantee. It's a gamble and a risk, but it's one we have to be willing to take. Without love, what is life? I know the one I was living before her and it was lonely. I know that we will face trials and tribulations together, but none of that matters to me. I want her here, I want her with me.

We stand there together, quiet and steady.

Neither of us know what will come next. Neither of us can possibly know what the future holds, but as long as I have her, none of that matters. She is what I want, all I need. I'm going to hold onto her for as long as I can.

And I'm going to love her until I'm nothing but ashes and dust.

EPILOGUE
ANDI

ONE YEAR LATER

I love quiet Sundays in the off-season with both of my guys.

No media, no team obligations. It's the kind of rare, perfect day we don't get during the hockey season. The kind where our little family gets to soak in the moments together. Soft and unhurried.

Carson first brought Matteo and me to Garnet Hollow last summer to spend time on the lake. It's a place his family always visited and he wanted to buy a home there to spend our summers together.

We found a property with a half-sunken dock and a crooked pine tree that looks like it's always bowing to the water. We settled on it three months ago and Carson immediately set to have all the work done so we could settle in as soon as summer began.

The dock was repaired and the interior of the house was updated and painted. A smile lifts my lips as I watch the sun catch the surface of the lake as I sink my bare toes into the mud and pebbles beneath the glass surface.

Matteo was exhausted from a full morning of swimming while Carson ran errands. He's curled up on the couch where he fell asleep during the movie we put on after lunch.

I took a quiet moment alone to walk down to the water. To breathe it all in. These are my favorite days, when Carson is home. When it's just the three of us, lost together in our own little world.

It feels like peace. It feels like home.

"Hey, Trouble." He pauses. "Can you come here?"

His voice penetrates my soul, demanding my attention. I turn toward the dock and find Carson standing there, just on the other side of the crooked pine. His hoodie is pulled over his head, sleeves pushed to his elbows.

Something about him feels off and it tugs at the base of my spine. His shoulders are tense, hands shoved in his pockets. His expression is unreadable, as if he's barely holding something in. My heart rate immediately spikes.

I wade out of the water, my breathing shallow. "What's going on?"

Carson is silent as I step up onto the dock with him. I watch him in confusion as he lifts his hands, gripping the sides of his hood and pulls it back away from his face. He turns his head to the side, moving his body so I can see the scrawling ink etched in his skin along his neck.

It's a fresh tattoo curving along his skin, edges tender and red as it's still healing. I step closer, my eyes scanning the script.

Andalina.

My eyes widen. "You tattooed my name on you?"

Carson glances at me, a ghost of a smirk dancing across his lips. "I did." His face falls, a frown tugging on his lips as he turns back to face me. His eyes slowly search mine. "You don't like it."

"No," I swiftly shake my head, emotion catching in my throat. "I love it."

He rolls his lips between his teeth to hide the grin that's pulling on the corners of his mouth. "Good," he says softly as he reaches for the bottom hem of his sweatshirt. "There's more."

My breath catches in my throat, the world tilting slightly as he lifts his sweatshirt, pulling it over his head, exposing his chest. Etched right over his heart is another tattoo, except this one is different. This one is written in my handwriting.

"With you, I'm home."

"That's . . ." I choke out, blinking back tears. "That's from the note I left you."

Carson takes a step closer, nodding as his gaze holds mine. "It was my first game of the season after you and Matteo officially moved in. It was the first time I had to leave you two after we evolved into this." He motions with his hands, taking another step closer. "I've kept it tucked in my skate and I look at it before every game, but I needed something permanent."

I close the remaining distance between us, pressing

my hand to the skin around his tattoo, careful not to touch the red skin. I touch it as if it might anchor me to the moment between us.

"You tattooed my name," I whisper, reaching one hand to tenderly touch his neck. "And my words."

"I'm committed to you, Andalina. You and Matteo are my priority. The two of you come first and I need you to know that. What we have is real and I never want a day where this isn't mine. Where you aren't mine."

Something cracks open inside my chest, raw and warm and deep.

And then Carson begins to sink onto one knee.

I momentarily forget how to stand, the world around us swaying like trees from the breeze dancing across the lake.

Carson's hand plunges into the front pocket of his pants, pulling out a small black velvet box. His gaze flashes to mine and tears immediately prick the corners of my eyes. He slowly opens it and my breath catches.

Nestled inside the box is the most perfect ring. It's not extravagant, it's not loud. It's an elegant, timeless, soft brushed white gold band with a delicate diamond that catches the sunlight.

"I want a life with you, Trouble. I want to go to bed every night with you in my arms. I want to wake up every morning next to you. I want all of the good days and all of the bad. I want you, Andalina. I want every fucking moment with you."

My chest tightens, my heart pounding against my ribcage. I've known from that first night together that

Carson is my home. There's always been an invisible thread between us, tugging us back to one another.

He takes a breath, steady, but shaking. "Will you marry me?"

"Yes," I breathe, without a moment of hesitation, although I'm barely able to get the word out. I swallow roughly, a soft laugh escaping me as tears spring from my eyes. "Yes," I tell him again, this time louder. "Yes, of course."

A smile breaks out across his lips and he slides the ring onto my finger. It fits like it's always belonged there.

He rises to his feet, arms sweeping around my lower back as he tugs my body closer to him. His lips immediately find mine, stealing the air from my lungs as he kisses me with a tenderness that drips into my soul.

He pulls away from our kiss and wraps his arms around my waist as he drops his forehead to mine. "I love you so much, Andi," he murmurs, his voice dancing against my eardrums. "Thank you for showing me that there's a life outside of the ice rink." He pauses. "There's a life right here, with you and Matteo."

"And we're not going anywhere," I tell him, my eyelids fluttering shut as I take a moment to breathe him in. A soft laugh falls from my lips as I lift my hand, pressing it against his chest. "I can't believe you tattooed my name and the words I wrote on your skin."

"You're my home, Andi," he breathes, lifting his head to press his lips to my forehead. "You always have been and you always will be."

The gentle breeze moves through the trees, the leaves swaying above.

"I love you," I say, the words soaking into the air around us. "Today, tomorrow, forever."

"I like the sound of that," he tells me, pulling me closer, until our bodies are flush together, melting into one another.

There was a time where I used to wonder if we would ever be anything more. If there was ever going to be a future for the two of us, where we fit together as perfectly as we do now.

But now, I no longer question any of that. Together is where we're supposed to be.

Carson Ford is my home. He's the place where my soul can rest.

And I am his.

WANT MORE?

Scan the QR code below for a Carson & Andi bonus scene!

WHAT'S COMING NEXT?

The final book in the Aston Archers series will be coming Fall 2025!
Make sure you're signed up for Cali's newsletter for an exclusive look inside!

Made with Flodesk

ABOUT THE AUTHOR

Cali Melle is a USA Today Bestselling Author who writes sports romance that will pull at your heartstrings. You can always expect her stories to come fully equipped with heartthrobs and a happy ending, along with some steamy scenes.
In her free time, Cali can usually be found living in a magical, fantasy world with the newest book or fanfic she's reading or freezing at the ice rink while she watches her kids play hockey.

ALSO BY CALI MELLE

ASTON ARCHERS SERIES

Make Your Move

Make Your Play

Make Your Save

Make Your Change

ORCHID CITY SERIES

Meet Me in the Penalty Box

The Tides Between Us

Written In Ice

Dirty Pucking Play

The Lie of Us

WYNCOTE WOLVES SERIES

Cross Checked Hearts

Deflected Hearts

Playing Offsides

The Faceoff

The Goalie Who Stole Christmas

Splintered Ice

Coast to Coast

Off-Ice Collision

<u>**STANDALONES**</u>

The Christmas Exchange

The Christmas Rebound

Tell Me How You Hate Me

The Art of Breathing